Ma...

ROCHELLE ALERS

NATIONAL BESTSELLING AUTHOR

Man of Fate

ARABESQUE®

Recycling programs
for this product may
not exist in your area.

MAN OF FATE

ISBN-13: 978-0-373-83160-9

www.kimanipress.com

Printed in U.S.A.

The BEST MEN series

You met Tessa, Faith and Simone—the Whitfields of New York and owners of Signature Bridals—in the WHITFIELD BRIDES series. Now meet three lifelong friends who fulfill their boyhood dream and purchase a Harlem brownstone for their business ventures.

Kyle Chatham, Duncan Gilmore and Ivan Campbell have worked tirelessly to overcome obstacles and achieve professional success, oftentimes at the expense of their personal lives. However, each will meet an extraordinary woman who just might make him reconsider what it means to be the best man.

In *Man of Fate,* high-profile attorney Kyle Chatham's classic sports car is rear-ended by Ava Warrick, a social worker who doesn't think much of lawyers and deeply mistrusts men. Ava expects the handsome attorney to sue her, not come to her rescue after she sustains a head injury in the accident. But Kyle knows he has to prove to Ava that he is nothing like the men in her past—a challenge he is prepared to take on *and* win.

Financial planner Duncan Gilmore's life is as predictable as the numbers on his spreadsheets. After losing his fiancée in the World Trade Center tragedy, he has finally begun dating again. In *Man of Fortune,* Duncan meets Tamara Wolcott—a beautiful and brilliant E.R. doctor with a bad attitude. As their relationship grows, Tamara begins to feel that she is just a replacement for his late fiancée. But Duncan knows that he has to put aside his pride if he's going to convince Tamara to be part of his life.

After the death of his identical twin years ago, psychotherapist Ivan Campbell is a "love 'em and leave 'em" guy who is afraid of commitment. But all of that changes in *Man of Fantasy* when he meets Nayo Goddard at an art gallery, where she is showing her collection of black-and-white photographs. Not only has she gotten Ivan to open up his heart to love again, she is also seeing another man. Ivan knows that he must prove that he is the best man for her, or risk losing her forever.

Yours in romance,

Rochelle Alers

A wise man will hear, and will increase learning;
and a man of understanding shall attain
unto wise counsels.
—*Proverbs* 1:5

Chapter 1

Kyle Chatham downshifted, maneuvering into an E-ZPass lane on the Robert F. Kennedy Triborough Bridge. Several cars ahead of him, traffic came to a standstill as a car stalled at the toll booth, eliciting a cacophony of horns and profanity-laced invectives from other motorists on the toll plaza.

A smile spread across Kyle's lips as he listened to the bawdy comments and watched as drivers flipped each other the bird. This was his city and he'd expected no less from New Yorkers. His motto when it came to his hometown was Either Love It or Leave It. His relatives from down South couldn't understand how he could live in a place that was so noisy and filled with throngs trying to navigate through crowded sidewalks and city streets. Even the brusque and sometimes rude manners of New Yorkers—who usually go about their business without even making eye contact or greeting others with a polite "good mornin'" or "evenin'"—takes some getting used to. He had lost track of the number of times he had to explain to visitors that New Yorkers didn't have time to dawdle or chitchat because they would never get where they were going. One thing he couldn't explain was the colorful language peppered with four-letter words that was uniquely a part of New York.

Kyle loved the city, and if someone offered him tens of millions of tax-free dollars to move, he would turn them down without batting an eyelash. He was Harlem—born and raised—and at thirty-eight years old, he still lived there.

There had been a time when he'd worked an average of eighty hours a week for a prestigious New York law firm handling high-profile cases ranging from corporate fraud to capital murder before he realized he was dangerously close to being burned out. He'd given Trilling, Carlyle and Browne—affectionately nicknamed TCB for "taking care of business"—ten years of his life, but had finally decided that if he had to work that hard, then it would be for Kyle Elwin Chatham.

Although he'd spent hours in his Park Avenue office overlooking the Waldorf Astoria and Grand Central Station, Kyle still found time to unwind with a very active social life. He dated, had a few long-term relationships and always set aside time to hang out with his closest friends, Duncan Gilmore and Ivan Campbell. The three had grown up together in the same public housing complex and they'd never lost touch with each other.

Faced with the most important decision he'd had to make, he tendered his resignation and spent the entire summer in Sag Harbor, Long Island, at a bed and breakfast, lying on the beach during the day and partying at night.

A fling with a local divorcée capped off what had become quite a memorable summer. He'd returned to his Harlem brownstone reinvigorated and ready to start practicing law again—this time for himself.

A year ago, he'd contacted Duncan and Ivan, offering to go in with them on the purchase of the brownstone. They planned to renovate the building and use it as professional office space for Kyle's law practice, Duncan's financial-planning services and Ivan's psychotherapy practice. Eight months later they toasted one another with champagne after the brass plate bearing their names and titles were affixed to the front of the three-story brownstone in Harlem's Mount Morris Historic District.

Traffic in his lane had come to a complete standstill. Either someone was in the wrong lane, had engine trouble or had run out of gas. Kyle reached over and pushed the volume button on the dashboard of his sports car and started singing at the top of his lungs. Not only did he know the lyrics to every Stevie Wonder song, but he also did a very good imitation of the blind singer-songwriter.

"Sing it, gorgeous!" a woman called out from the open window of a sport utility vehicle in the next lane.

Nodding, Kyle winked at her as he continued to sing. "Superwoman" and "Living for the City" were his favorites. His musical taste was eclectic, running the gamut from blues and classic jazz to R&B, and he had to thank his father and uncles for that. Every time there was a family gathering, the Chatham men engaged in their favorite pastime: comparing the latest additions to their growing music libraries.

Kyle had surprised his father one Christmas with an MP3 player with selections he had converted from his father's record collection and cassettes. Elwin Chatham—a highly decorated Vietnam vet—sat stunned as his eyes filled with tears after he plugged the MP3 player into a tuner to hear the music of his youth.

The honking increased as Kyle glanced up at the rearview mirror to gauge if he had enough room to maneuver around the vehicle in front of him to get into another lane. It took a full three minutes before he was able to make it through another toll booth and onto the roadway that would take him into Manhattan.

It was a warm Saturday night in June and the sidewalks and roadways in East Harlem were as crowded as if it were Monday-morning rush hour. Neither the bumper-to-bumper crosstown traffic nor the pedestrians ambling across the wide avenues, oblivious to the traffic lights, could dispel Kyle's good mood. He'd spent the evening in Mount Vernon, a guest at the wedding of Micah and Tessa Whitfield-Sanborn.

As a graduate of Brooklyn Law School, Kyle had been a mentor to NYPD Lieutenant Micah Sanborn when he attended law school as a part-time student. Micah had graduated at the top of his class, passed the bar on his first attempt and went on to work as a Kings County assistant district attorney. Kyle had offered Micah a position in his private practice, but the former police officer declined, saying he didn't have the temperament to work in the private sector.

No one was more surprised than Kyle when he received the wedding invitation, since Micah never seemed to be serious about any woman, certainly nothing that would lead to marriage. But when he was introduced to Tessa Whitfield he knew why Micah was marrying the wedding planner. Tessa was intelligent, elegant *and* stunningly beautiful.

Tessa had everything Kyle was looking for in the women he'd dated over the years. As a teenager and in his early twenties, it had been sex. But as he matured he realized sex was only one aspect of a satisfying relationship. It was important, but not as important as communicating with each other out of bed.

He never took a date with him to a wedding because he didn't want to send the wrong message. He wasn't anti-marriage or commitment-phobic. It was just that he hadn't found *that* certain someone, a woman who complemented him.

Kyle was ambitious, generous and fun-loving, but he was also moody, possessive and, at times, irritable and tactless. He was waiting for the time when he'd be able to balance his career and personal life, and he was close to achieving that.

Thankfully there was no pressure to have grandchildren. Between his younger sister and brother, Elwin and Frances Chatham had two grandsons and two granddaughters. Life was good, and he intended to enjoy it to the fullest.

Ava Warrick didn't know what else could go wrong. Her week had begun badly when she'd overslept—something she rarely did. She'd missed an important meeting with the mental health agency's medical director, and now it was her weekend to be on-call and she'd gotten a call from a social worker at Harlem Hospital that one of her clients had been admitted to their psychiatric unit.

"Don't you dare stop!" she screamed at the driver in the convertible sports car in front of her own. He'd slowed within seconds of the light changing from green to yellow. "Dammit!" Ava hissed between clenched teeth.

Her attempt to go around the two-seater was thwarted when a Cadillac Escalade came out of nowhere and she was forced to hit the brakes, but not soon enough to avoid slamming into the rear of the sports car. The driver's-side air bag in her car deployed and she sat dazed and unable to see beyond the fabric pressed against her face.

Kyle put his Jaguar in Park, shut off the engine and got out. It wasn't often that he took the antique convertible out of the garage except when he had to travel outside the city, but he knew without looking that it had sustained some rear-end damage. He'd invested a lot of money in the Jaguar XKE with ground-up restoration. His skilled mechanic had installed a new tan-leather interior, totally rebuilt the engine and outfitted it with new Dayton Wire Wheels.

The car's body gleamed with a new coat of sapphire-blue paint, making it better than it was the day it was built. He'd lost count of the times people had offered to buy the convertible from him, but Kyle had waited too long for a vehicle that suited his temperament and lifestyle to turn around and sell it.

He approached the driver's-side window of the car that had hit him and found a woman, her face pressed against the air bag. His concern for his vehicle shifted to the driver. "Are you all right?"

"Open the door," came her muffled reply.

Kyle pulled on the door handle, stepping back when the driver managed to slip from behind the wheel unassisted. The young woman swayed slightly but righted herself before he could reach out to steady her.

"Do you have any idea how fast you were going?" he asked.

Ava pressed her back to the door of her brand-new Maxima. She hadn't had the car a week, and now she was in an accident. She'd driven her last car, a twelve-year-old Maxima with more than one hundred thousand miles on it, into the ground without a single mishap.

Within seconds the pain in her head was replaced by a blinding rage that made it almost impossible for her to speak. "I…I know how fast I was going. You were the one slowing down to a crawl at least twenty feet before the light changed. If you can't drive on city streets, then you should keep the hell off the road."

Kyle's eyes widened as he glared at the woman who seemed to blame him for causing the accident. "Hel-lo, you were the one who hit me, not the other way around."

"I wouldn't have hit you if you didn't drive like—" Her words stopped when she felt a rush of bile in the back of her throat.

"Yo, man, I saw the whole thing. If you need a witness, then I'm it."

Kyle turned to find an emaciated-looking man holding up the front of his pants with one hand while he'd extended the other, seemingly for a handout. "Beat it!"

The panhandler lowered his hand. "Damn, brother, there's no need to go mad hard. I'm just trying to help out."

"Help out somewhere else." Walking back to his car, Kyle surveyed the damage. Except for a dent in the fender, his vehicle hadn't sustained any serious damage. But the right side of the Maxima's front bumper rested on the roadway. Reaching for the cell phone in the breast pocket of his shirt, he dialed two numbers: one to report the accident to the police and the other to his mechanic.

Ava's gaze narrowed when she stared as the tall, slender man approached her. "I'll pay for the damage to your car."

"It's too late, miss. I just called the police."

"Why the hell did you do that?"

"Look, miss—"

"Miss Warrick," Ava said. "It's Ava Warrick. And as I said, I would've paid out-of-pocket for the damage to your car."

Kyle lifted his eyebrows. "What about your car? It has a lot more damage than mine."

"I have a friend who owns a body shop," she said.

"You should've said that before I made the phone call."

"You didn't tell me you were going to call the police," Ava countered.

"That's because I didn't have to," Kyle retorted nastily. "After all, you did hit *my* car."

Ava knew she wasn't going to be able to drive her vehicle. She rounded the car, opened the passenger-side door, reached into the glove compartment for the vehicle's registration and insurance information and sat down to wait for New York's finest. She didn't know if the pain in her head was anxiety from the accident or the impact of the air bag.

"Where's your friend's shop?"

Her head came up, and she found herself staring up into the dark face of the most handsome man she'd seen in years. To say he was tall, dark and handsome was an understatement. He claimed an angular face with high, chiseled cheekbones. There wasn't enough light to discern the color of his deep-set, slanting eyes. He had a strong nose with slightly flared nostrils and a firm mouth with a full lower lip. Her gaze moved from his square chin up to his close-cropped hair and reversed itself to wander slowly down the front of a crisp white shirt with French cuffs and a pair of tailored trousers and imported leather footwear.

"It's in Flatbush."

"Start dialing, Miss Warrick, because Flatbush is not around the corner." Kyle hoped her friend would come from Brooklyn before they were able to settle the accident report. Otherwise, she might become another police statistic if some criminal decided to rip her off despite the neighborhood's rapid gentrification.

Moving as if she were in a trance, Ava searched into her cavernous leather bag for her cell phone. She scrolled through the directory for her friend's number, but before she could depress the button her vision blurred. Then without warning everything faded to black.

Kyle reacted quickly as Ava slumped against the leather seat. Reaching over, he righted her, but her body was as limp as an overcooked noodle. Her car had collided with his, yet he hadn't thought about whether she had injured herself.

The possibility that Ava might have sustained a serious injury took precedence over the damage to either of their cars and he knew she had to get to a hospital right away. Reaching over, he touched her cheek, which was moist. He glanced down at her chest to see if she was still breathing, and noted thankfully that she was.

"Ava," he said, calling her name softly. "Come on, beautiful, wake up. That's it. Talk to me."

Kyle was afraid she'd suffered a concussion and he remembered reading somewhere that people with head injuries shouldn't be allowed to go to sleep. He exhaled an audible sigh when her eyelids fluttered wildly.

Ava tried focusing on the face inches from her own. "What happened?"

"You must have passed out for a few seconds," Kyle explained.

She pressed the heel of her hand to her forehead. "I don't know what hurts more—my head or my face."

"You probably had your seat too close to the steering wheel."

Opening her hand, Ava stared at her cell phone as if she'd never seen it. "You were going to call your friend, but there's no time for that," Kyle continued.

She blinked as if coming out of a trance. "What are you talking about?"

He saw flashing lights from a police cruiser coming in their direction. "The police are on their way and when they get here I'm going to have them call for an ambulance."

Ava sat up straighter, but more pain shot through her head, bringing with it another wave of dizziness. "I don't need a doctor."

"Yes, you do. When my mechanic gets here I'm going to have him tow your car to his garage, and I'll follow the ambulance in my car."

When Ava had gotten into her car she hadn't thought that instead of going to visit a patient she would become one. "It's just a headache."

Kyle's expression was grim. "It has to be more than a headache if you passed out."

Any attempt at smiling brought more stabbing pain for Ava. "Do you want me to go to the hospital because you're afraid I'm going to sue you? After all, New York has a no-fault insurance."

Hard-pressed not to laugh, Kyle gave the woman a long, penetrating stare. He hadn't lied when he'd said she was beautiful, because she was. Not beautiful in the traditional sense, but stunning nonetheless.

Ava Warrick's short, fashionably styled hair and her skin were her best assets. Her dark brown complexion was the color of milk chocolate, its flawlessness reminding him of whipped mousse. He forced himself not to look below her neck where a scoop-neck T-shirt revealed a hint of cleavage and generous hips in fitted jeans.

"Not in the least."

Time seemed to go by in slow motion even though it was only minutes until the mechanic arrived with a tow truck, followed by the police cruiser. Kyle instructed the mechanic to tow Ava's car, then told the police officers that Ava needed to be transported to a hospital. A female officer, who looked young enough to have been a recent police-academy graduate, called for an ambulance while her partner completed the accident report.

Ava's protests that she didn't need medical assistance were ignored when the ambulance arrived and the paramedics assisted her inside and closed the door. She lay down on the gurney, gritting her teeth each time the vehicle hit a bump in the roadway. If she hadn't needed a doctor before, she clearly did now. By the time the ambulance driver had maneuvered into the area leading to the emergency room and the gurney was lowered to the ground, the nausea and pain vanished as she slipped into a comforting blackness.

Kyle alternated between pacing the floor and reading the sports pages of the *Daily News,* which someone had left on a chair in the E.R. waiting room. He didn't know why he'd followed Ava Warrick to the hospital except maybe to reassure himself that she would be all right. He realized his actions had come from his father's endless preaching that men were placed on the earth to protect women, something he'd never forgotten.

Elwin Chatham should've been a preacher instead of a railroad chef. Whenever he was home his booming voice echoed throughout the apartment as he lectured his three children about making bad choices that could result in them either going to prison or to an early grave.

Kyle had always thought his father talked just to hear himself talk. But his warnings were realized when at fourteen, Kyle, hanging out with the wrong crowd, landed in a juvenile detention center. The single episode was a wake-up call that Elwin hadn't been just beating his gums, but wanted the best for his children. And as the eldest, Kyle was expected to set a good example.

"Mr. Chatham?"

Kyle's head came up when he heard someone call his name. Rising to his feet, he saw a tall, gangly doctor with a mop of light brown hair falling over his forehead standing a few away. "Yes, I'm Mr. Chatham."

The doctor extended his hand. "I'm Dr. LaMarca, and I've just completed my examination of Ms. Warrick."

Kyle took the proffered hand. "How is she?"

Bright-blue eyes met his warm brown ones. "I'm recommending that we keep her overnight for further tests."

A frown settled on Kyle's face. "What type of tests are you talking about?"

"Ms. Warrick has suffered a concussion—"

"It's only a concussion?" he asked, interrupting the doctor.

Dr. LaMarca nodded. "Yes. In order to rule out any other neurological damage I've ordered Ms. Warrick to undergo a CT scan."

His frown deepened. "You suspect her injury may be more serious?"

"Mr. Chatham, I'm requesting the scan to err on the side of caution. I've seen patients who've been diagnosed with a mild concussion end of up with something a lot more serious because the examining doctor failed to order a brain scan."

"When are you going to do the scan?"

"Not until tomorrow morning. The only neurosurgeon on staff at the present time is in surgery. Ms. Warrick will stay overnight, and will be released if the scan comes back negative for neurological injury."

"Did you tell her that she has to remain overnight?" Kyle asked.

A deep flush crept up the doctor's neck to his hairline. "Yes, I did. Unfortunately Ms. Warrick wasn't receptive to the idea until I outlined the seriousness of her injury."

Kyle's eyebrows lifted. "Injury? She got hit in the face with an air bag."

A wave of doubt had crept into Kyle's mind when he'd thought that perhaps Ava Warrick was trying to make something more of a simple fender-bender. After all, she was the one who'd mentioned New York's no-fault insurance law. He quickly changed his mind when he recalled her reluctance to seek medical assistance. He was the one who'd insisted she go to the hospital.

"When you see her face it looks like she has been hit with a baseball bat."

"May I see her?"

The doctor nodded. "I'm hoping you can convince her that she should stay and have the scan."

Kyle followed the doctor across the waiting room, where mothers sat cradling their sick children and a group of teenagers huddled together, talking and awaiting news of their friend who'd come in bleeding from a gunshot wound.

He made his way down a corridor to an area where curtains cordoned off a row of stretchers into examining rooms.

Dr. LaMarca stopped and swept back a curtain. Ava Warrick sat on a chair, eyes closed and hands clasped in her lap. The right side of her face was bruised and swollen, and Kyle doubted whether she had complete vision in her left eye.

Moving quickly, he went to his knees and took her hands. They were ice-cold. "I'm sorry, Ava." Now he knew why the doctor had recommended a brain scan.

Ava opened her eyes when she felt the warmth of the hands cradling hers. It took her a full minute before she recognized the man hunkered in front of her. He was the one whose car she had rear-ended.

"I want to go home, Mr...." Her voice trailed off when she realized she didn't know his name.

"My name is Kyle Chatham, and no, you can't go home tonight."

"Why not?"

"The doctor wants you to have a CT scan."

Ava blinked slowly. "Why?"

"To make sure there isn't another problem."

She closed her eyes. "The only problem I have right now is a mother of a headache."

"You have more than a headache. You suffered a concussion."

Her eyes opened again. "What I have is a *slight* concussion."

"What you have is an injury to the brain which interferes with your cerebral functioning. Simple or severe—it's still the same thing."

"Don't tell me you're a doctor."

"No. I'm a lawyer."

"I guess you're going to sue me for dinging your little car."

"My *little* car happens to be a classic Jaguar XKE." Ava shook her head then chided herself for not remembering how much it hurt just to move her head. "That means nothing to me."

Rising to his feet, Kyle glared at her. "Of course it doesn't mean anything to you, because if it did then you wouldn't have been trying to run the light."

Resting her fingers on her forehead, Ava gently massaged her temples. "I wasn't running the light, Kyle. It was still green."

"It had just changed to yellow."

She lowered her hands. "I'm not going to argue with you. I'm going home."

Kyle knew he had to act quickly, or Ava would walk out of the hospital. "If you leave here I *will* sue you."

Ava went completely still, not wanting to believe she was being threatened. Her chin lifted and she stared up into the steady gaze of a man who, up until an hour ago, she hadn't known. Everything about him reeked of power: his voice, his body language. She stared at the shirt with French cuffs that bore his monogram. The silver buckle on the black alligator belt around his slender waist was also monogrammed.

"You wouldn't," she whispered.

A hint of a smile tilted the corners of Kyle's mouth. "Hell, yeah, I would if you decide to walk out of here."

"What's with you?" Ava asked. Her fingers curled into tight fists. "My insurance company will pay for the damage to your little *classic* car, and I give you my word that I'm not going to..." Her words trailed off again, this time as a rush of bile filled the back of her throat.

Clapping both hands over her mouth, she scrambled off the chair as Kyle reached for a plastic kidney-shaped bowl and pushed it under her chin. Vomiting left Ava gasping for air, her eyes filled with moisture and her throat raw and burning.

Reaching into the pocket of his suit trousers, Kyle handed her a handkerchief and watched as she touched it to her mouth. "Do you still think you're ready to go home?"

"No," she moaned.

He eased her off the chair and helped her onto the stretcher. "Lie down, Ava. I'm going to get you some water."

For the first time since meeting Kyle Chatham, Ava didn't have a comeback. She lay on the stretcher, closed her eyes and awaited his return. The E.R. doctor who'd examined her had suggested a scan to rule out bleeding in the brain, and she'd refused his recommendation.

Her vision was blurred, she'd passed out and now she was vomiting—all of the symptoms associated with a concussion.

She didn't want to believe an air bag could cause such a serious injury. But when she thought about the air-bag warnings about infants or young children riding in the front seat leading to serious injury or death, she knew the doctor's recommendation was best. Ava had become a patient in the very same hospital as the client she'd been rushing to see.

Kyle returned with a bottle of water he'd gotten from a vending machine and handed it to Ava. The bruising and swelling in her face did little to detract from her attractiveness. Despite all that had happened to her, not a strand of her hair was out of place. He watched as she put the bottle to her mouth and took furtive swallows.

"Is there anyone you want me to call to let them know where you are?" he asked Ava.

She lowered the bottle. "Yes." Ava gave him the telephone number to the Upper West Side family services center. "When the answering service picks up please tell them to contact Dr. Mitchell and let her know that someone will have to cover my caseload and that I'll be out for a couple of days."

Kyle stopped writing on the piece of paper he'd torn from a pad advertising a drug for hypertension. "It's going to take more than a couple of days for your bruises and swelling to go away. What if I tell them you'll return once you get medical clearance?"

"Tell them whatever you think is best, counselor."

Smiling, he winked at her. "Thank you. Who else do you want me to call?"

"That's it."

"What about your folks?"

"My mother lives in D.C. and my dad in North Carolina, so there's no need to call and upset them."

"What about your husband or boyfriend?"

The seconds ticked off before Ava said, "I don't have a husband *or* a boyfriend."

"My mechanic towed your car to his garage. If you still want your friend to take care of the repairs then I'll give you the name and address of the garage so he can come and pick it up."

Ava closed her eyes again when pain shot through the left side of her face. "Your mechanic can take care of the repairs. He can't rip me off too much because the insurance adjusters won't approve it."

Kyle leaned forward and glared at her. "My mechanic happens to be *my* cousin and he's not going to jeopardize his business or reputation by ripping off a customer."

Ava returned the hostile stare with one of her own. "I've lived in this city long enough to know everyone has some sort of a hustle. And I'm willing to throw shyster lawyers into the mix."

Throwing back his head, Kyle laughed. "I can assure you, Ms. Warrick, that I'm not one of those so-called shysters."

"But you do have a very successful practice."

He sobered quickly. "Are you stating a fact or asking a question?"

"Both. Struggling attorneys don't wear custom-made shirts or monogrammed accessories."

"I'll admit to having my shirts custom-made, but the belt is a gift from former colleagues who surprised me when they learned that I was leaving to start up my own practice."

"Where is your law firm?"

"Right here in good old Harlem, USA."

"Where did you work before?"

"I worked for a major Park Avenue law firm."

Ava whistled. "That's pretty expensive real estate. Do you—" Whatever she was going to say was preempted when Dr. LaMarca returned.

"We have a bed for you, Ms. Warrick. An orderly will be here in a few minutes to take you to your room. If there's anything of value in your purse I suggest you give it to your boyfriend for safekeeping."

She opened her mouth to inform the doctor that Kyle Chatham was *not* her boyfriend but a stranger— a stranger she'd entrusted with her brand-new car *and* information about where she worked. She'd had to trust him since her family was too far away to be of any help. Her younger brother was aboard a navy submarine somewhere, while her older brother was a warden at a maximum-security prison in Texas. Her sister, Aisha, was at home in Maryland awaiting the birth of her first child.

"When do you think I'll be discharged?" she asked the doctor.

He smiled and a network of tiny lines fanned out around his eyes. "I've scheduled the CT scan for eleven. If it comes back negative, then you can expect to be discharged by noon."

"I'll get here around eleven-thirty in case they finish early," Kyle volunteered.

Reluctantly she handed Kyle her leather handbag with her keys, cell phone and wallet. She'd left most of her cash and credit cards at home when she'd gotten the call from the answering service. The curtains parted and an orderly came in pushing a wheelchair.

Kyle usurped the orderly's responsibility by reaching over and lifting Ava effortlessly off the stretcher and onto the chair. He dropped a kiss on the top of her fragrant hair. Smiling, he winked at her. "I'll see you tomorrow, sweetheart."

Ava flashed a sexy smile. "Thank you, Kyle."

The last thing Ava remembered when she closed her eyes after getting into bed was Kyle calling her sweetheart. She knew he'd done it because the E.R. doctor believed they were involved. They were involved, all right, but it wasn't romantically.

She'd had two long-term relationships and each had ended badly.

Her first love had been a fellow college student, and their relationship ended within days of graduation. Ava had waited six years before giving her heart to a man she thought was her soul mate, but in the end he'd become her worst nightmare.

That long-term relationship had ended badly when her former lover began stalking her. It had taken a restraining order from the police to stop the harassing telephone calls and to prevent him from showing up at her office unannounced. It was only when she changed jobs and moved from her Lower East Side apartment to Morningside Heights that she was able to put Will Marshall behind her.

Six months ago when she'd celebrated her thirty-fourth birthday, she'd vowed to remain a single woman for the rest of her life rather than deal with another immature, insecure brother.

Kyle's endearment lingered on the fringes of her mind until Ava succumbed to a numbing sleep that kept the blinding pain at bay, at least temporarily.

Chapter 2

Kyle maneuvered into the carriage house that was attached to his brownstone. Along the street were townhouses, carriage houses and Georgian-style brownstones that made up the neighborhood known as Strivers' Row. Originally, he'd bought the property as an investment and for the tax write-off, but then changed his mind. He'd decided not to rent the expansive triplex, but to live in it himself. He was still ambivalent about whether he would eventually rent the one-bedroom rental duplex with a downstairs basement.

Working with Duncan Gilmore, his friend and investment adviser, Kyle's net worth had soared and when the Strivers' Row townhouse was put on the market, he'd met with the real estate agent, checkbook in hand. When the real estate agent showed him the property, she'd suggested that he live in one section of the townhouse and use the other part for his private practice. Kyle knew the beautifully renovated six-bedroom, six-bathroom, three-story townhouse was much too large for one person but he'd come to value his privacy and didn't want clients to know where he lived. Having worked for a prestigious corporate law firm had its advantages and disadvantages, the former being a generous six-figure salary and year-end bonuses. But it also meant having little time for himself.

Three years later, he and his childhood friends—Duncan and Ivan—bought another Harlem property, this one in the historic Mount Morris neighborhood.

Kyle deactivated the security system and walked into a small area between the kitchen, pantry and the first-floor deck. Kicking off his slip-ons, he left them on a mat and walked into the kitchen to put the gift-wrapped box containing a slice of wedding cake, a souvenir from Micah and Tessa's wedding, on the refrigerator shelf. After placing Ava's handbag on the granite countertop, he checked the wall phone. The display read: No Missed Calls. It wasn't often someone called his house, except for family members. No news was good news.

He had a habit of calling his parents on Sunday evenings for an update on what was going on in the family. The calls were actually not to hear the latest family gossip but to reassure his mother that he was alive and well.

Frances Chatham had been the most concerned when he revealed he was leaving his position with the corporate law firm to set up his own practice. She went on about his decision to give up a position that she and her contemporaries had struggled for so that he could have his piece of the American dream. What Kyle had to remind his mother was that he *was* a child of the Civil Rights Movement *and* had realized the American dream. He could choose where he wanted to practice law, and working to help those who couldn't afford the high-price, high-profile lawyers had always been a lifelong dream, and like the late Johnnie Cochran, Kyle wanted to champion and defend the underserved.

Throwing his suit jacket over his shoulder, he climbed the staircase to his bedroom. He wanted to take a shower and wash away the antiseptic smell associated with hospitals. Kyle hadn't wanted to think about Ava Warrick because he couldn't understand why he'd insinuated himself into the situation. Without thinking he'd slipped into the role of counselor with the intent of protecting his client.

Perhaps his eagerness stemmed from the fact that she had a brand-new car and he didn't want to leave her on the street waiting for her friend to come from Brooklyn. And if she wasn't able to contact her friend then she'd be at the mercy of any tow truck company out to make a quick buck. He'd gleaned from her driver's license that she lived on the Upper West Side, putting her three stops from his 135th subway station.

Walking into the master bedroom, he drew the silk drapes over the French doors leading to a Juliet balcony. Solar lamps lit up the backyard around an expansive deck surrounded by a flower garden with a stone fountain. Summer was already here and Kyle hadn't been outdoors to enjoy the warmer weather. All of his waking hours were spent working on a criminal case in which his client was implicated in the armed robbery of a bodega. Despite the D.A.'s overwhelming evidence against the teenager, Kyle believed the boy when he said he was innocent.

Emptying his pockets of loose change, a money clip and a small leather case with his driver's license and credit cards, he left them on the side table in an adjoining dressing room. He switched on the cell phone he'd turned off before entering the hospital. Seconds later it chimed a distinctive tone to let him know he'd missed a call. Scrolling through the features he groaned when he recognized the number. Kendra Alexander had called him three times.

Kyle had dated Kendra for a month, then told her that they had to stop seeing each other when she began to show signs of being emotionally unstable. His suggestion that she seek professional therapy was followed by a barrage of expletives he hadn't known existed, followed by inconsolable sobbing.

He'd referred her to his friend Ivan, a therapist, who

after a psychological evaluation referred her to a psychiatrist since she needed medication to control a bipolar
disorder. Even on medication, Kyle knew he wasn't
ready to deal with Kendra. If she'd been his wife then
he would've taken care of her, but he already had to deal
with his clients, who often had psychological, physical
and emotional problems. Everyone who was referred to
him was in crisis, and most of the time they didn't have
enough money for the initial consultation fee. He could
count on one hand those he had on retainer.

Before he even set up his practice, he knew the kinds
of problems he would encounter in a community like
Harlem with its widening gap between the haves and
have-nots. Brownstones that had once sold for five and
six figures now sold for millions.

Punching in the PIN for his voice mail, he listened
to the messages from Kendra: "Hi-eee, this is Ken. Call
me." Shaking his head, Kyle smiled, wondering why a
woman as feminine as Kendra would refer to herself
with a masculine name. "Call me, Kyle, when you get
this message." His smile grew wider. "I have a surprise
for you, so pul-lease call me back." He was tempted not
to listen to the last message because he really didn't
want to deal with anymore surprises—at least not for
twenty-four hours. Becoming a knight in shining armor
for Ava Warrick was enough. "I can't wait for you to call
me back, so I'm going to tell you that I'm pregnant and
I'm getting married next weekend. I know it is short
notice, but I'd love for you to come to the wedding. It's

going to be at my sister's house in Staten Island, so I hope you can make it."

Kyle's smile grew even wider. Although he wouldn't attend the wedding, he planned to send a gift card.

Remembering Ava's request to call her job, he reached for the number on the slip of paper he'd put into the breast pocket of his shirt. It took less than a minute to call the answering service and relay Ava's message, making certain the operator understood that Ava wouldn't return to work until she received medical clearance. He plugged the cell phone into a charger, stripped off his clothes, leaving them on a padded bench, then made his way into the marbled master bath with its heated steam shower, double sinks and tumbled marble floor.

He brushed his teeth, showered and after drying his body returned to the bedroom and fell across the crisp sheets. Although he'd closed his eyes, Kyle could still see Ava Warrick's bruised and swollen face. It was a long time before the image faded and he fell into a deep, dreamless sleep.

Ava returned to her room to find a strange man staring at the flickering images on an overhead television screen. He'd turned on the television, but the volume was turned down. It took her seconds to realize the man was Kyle Chatham. She hadn't recognized him in a pair of faded jeans, running shoes and a navy-blue golf shirt.

She'd had a CT scan, followed by a consultation with a neurosurgeon who'd reassured her that the pictures of her brain showed no evidence of bleeding or swelling. His recommendation: rest. The doctor cautioned her to avoid aspirin, as it increased the risk of bleeding. He'd also given her a referral to a neurosurgeon whose office was in her neighborhood.

"Are you going to need the chair?" the orderly asked Ava as she tried to stand.

"No," she said, pushing to her feet. "I think I'm good."

Kyle stood up when he heard Ava's voice. When he'd gotten up that morning he'd tried remembering if she had a trace of a southern accent. He recalled her saying her mother lived in D.C. and her father in North Carolina, which meant she had southern roots. The bruises on her face were darker, almost purple, but some of the swelling had gone down.

Picking up her handbag, he closed the distance between them and cupped her elbow. "Good morning."

Ava attempted what passed for a smile, but even the slightest gesture made her face ache. "Good morning, Kyle."

His eyebrows lifted. "Oh, you remember my name?"

"Yes, I do."

Not only had she remembered his name but also his face. He hadn't shaved and the stubble on his jaw enhanced his blatant masculinity. She wanted to tell Kyle that what she wanted to forget was the image staring back at her when she stared into the mirror earlier that morning. The skin around her left eye was frightfully swollen and a hideous bruise running from her eyebrow to her jaw made her look as if she'd been hit by a professional boxer.

"How are you feeling?" he asked.

Ava studied the man, who, despite her hitting his car, had come to her rescue. He'd assumed responsibility for towing her car and seeing that she'd received medical treatment.

"A lot better than I look."

"The bruises and swelling will go away in a few days," he said, reassuringly.

"That's what the doctor said."

"What else did he say?" Kyle asked.

"I'm going to have to rest, because healing is going to take time."

"What about your headaches?"

"I can take either acetaminophen or ibuprofen, but no aspirin. That's Tylenol, Advil or Motrin," Ava explained when Kyle gave her a puzzled look.

"Do you have any at your place?"

"Yes."

Kyle tightened his hold on her arm. "I believe you'll have to settle your account before you're officially discharged."

Ava closed her eyes again when a sharp pain settled over her left eye. "I'm ready." She was ready to go home, take a shower and get into her *own* bed.

Leaning heavily against Kyle for support, she followed him into the elevator. It was another twenty minutes before she settled the bill and found herself outside the hospital. Reaching into her bag, she took out a pair of sunglasses and slipped them on.

"I'm parked around the corner," Kyle said. He tightened his hold on her waist. "Take your time, Ava," he cautioned softly.

"If I walk any slower I'll be standing still," she countered.

"You're supposed to take it easy," he retorted. "The doctor's recommendation indicated that someone should check on you for at least twenty-four hours, and you may need to be awakened every two hours to make sure you're conscious. Do you have a neighbor or friend who can do that?"

"No. What I'll do is set my clock."

"What if you don't hear the clock?"

"Then I guess I won't wake up."

Kyle glared down at her. "That's not funny."

"Neither is having a concussion. I can't remember the last time I was sick. I managed to get through high school without missing a day of classes."

"I guess that's why you're such a stubborn patient."

Ava knew she was in no shape to engage in any verbal sparring with Kyle Chatham so she gritted her teeth and swallowed the sarcasm poised on the tip of her tongue. Even though she'd rear-ended him, Kyle was partially to blame because he'd slowed down too quickly. The sunglasses did little to block out the brilliant summer sunlight which only intensified her headache. It was only when he settled her in the low-slung sports car that she was able to close her eyes.

"How far downtown do you live?"

She opened her eyes and stared through the windshield. "I'm on Riverside Drive between 112th and 113th."

"I'll try to avoid the potholes."

Ava smiled, but it resembled a grimace. "Thank you." Those were the last two words she said as she closed her eyes again and settled back against the leather seat that smelled brand-new.

Whenever he stopped for a red light, Kyle glanced furtively at his passenger. He didn't know what to make of Ava Warrick. As she was being discharged, he'd learned that she was thirty-four, single and a certified social worker. She worked for an agency that provided social and psychiatric services to women and their children.

He knew she was trying to put up a brave front, but whenever she thought his attention was elsewhere, he saw her clench her teeth or ball her fingers into a fist. Her comment about making it through high school without an absence spoke volumes: she set unrealistic goals for herself.

Kyle wanted to tell her that he'd "been there, done that," working eighty-plus hours a week. When he was lead counsel on a case once, he'd locked himself in his office for thirty-six hours straight, leaving only to shower in the executive restroom and to change his clothes. His secretary ordered in for him, and when the day came for the trial he was running on pure adrenaline.

He won the case and the next day he flew down to the Caribbean, checked into a hotel room and slept around the clock. The billable fees and the firm's share from the suit earned him a six-figure bonus but the accolades weren't enough to make up for the stress and burnout.

He drove across 135th Street then turned south onto Broadway. Students from Columbia University filled the streets along with neighborhood residents taking advantage of the warm summer weather. Ava still hadn't stirred when he maneuvered onto Riverside Drive, thankful to find a parking space along the tree-lined street overlooking the Hudson River.

Reaching over, Kyle shook Ava gently. "We're here."

Ava awoke, her eyelids fluttering wildly. "That was quick."

"Nothing but the best from the Chatham car service," he said jokingly.

"I'm sorry I've caused you so much trouble."

"Don't apologize. Accidents happen."

"I know, but I want to make it up to you."

Shifting on her seat, Ava stared at the man beside her. When she'd come to New York from Washington, D.C., as a college freshman, her roommate had warned her that New Yorkers were known for minding their own business. If it didn't concern you then don't get involved. Kyle Chatham had broken that rule.

But the World Trade Center tragedy and the city's

campaign of See Something, Say Something changed a lot of New Yorkers. People had a different attitude. After living in the city for the past sixteen years, Ava still didn't feel she was a part of the pulsing metropolis.

Kyle smiled, the gesture so sensuous, Ava found herself catching her breath. "*Thank you* will be enough."

"No, Kyle, *thank you* is not enough for what you've done for me. You could've left me to fend for myself, but you didn't."

"I would've done the same for anyone."

"Even a man?"

"Well, maybe not."

"So, you did it because I'm a woman?"

The seconds ticked off. "Yes," Kyle confirmed. "It's because you are a woman. Do you see that as a problem?"

"Not in the least. It's refreshing to know that there are still good black men around."

He inclined his head. "Thank you. I take it you haven't met too many you can call 'good black men.'"

"I don't know what it is about me, but I seem to attract the worst."

Kyle winked at her. "Don't beat up on yourself, Ava, because dudes go through the same thing."

"You have it better than most women. You have a wider pool to select."

"That, Miss Warrick, is debatable. Which building is yours?" he asked, changing the topic.

"It's the one closest to 112th."

The co-op apartments in the pre-war, high-rise

building facing the river had spectacular views of the river and New Jersey. The building had retained its original architectural details and had a canopy-covered entrance with a full-time doorman. Ava had thought she was blessed when a former Columbia University professor offered to sublet his apartment for two years when he and his wife accepted teaching positions in Saudi Arabia. She sat, waiting for Kyle to come around and help her out of the car. He opened the passenger-side door, extended his hand and pulled her gently to her feet. His arm went around her waist as he led her across the street to the entrance of her apartment building.

The expression on the doorman's face was shock. "I was in an accident last night," she explained.

The doorman's gaze went from Ava to the tall man supporting her body. "Are you all right, Miss Warrick?"

"I'm sure I will be in a few days, Max. Thank you for asking."

"If you need anything, please call me."

"Thank you."

If you need anything, please call me, Kyle mused. Max was staring at Ava as if she were a frothy concoction he wanted to devour. He knew firsthand that New York City doormen knew as much about their building's tenants as the FBI. They were aware of who came and went, which magazines they subscribed to and who had a problem making their mortgage payments and maintenance fees. The reason he'd sold his condo to buy the townhouse was because his doormen knew too much of his business. The straw that broke the proverbial camel's back was when one of the nighttime doormen called his then-current girlfriend by a former girlfriend's name. Unfortunately the name was the same as her best friend's, and she'd accused him of creeping. Despite having dated a lot of women he'd never cheated on any of them.

He led Ava into the vestibule and across a richly appointed lobby to a bank of elevators. The doors to one car opened, they walked in and Ava pushed a button. The doors closed, the elevator rose smoothly, quickly and stopped at the fifteenth floor.

Kyle went completely still when the doors opened. He stared at wall-to-wall glass and a curving staircase leading to an upper floor. He knew he would've kept his condo if it had been a duplex with these panoramic views of the city.

Ava walked out of the elevator and dropped her handbag on a side table in the foyer. "I've been apartment-sitting for the past year," she said over her shoulder.

He stared at her hips in the fitted jeans as she crossed the parquet floor to draw the drapes. The night before, he'd deliberately ignored her lush body in the revealing jeans and T-shirt because her injuries took precedence. But now he was able to stare at her—all of her, finding everything about Ava undeniably feminine. She wasn't tall or short, heavy or too slim, but her full breasts and hips categorized her as a curvy woman.

"Where did you live before?"

Ava turned and gave him a long, penetrating stare. "I shared an apartment in the East Village."

"Was your ex-roommate a man?"

"How did you know?"

"If it'd been a woman you wouldn't have hesitated."

Ava sat down on a tapestry-covered armchair, resting her feet on a matching footstool. "You're really perceptive."

Kyle approached her and sat on a silk-upholstered Louis xv bergère. "It comes with being an attorney."

Pressing the back of her head to the chair, Ava closed her eyes. "Are you a good attorney?"

"That's something you would have to ask my clients."

She opened her eyes and smiled. "My, my, my, aren't you modest?"

"Why would you say that?"

"Most lawyers I know are brash, aggressive and pretentious."

Kyle bit back a smile. "You're tarring lawyers with a pretty broad brush."

"You don't deny that you're an arrogant lot?"

"I can't speak for all of us, Ava. But on the other hand, the same can be said for social workers."

"What about us, Kyle?"

"You're a bunch of bleeding-heart liberals who believe they have all the answers to the world's social ills."

"Try sensitive, compassionate and benevolent."

Looping one leg over the opposite knee, Kyle stared at the toe of his running shoe. He'd forgotten to add *feisty.* Bruised and obviously still in pain there was still a lot of fight in the sexy social worker. "Perhaps we can debate the merits of our professions over dinner or drinks—whichever you prefer."

Ava recognized the silent expectation in the deep-set, slanting, catlike warm-brown eyes. Unable to tear her gaze away from Kyle's chiseled cheekbones and close-cropped black hair with a sprinkling of gray, she wanted him to leave so she could get into bed. But she also wanted him to stay because it'd been a long time since she'd had the opportunity to talk to a man who wasn't involved with the women or children on her caseload.

"Are you asking me out, Kyle Chatham?" He flashed the sensual smile she found so endearing.

"What does it sound like, Ava Warrick?"

She smiled through the dull throbbing in her head. "It sounds like a date."

"Then it is. You were the one who said you wanted to make it up to me, and you can if you have dinner with me. Of course, when you're feeling better," he added.

Ava massaged her temples with her fingertips. "Okay."

Pushing to his feet, Kyle walked over to Ava and cradled her chin in his hand. "Don't bother setting your clock. I'll call you."

"There's no need for you to do that."

"Yes, there is," he countered. "Someone's supposed to check on you every two hours for the next twenty-four. Either you give me your number or I'll hang out here until tomorrow."

"Haven't you done enough for me?"

"I just want to make certain you won't renege on your promise to make it up to me."

Ava swiped at his hand. "I never would've said so if I didn't mean it."

"That's why I intend to keep you honest."

"Oh, no, you didn't. It's not too often that *lawyer* and *honest* are uttered in the same breath."

"See, Ava, that's why we have to talk." Reaching into the pocket of his jeans, Kyle took out his cell phone. "Come now, give me the number to this place and your cell." He programmed her name and both numbers, then leaned over and helped her stand. "Come and lock the door. I'll talk to you in a couple of hours."

She walked Kyle to the door, opened it and then closed it behind him. Ava tried putting what had happened over the past twelve hours into perspective but everything seemed to merge before coming apart like a thousand pieces of a jigsaw puzzle. She knew she had to rest and wait for the pieces to come together.

It took twice as long as it normally did for her to shower and ready herself for bed, and instead of climbing the staircase to the second-floor bedroom, she selected one off the alcove near the kitchen. Carrying a cordless extension, she got into bed, pulled a sheet and lightweight blanket over her body and closed her eyes.

The incessant ringing of the telephone penetrated the comfort of her deep sleep, forcing Ava to open her eyes. The shades in the room were drawn, making it impossible for her to discern the time of day. Patting the mattress, her fingers curved around the receiver. She managed to find the Talk button after several attempts.

"Hello." Her voice, still heavy from sleep, had dropped an octave.

"Ava, it's Kyle."

A dreamy smile parted her lips. His deep voice came through the earpiece like watered silk. "How are you?"

"I'm good, Kyle."

"You sound sleepy. Did I wake you up?"

"Yes."

"Good."

"Good?" she asked.

"Yes. That's means you're conscious."

"I was sleeping, not unconscious, Kyle."

"Thank goodness for that. Do you want me to call you again in another two hours?"

Ava sighed softly. "Call me again in four hours."

"Are you sure?"

"I'm very sure, counselor." She smiled when his laugh caressed her ear. "Thank you for checking up on me."

"You're very welcome. I'll talk to you later."

A click signaled that Kyle had hung up. Ava lay staring up at the shadows on the ceiling. She didn't know why the lawyer had taken an interest in her well-being, and she didn't want to believe he had an ulterior motive. When it came to men, her batting average hovered close to triple zeros.

It'd been more than a year since her last date and two years since a man had shared her bed. The only thing she'd missed when she'd ended her relationship with Will Marshall was the intimacy. The lovemaking between them ran the gamut from hot to cold depending on their interaction, yet there had never been a time when they got into bed together that they didn't cuddle. Waking up, limbs entwined, was the perfect way to begin a day.

Ava knew she would've continued to cohabitate with her live-in lover if he hadn't felt the need to monitor every aspect of her life. After a while she felt as if she were a parolee having to check in with her parole officer. In the end she had to leave Will or she would have fared no better than the victimized women she counseled.

She didn't want to repeat her mother's mistakes. Alice Warrick had fallen in love with and married a man to whom she'd surrendered her will. Charles Warrick made every decision for his wife and children until their youngest left home to go to college. A week later, Alice served her husband with divorce papers, citing emotional abuse and lack of communication. Alice's decision to take control of her life was the impetus for Ava to leave her job as an elementary school teacher and go into social work.

The pounding in her forehead intensified, and Ava knew she had to get up and take some Tylenol. She'd predicted that she'd be out of work for a couple of days. But with this severe pain that made it nearly impossible to think clearly, she knew it would be longer. The note the neurosurgeon had given her said she'd be unable to return to work until she was medically cleared.

Ava went into the bathroom and after swallowing two Tylenol capsules with a full glass of water, she returned to the bedroom to lie across the bed. The medication worked quickly and when she closed her eyes she forgot about the pain and the incredibly handsome man who'd unknowingly become her knight in shining armor.

Chapter 3

Kyle walked out of his brownstone and into a blanket-ing fog so thick it was virtually impossible to see more than a few feet in front of him. The humidity intensified the different odors of the big city—the smell of fuel from passing cars and buses was magnified in the thick air.

In the past he'd taken the subway downtown to his office, but the days of taking the iron horse to work was relegated to the past. The brownstone where he'd set up his office was less than a mile away, and he usually made the walk from 139th Street and Frederick Douglass Boulevard to 121st Street and Adam Clayton Powell Boulevard in under half an hour.

On the days he jogged, he made it in ten minutes. The

closet in his private office was filled with suits, slacks, shirts, jackets, ties and underwear. An adjoining full bathroom was stocked with his favorite cologne and grooming supplies.

Lately Kyle found himself spending more hours at the brownstone than he did at home. His caseload had doubled after he'd won a high-profile case—the accidental shooting death of a teenage girl by a bank guard trying to prevent a robbery. Kyle brought a suit against the bank *and* the security company for negligence because the retired police officer had failed to go for his mandated firearms training update.

He'd expected a long and drawn-out litigation until he'd uncovered information that the guard, who wore glasses, hadn't had an eye exam in more than five years. Rather than go through a lengthy trial, the case ended with a multimillion-dollar settlement to the parents of the dead child, who was a musical prodigy. The case was closely followed by the local dailies. Rarely a week went by when Kyle's name or photo didn't appear in the *New York Amsterdam News,* and winning the case turned him into a local celebrity.

He'd gotten out of bed before his alarm went off because of the disturbing dream he'd had about losing a case in which his young client ended up serving a long prison term. After several attempts, he got out of bed, went into his den and watched a video of last year's Super Bowl and the 2008 World Series highlights.

* * *

Kyle made it to the corner and flagged down a passing taxi. He didn't mind walking in the rain or snow, but not fog. There was something about not being able to see where he was going that was unnerving. Settling into the back seat, he gave the cabbie the address and the cross streets. The weather made it impossible for motorists to go more than a few feet before having to stop for a red light. The cabbie signaled then maneuvered around a bus, tires spinning and slipping on the oil-slick roadway.

"Slow down, my man," Kyle called out from the rear of the cab. "I'm not in that much of a hurry."

Every Monday he went into the office two hours before his staff arrived to review open cases before their weekly staff meeting. He'd started up his practice sharing a full- and a part-time receptionist and the cost of a cleaning service with Ivan and Duncan. Then he'd added a full-time paralegal, an office manager, a legal secretary and recently, a part-time paralegal who'd once worked as a court stenographer. A former colleague had asked to join the firm as a partner because he, too, had tired of the heavy workload at corporate law firms, but Kyle told him that he would have to get back to him. Jordan Wainwright was a highly skilled litigator, but the question was, did he have the sensitivity to work well with the residents of the Harlem community?

The cabbie executed another maneuver, prompting Kyle to knock on the partition. "Hey, brother, your tip depends on you getting me to where I want to go look-ing the same as I did when I got in this taxi." Thank-fully the driver got the message and slowed down. Kyle didn't want a repeat of Saturday night's visit to the hospital.

As promised, he called Ava four hours later, knowing her sleepy, husky voice would send shivers up his spine. There was something about her that had him thinking what his grandmother referred to as "impure thoughts." Impure or not, Ava Warrick had him thinking about her when he least expected to.

Reaching into the pocket of his suit jacket, he pulled out his cell phone and punched speed dial. The tele-phone rang three times before he heard her voice.

"Hello."

Kyle smiled. "Good morning, sunshine."

"Where are you, Kyle?"

"Why?"

"I'm asking because I'm looking out the window and the fog is so heavy I can't see across the river."

"I'm in a cab on my way to work."

"Why so early?"

"I always go in early on Mondays. How are you feeling?" he asked.

"I'm much better than yesterday," Ava admitted. "I just have to be careful that I don't bend over. When I do it feels as if all of the blood in my body is rushing to my head."

"Don't try to do too much too soon."

"Okay, Daddy."

Kyle frowned. The last thing he wanted to be was her father. "I don't mean to sound like your—"

"You could never be my father, Kyle," Ava snapped, interrupting him.

"I didn't mean it that way."

There came a beat before Ava said, "I'm sorry I snapped at you. You didn't deserve that."

"Apology accepted. What are you doing for dinner?"

"I plan to eat leftovers."

"Forget about the leftovers. I'll bring dinner."

"You don't have to, Kyle."

He smiled. "But I want to. What don't you eat?"

There came another pause. "I don't like yellow squash," Ava admitted.

Kyle laughed. "I'll be certain to leave it off the menu. Expect me sometime after six."

"I'll be here waiting."

I'll be here waiting. Ava's promise was etched in his mind even after he ended the call. Kyle knew he wanted to see her again as much to see if she was all right as to assuage his curiosity about a woman who piqued his interest in a way no one had in a very long time.

She wasn't as beautiful as some of the women he'd dated, yet she claimed her own special beauty that he found irresistible. She was outspoken, a trait he admired in a woman, and she was intelligent, something that was requisite for any woman with whom he found himself involved.

"You can let me out here," Kyle instructed the driver.

He handed him a bill, exited the cab and sprinted the short distance to the brownstone. The three-story structure had come with twelve rooms, nine of them bedrooms, as well as four bathrooms and multiple fireplaces.

Kyle, Ivan and Duncan had hired an architect to re-configure the nineteenth-century landmark structure from personal to business use. They'd added an elevator and the vestibule was expanded into a waiting area with comfortable leather furniture, wall-mounted flat-screen televisions and potted plants. During the winter months a fire roared around the clock in the huge fireplaces.

Duncan's financial planning firm occupied the first floor, Kyle's law practice the second and Ivan's psycho-therapy practice was on the third. The street-level space was transformed to include a gym with showers, a modern state-of-the-art kitchen, a dining room and a game room.

Kyle climbed the stairs to the entrance, unlocked the front door and disarmed the alarm. Closing the stained-glass doors behind him, he reset the alarm and took the stairs to the second floor instead of the elevator. He was seated behind his desk, perusing a case file when his legal secretary stuck her head through the partially opened door.

"Good morning, Kyle."

He glanced up, smiling. Cherise Robinson's neatly braided sandy-brown hair framed a light brown face with an abundance of freckles dotting her nose and cheeks. Her cheeks were bright red, which meant she'd spent some time in the sun.

Cherise had come highly recommended by an elderly neighborhood attorney who'd suffered a mild stroke. On the advice of his wife and doctor, the attorney had decided to retire. Kyle hired the man's legal secretary, paralegal and office manager. Not only had the three worked together for many years, but they knew the ins and outs of a legal practice.

"Good morning, Cherise."

"What time is this morning's staff meeting?"

He glanced at the clock on the credenza. It was eight-fifty. "Is everyone here?" Although usually easygoing, Kyle was finicky when it came to being punctual. He allowed for the occasional bus or subway delays, but not the mundane excuses of oversleeping or broken alarm clocks. He paid his employees well and expected nothing short of perfection from them.

"All present and accounted for."

"Tell them we're meeting at nine-thirty."

She nodded. "I'll let everyone know."

Kyle returned his attention to the file in front of him. He'd spent the past ninety minutes reading and rereading all the notes on the case of a nineteen-year-old boy charged with robbing and assaulting the owner of a local bodega. The owner of the store had identified his client in a lineup as the one who'd hit him across the face with a gun, fracturing his jaw and knocking out teeth, before jumping the counter and taking several hundred dollars from the cash register. His client, despite having protested his innocence, had had an argument with the store owner the day before, telling him he was going to "come back and get him."

Although he had witnesses who said his client was with them during the time of the robbery, the A.D.A. claimed the pictures from a closed-circuit camera put his client at the scene. Initially, the hard-nosed assistant district attorney refused to grant bail until Kyle insisted that his client didn't pose a flight risk. Unfortunately his client's witnesses weren't model citizens, all having priors for petty crimes.

Kyle knew there was something his client was withholding from him, but so far he hadn't been able to crack the hard shell the teenager had affected so as not to appear "soft" to his "boyz." It wouldn't matter whether he was hard or soft once he was sent upstate to a prison with men who'd been incarcerated more years than he'd been alive.

There was something about the teenager that reminded Kyle of himself when he'd run with the wrong crowd. Elwin's "you'll come to no good end" echoed in his mind. The difference was that at fourteen he was a juvenile and therefore he'd been given a second chance. But if he didn't find something to prove Rashaun Hayden's innocence, then the boy would become another one of the growing number of young men warehoused in state prisons.

A slight frown creased his forehead. Leaning over, he punched the speaker button on the telephone console. "Cherise, please get in touch with A.D.A. Clarkson and tell him I need a set of photos from the Hayden robbery."

"I'm on it, Kyle."

"Thank you, Cherise."

Kyle had glanced at the grainy photos, but thought they needed closer examination. He closed the file. The trial was scheduled to begin in another month, but four weeks wasn't enough time to prepare a case when most of the evidence pointed to Rashaun's guilt.

He went through the other files, reading the updates until Cherise returned to tell him that everyone had gathered in the conference room. "I'll be right in."

Pushing to his feet, Kyle gathered the files, walked out of his office and into the conference room where he held meetings and met with clients and their family members. A gleaming cherrywood table and eight leather-covered chairs sat in the middle of the large room. One wall of built-in shelves was stacked with law books and journals. A trio of tall windows occupied another wall, while the remaining two were brick, one with a large working fireplace. An assortment of breakfast breads, fresh fruit, pitchers of freshly squeezed juice and carafes of coffee and hot water for tea filled a corner table.

The office manager had gotten the staff to donate a few dollars each week to have breakfast in the office to offset the exorbitant prices for specialty coffees and sweet breads until Kyle instructed her to take the money out of the office petty cash.

He filled a cup with coffee, adding a dollop of cream, and carried it to the table, which had been covered with place mats to protect its surface. Sitting down, he stared at his staff. Kyle marveled at the fact that he'd inherited an intelligent, experienced group of people who came to work on time and utilized their skills to grow the practice. With the exception of Cherise, who'd recently celebrated her thirty-fifth birthday, everyone else was older than him.

He opened a file. "We're going to start with Hector Lonzo's hit-and-run." Kyle looked at Mercedes Quiñones, the full-time bilingual paralegal. "Did you get Mr. Lonzo's wife's statement?"

Mercedes nodded. She'd recently cut her curly black hair, much to the chagrin of her husband of twenty-eight years, because she claimed long graying hair made her look older. "I spoke to her late Friday night. I have everything on tape, and I just have to translate it."

Kyle smiled. "Good."

It took less than an hour to go over the case-file updates, and when everyone stood up to leave the room Kyle asked Cherise to stay. "I need you to send a bouquet of flowers to someone." He scrawled Ava's name and address on a sheet of paper, handing it to her.

Her reddish eyebrows lifted. "What kind of flowers do you want?"

He thought for a moment. "See if they have peach-colored roses. If not, then pink. The message should read: Hope you are feeling better, and my name."

"How many roses do you want to send, Kyle?"

"Two dozen and I'd like them delivered before this evening."

"I'm on it."

A hint of a smile parted Kyle's lips at Cherise's trade-mark rejoinder. "I know you are," he said.

She blushed furiously then turned and walked out of the room. Kyle knew he'd embarrassed her but he hadn't meant to. When he'd bragged to Duncan and Ivan that his employees were superior to theirs it had begun an undeclared cold war among the childhood friends. Kyle felt closer to Ivan and Duncan than to his career-army-officer brother Kenneth, with whom he seldom spoke. Although Kenneth was stationed stateside, it was his sister-in-law who sent Kyle Christmas cards with up-dated pictures of his school-age nephews. His sister Sandra had a special place in his heart. She'd recently moved to Arizona with her husband and toddlers, and never failed to e-mail pictures of her adorable little girls.

He'd poured his second cup of coffee when Duncan Gilmore walked in. Duncan was the most complex of the trio. An even six feet, he cut an incredibly handsome figure in his Brioni suit and accessories. However, all of the sartorial splendor couldn't disguise the sadness in Duncan's beautifully modulated voice and occasion-ally too-bright smile. Women of all races and ethnic groups were drawn to his olive coloring, chiseled fea-tures and close-cropped curly black hair.

His friend had suffered a series of losses, beginning with his single mother, who died from a blood clot in her lung the year Duncan turned fourteen, to losing his fiancée on September eleventh. Having never known his father, Duncan had gone to live with a school-teacher aunt in Brooklyn who had recognized his mathematical genius and encouraged him to work beyond his potential. He graduated with honors from Brooklyn Technical High School, then enrolled in Baruch College for a degree in business. He had returned to college five years later to earn an MBA from Pace University.

It'd been eight years since Duncan had lost the love of his life, and he had yet to form a lasting relationship with any of the women he dated. He had been the least commitment-shy of the three, but that had changed.

Kyle was shocked when Duncan had announced after his fiancée's death that he intended never to marry or father children. Ivan went from being a friend to being a therapist, but Duncan had refused to listen to him. They'd allowed their friend to grieve in private, and nearly eight years later he was still grieving.

The two men bumped fists, a gesture they used when greeting each other. "What's up, DG?" Kyle asked Duncan.

"That's what I came to ask you," Duncan countered. "How was the wedding?"

Kyle smiled. "It was spectacular. The bride was beautiful, the groom handsome and the bridal attendants were luscious-looking."

"Did you meet anyone?" Duncan asked, smiling.

"The bride's sister was really gorgeous, but unfortunately I didn't know at the time I was trying to hit on her that she was already taken."

"I guess you win some and you lose some."

"It's okay, because she's what I consider geographically undesirable. The lady lives in White Plains."

Duncan whistled softly. "Westchester County roads can be a bitch. Some of their parkways flood quickly and the one time I tried driving along one of the local roads in the snow I almost wrecked a rental car."

Attractive lines fanned out around Kyle's eyes when his smile widened. "I don't have a problem dating Big Apple sisters or those from the other boroughs." Duncan nodded, but didn't say anything. "What are you doing for the Fourth?" This year the Fourth of July fell on a Saturday and Kyle planned to close his office that Friday and not reopen until Tuesday to give his employees a four-day holiday weekend.

Duncan picked a stray raisin off the table and popped it into his mouth. "Right now I'm open, but Ivan mentioned something about having a cookout at his place."

Ivan owned a brownstone in the Mount Morris Historic District two blocks from their offices. "If he doesn't want to do it, then I will," Kyle volunteered. "I haven't sat outside or used the grill since last year."

Resting a hand on Kyle's shoulder over a starched white shirt, Duncan leaned closer. "Please tell Ivan you'll do it. If I have to eat another hockey puck masquerading as a hamburger I'm going to go ape-shit and hurt Dr. Ivan Campbell. The man can't cook for nothing!"

"Hear! Hear!" Kyle intoned, bumping fists with Duncan. "That settles it. We'll hang out at my place."

Duncan flashed a wide smile. "Thanks, buddy. You just saved a thirty-year friendship." He glanced at his watch. "I have to meet a client in a few minutes. We'll talk later."

Kyle waited for the financial planner to leave before gathering his files and returning to his office. There was something Mercedes had said that made him believe Rashaun Hayden was covering for someone, someone who might have threatened him if he decided to snitch. The street code of "snitches get stitches" prompted many defendants to take the rap for someone else.

The elder Haydens had emptied their bank account to hire private legal counsel for their only child, feeling that a public defender wouldn't fight to keep their son out of jail. Kyle was charging them half his hourly fee because he believed Rashaun was innocent. Sitting down at his desk, he picked up the phone and dialed the Hayden residence. Rashaun answered after the second ring.

"Hey, this is Ras."

"It's 'Hello,' Rashaun. How do you expect a jury to believe you when you come across like that?"

"I'm sorry, Mr. C. I thought you was one of my boys."

Kyle wanted to ask the teenager if he cut English classes, because he invariably screwed up his verb tenses. "The name is Chatham, not C, and, Rashaun, I need to see you."

"When, Mr. Chatham?"

"I want you to ask either your mother or father to call me so I can set up an appointment."

"Do I have to come?"

"Yes, Rashaun, you *have* to come."

"What do you want to talk about, Mr. Chatham?"

Kyle leaned back in his executive chair. There was a thread of anxiousness in his client's voice that hadn't been there before. "You'll find out when we all meet."

"Have you found out who really jacked up that lying bitch?"

"I want you to listen real good, Rashaun, because I'm only going to say this once. Clean up your mouth or I'll have the judge revoke your bail and you'll find yourself back in Rikers at the mercy of some inmate who'd be happy to make *you* his bitch before he passes you around to his buddies for cigarettes."

There was complete silence on the other end of the line. Kyle knew he had gotten through to the cocky young man who believed doing a "bid" would enhance his street cred. What Rashaun failed to understand was that going to prison was not a walk in the park. He was facing a sentence of ten to fifteen years, with the possibility of parole in eight years. And a lot could happen to him in eight years.

"Now that I have your attention, please let your parents know I called and that I want them to contact me as soon as possible."

"Yes, Mr. Chatham."

"Thank you, Rashaun."

Kyle ended the call, annoyed that he had to go there with the young man. He didn't know where Rashaun had gotten the idea that going to prison was a badge of honor. Kyle had grown up with boys who'd gone to prison, only to return either hardened or broken men. Some were never able to assimilate afterwards and become a part of society, shut out from certain jobs because of their criminal backgrounds.

The intercom rang and he pushed the speaker button. "Yes, Cherise?"

"I ordered the flowers. They'll be delivered to Miss Warrick before three today."

"Good." Kyle made another call to the owner of one of his favorite neighborhood restaurants.

"Good morning. This is Leroi's"

"Good morning, Pearl. This is Kyle Chatham. Is your husband available to come to the phone?"

"Sure, Kyle. Leroi's right here."

"What's shaking, brother?" said a deep, booming voice.

"I need a favor."

"Name it," Leroi said without hesitating.

"I want to buy a steak from you."

"Buy a steak or you want me to cook a steak?"

Kyle knew Leroi probably thought he was losing his mind. "I want to buy two uncooked strip steaks from you. I'd prefer if they were aged." He usually ordered his steaks directly from Peter Luger's butcher shop, but the dry-aged strip and porterhouse steaks in his freezer were frozen solid. He'd suggested to Duncan they have the cookout at his place because it'd been a while since he'd entertained outdoors and he wanted to broil those steaks before they developed freezer burn.

"How large do you want them?" Leroi asked?

"Not too large." Kyle planned to make steak au poivre.

"I have a few aged ones weighing approximately sixteen and twenty ounces."

"Don't you have anything smaller?"

"Nope. It sounds like a lot of meat, but it won't be after you broil it."

"Wrap up two for me, and I'll pick them up around five."

"I can have someone run it over to you, Kyle."

"You don't have to do that, Leroi."

"Yeah, I do. After all, you helped me out when you got that fraud to drop her lawsuit when she claimed she found bugs in her salad. I'm sending the steaks and think of them as a gift from me and the missus."

"Only this time, Leroi."

"No problem, brother."

Kyle hung up. Normally he wouldn't accept a gift or gifts from his clients, but he knew it was useless to argue with Leroi, *and* he needed a premium cut of thawed beef.

The morning and afternoon passed quickly for Kyle. He stopped long enough to order a Caesar salad with grilled chicken from a nearby deli. Mrs. Hayden returned his call, and he set up an appointment to meet with her, her son and husband the following week.

Tonight his focus was on seeing Ava again. He stopped at a local grocer to pick up what he needed to go with his steak dinner, and then he hailed a taxi to take him to Morningside Heights.

A different doorman was on duty when he stepped out of the taxi. He gave the man his name, waiting while he called Ava's apartment. "Miss Warrick is expecting you, Mr. Chatham."

The doors to an elevator opened as he approached and Kyle stepped inside and punched the button for the fifteenth floor. When the doors opened and he saw Ava Warrick standing there waiting for him, he hadn't realized how much he'd missed her or how fast his heart was beating.

Chapter 4

Ava gave Kyle a dazzling smile. "What on earth did you bring?" she asked, pointing at the shopping bags he held in each hand.

Kyle winked at her. "Dinner."

It'd been a little more than twenty-four hours since he'd last seen Ava, and she'd changed dramatically. Her hair was a mass of tiny curls that hugged her head like a cap. She wore a pair of black cropped pants that showed off her shapely legs, black ballet-type flats and a white sleeveless V-neck blouse that displayed toned arms and shoulders. There was still a hint of swelling along the left side of her face and the angry bruise was changing color from deep purple to a sickly greenish-yellow.

Ava reached for one of the bags, but Kyle tightened his grip on the handles. "I've got this."

She flashed an attractive moue. "Oh, it's like that?"

Lowering her head, he pressed his mouth to her un-injured cheek. "Yes, it is. Where's the kitchen?"

"Follow me." Ava led the way through a hallway and into one of the two kitchens in the duplex.

Kyle walked into a kitchen designed for cooking and entertaining. Hollyberry-red cabinetry was a shocking contrast to stainless-steel appliances and neutral-colored walls, granite gray-and-black countertops and back-splashes resembling a mosaic. There was a built-in microwave/convection oven, sub-zero fridge, a wine cellar and a side-by-side commercial refrigerator.

"I love your kitchen." He was unable to disguise the surprise in his voice.

Folding her arms under her breasts, Ava leaned a hip against the countertop. "I wish I could claim it as mine. I'll live here until next summer. After that I'll have to look for another apartment. I've been thinking about buying a co-op but I'm not certain where I'd like to live."

Kyle took off his suit jacket and hung it over the back of a stool. Removing his cufflinks, he rolled back his cuffs and began emptying the canvas bags. "Where are the owners?"

"They're involved in a project in Saudi Arabia. Pro-fessor Servinsky lived in this apartment with his first wife for more than twenty years before she passed away in her sleep. After several years he began dating his neighbor, who was also a widow. He didn't want to give up his apartment and it was the same with her, so they renovated, turning the two into a duplex. There are three bedrooms on this floor and three upstairs. Each also has a small bedroom off the kitchen, commonly known as the maid's room. Mrs. Servinsky removed the wall between two upstairs bedrooms and set it up as a solarium."

"Where do they sleep?"

"They sleep down here and entertain upstairs."

"Where's your bedroom?"

"Upstairs. I'll show you around later," Ava promised. "Would you like some help?"

Kyle gave her a sidelong glance as he emptied plastic bags of cucumbers, bell peppers, a lemon, tomatoes, scallions and baking potatoes into the sink. The contents of the other bag yielded small containers of fresh mint, garlic, feta cheese and bottles of olive oil and red wine. Her gaze widened when he unwrapped strip steaks with a liberal amount of marbling.

"No. I want you to sit and do absolutely nothing. How do you like your steak?"

"Well done." The seconds ticked off as she watched Kyle navigate his way around the kitchen as if it were something he did often, opening cabinets for bowls and platters and a drawer with an assortment of knives.

Unable to tolerate complete silence, Ava got up and turned on the radio positioned under a cabinet. The melodious sound of Whitney Houston singing "You Give Good Love" filled the kitchen.

Shifting, she stared at the width of Kyle's broad shoulders under the white shirt. "I want to thank you for the flowers. They're beautiful."

The flowers had been delivered to the apartment when she'd been on the telephone with her supervisor. Earlier that morning she'd scanned the doctor's note and faxed it to her office. Within an hour she was inundated by a number of telephone calls from her coworkers asking if she was okay or if she needed them to do something for her. The outpouring of support was somewhat unexpected because the atmosphere in the agency had been somewhat strained under the current administration. Threats of resignations were rampant, and Ava was seriously considering looking for another position at the end of the year. She'd had another offer to work for a private agency, but hadn't wanted to leave the city-funded agency and the disenfranchised clients who came with a myriad of social and mental-health issues.

He inclined his head in acknowledgment. "I'm glad you like them."

She approached Kyle, watching as he manipulated the pullout kitchen faucet, rinsing the vegetables. The heat from his body and the subtle scent of his cologne wafted into her nose. He looked and smelled good.

"Where did you learn to cook?"

Kyle gave Ava a quick glance. "Before my dad retired, he worked as a chef for the railroad. My mother loved when he was home because she didn't have to cook. Once we were tall enough to look over the stove he taught his children."

"At what age did you learn?" Ava asked.

"I had to be eight or nine. My younger brother flat-out refused, while my sister and I became proficient enough so that we could put together an entire meal by the time we were teens. Are you an only child?" Kyle asked, deftly switching the topic from himself to Ava.

"No. There're four of us: two boys and two girls. My older brother is a warden at a prison in Texas and my younger brother is a naval officer. The last I heard is that he's aboard a submarine somewhere in the world. My sister Aisha is nine months pregnant and she and her husband are waiting for the birth of their first child."

"What does your sister do?"

"She's a teacher."

"How many grandchildren will it make for your parents?"

"It will be their first. Curtis—he's the warden—just got married last year but I believe he and his wife have decided not to have children, while Calvin professes to be a confirmed bachelor."

Kyle washed and blotted the moisture from the steak with paper toweling. "What about yourself?"

"What about me?" Ava asked, answering his question with one of her own.

"Were you ever married, or have you come close to marrying?"

"No."

"Do you want to get married?" he asked.

"No," Ava repeated.

Kyle stopped rubbing sea salt, fresh cracked pepper-corn and Dijon mustard onto the steaks and dredged each side with pepper and olive oil. "I always thought most women wanted to marry and have children."

Resting her elbows on the glass-topped table next to the sink, she stared directly at his distinctive profile. "I suppose I'm not like most women."

"Don't you want children?"

She nodded. "Yes."

"But you don't want to marry? She nodded again. "You plan to be a baby mama?"

A hint of a smile curved her mouth. "No. What I'd be is a single mother."

Kyle's eyebrows lifted. "Is there a difference?"

"Of course there is," Ava stated emphatically. "A baby mama is a woman without a husband or a man in her life. A single mother can be divorced, widowed or she can adopt a child without the benefit of marriage."

"Do you intend to adopt?"

"Yes. There're so many of our children languishing in foster homes that it's criminal. Once I have a perma-nent residence I plan to go through the adoption process for a school-age child."

Kyle stared at Ava, his admiration for her surpassing his interest in her as a woman. He found her physically appealing, but her intelligence and sense of purpose as

to what she wanted to do with her life were pleasant surprises. He'd met so many women whose sole focus was
landing a "good black man" that he'd stopped asking
them what they wanted for their futures. It was as if
they'd all gone to the same school and taken the same
courses. Despite their complaints, there were a lot of
available good black men if only they looked in the
right places, *and* more importantly, were not willing to
settle for anything in a pair of trousers.

He'd cautioned his sister, Sandra, to stay out of the
clubs if she was looking for someone with whom she
could plan a future, because he'd been there and done
that. Most times he'd trolled the clubs looking to pick
up someone for a one-night stand or brief encounter.
That had been a time in his life he'd rather forget
because each time he ended a relationship he lost a little
bit of himself in the process. After a while Kyle realized
if he didn't intend to commit to a relationship of long
duration, then he had to be forthcoming and let the
woman know that.

Once he was able to state his intentions he was able
to date women without any guilt or angst about taking
advantage of them. Most of them gave him his walking
papers; one told him that she was more than happy with
her single status. They had dated exclusively for a year
until her job forced her to relocate to Tampa, Florida.

"You're an extraordinary woman."

"You know nothing about me."

"I may not know all about what makes Ava Warrick

who she is, but I find you very different from a lot of other women I've met."

"Don't you mean 'slept with'?"

Kyle went completely still and glared at her. "Is that what you believe? That I sleep with every woman I either meet or date?"

"Don't you?" Ava asked, answering his question with one of her own.

A smile softened his even features. "I wish."

Ava's jaw dropped. "You what?"

"I wish I had the opportunity *and* stamina to sleep with every woman I've ever known."

"You have ED?"

Kyle looked stunned. "I do *not* have erectile dysfunction!"

"Well, don't act so put out, Kyle," she countered. "You're the one who said you don't have the stamina."

"I'll turn thirty-nine in August and I don't mind admitting that I can't go as often as I did at nineteen, but for someone approaching middle age I've had very few complaints."

"Are you bragging or stating a fact?"

Wiping his hands on a cloth towel, Kyle ran a forefinger down the length of Ava's nose. "That *is* a fact. Because an idle mind is the devil's workshop I'm going to ask you to help me out here."

Ava jumped up. "Thanks. What do you want me to do?"

"I need you to cut the pepper into strips, quarter the tomatoes, and slice the cucumber and scallions for the salad. I hope you have black olives, because I forgot to buy them."

She opened a narrow cabinet with rows of spices and condiments, shifting cans and bottles until she found a can of black olives. "Black olives coming up. Do you want me to slice them or leave them whole?"

"Whole."

The segment of all-music radio that was playing featured female vocalists: Aretha Franklin, Alicia Keys, Anita Baker, Dionne Warwick and the incomparable Etta James. Ava found herself singing along with the familiar lyrics as she sliced and diced the ingredients for a Greek salad into a glass bowl, which she then placed on a shelf in the refrigerator.

"Tell me about Kyle Chatham," she said after a comfortable pause.

Kyle moved closer, his arm touching her shoulder. "There's not much to tell."

Tilting her chin, Ava met his amused stare. "Then tell what little there is."

"Why, Ava?"

Her eyebrows lifted slightly. "I'm surprised you have to ask why."

"But I am asking, sweetheart."

She ignored the endearment. "Because I'm interested in you."

"I'm not going to ask you to translate *interested*. What do you want to know?"

"Where were you born? I'd like to know a little

about your childhood, and why you decided to become a lawyer."

"Do you plan to do a psycho-social on me?"

Wrinkling her nose, she made a face. "No!"

Kyle placed two foil-wrapped potatoes on a shelf in
a preheated eye-level oven and closed the door. Wiping
his hands, he anchored his arms under Ava's shoulders
and sat her on the stool with his jacket. Pulling over a
matching stool, he sat across from her, his penetrating
gaze taking in everything about Ava Warrick in one
sweeping glance.

She claimed he didn't know her, but what he knew and
saw he liked—a lot. Ava wasn't silly, insipid or attempting to go out of her way to try and impress him. She was
outspoken and confident—traits he admired in a woman.

"I was born in Harlem thirty-eight years ago. My dad
worked for the railroad and my mother was a stay-at-
home mom. We lived in public housing. I was exposed
to things a young child had no business seeing or hearing. Heroin swept through the neighborhood like a
twister, but instead of touching down and leaving it
stayed. After a while I lost track of the number of kids
I'd gone to school with who went to prison for selling
drugs or ended up in the morgue either from an overdose
or because they got stupid and messed up with someone's supply or money.

"I called my father the preacher, because whenever
he came home he gathered his kids together and went
on about the evils of drugs and running with a bad

crowd. After a while I knew what he was going to say and could repeat it verbatim. I always hung out with two boys I met when we were in the same second-grade class. Duncan Gilmore and Ivan Campbell were different because they'd rather stay home and read books than shoot hoops. Today they would be called nerds or dorks, but it paid off because both are very successful."

"What do they do?" Ava asked.

"Ivan is a psychotherapist and Duncan is a financial planner and investment adviser."

"Are you saying you're not successful, Kyle?"

He ducked his head. "I do okay," he said modestly. "We hung out together in school and at one another's apartments. But everything changed when Ivan's twin brother was killed in a drive-by shooting. The horror was that Jared died in Ivan's arms. A year later Duncan's mother died and he went to live with an aunt in Brooklyn. Ivan, Duncan and I swore an oath at his mother's funeral that we would never lose touch with one another.

"With Duncan living in Brooklyn and Ivan refusing to come out whenever he wasn't in school I started hanging out with kids who did everything from snatching purses to following and shaking down people after they'd left check-cashing places."

"How old were you?"

"Fourteen."

"Did you ever steal from someone?"

Kyle shook his head. "I just stood around and watched because I thought they were really cool. It was like watching a bunch of Billy the Kids in action. They had no fear when they walked up on someone and demanded their money. The hero worship ended one night when one of them threw a brick through the plate-glass window of a corner store. He ran, but I was too stunned to move. Usually they talked about what they were going to do, but this night one of them had picked up a brick from a vacant lot. None of us knew he was going to throw it through that store window. A police cruiser was coming down the block at the time and yours truly wound up in cuffs.

"The precinct sergeant knew my dad, so he called my home to tell him I was in the lockup. They trans-ferred me to a place where I was processed as a juvenile delinquent. When I was taken to juvenile court the next day it was the first and only time I saw my decorated Vietnam-veteran father break down and cry. At fourteen, I'd thought myself a man because my voice had changed and I was taller than my dad, but seeing him like that changed me inside. Suddenly all of his preaching made sense. He hadn't gone to war, done unspeakable things, to come home and regret fa-thering a child.

"I was assigned a youth counselor who asked the family court judge to give me a second chance. I was more fright-ened by the judge sitting on the bench in his black robe than by spending time in a juvenile detention center. He had shockingly white hair, black eyebrows and piercing black eyes that looked like a bird's. When he leaned forward to stare down at me he looked like an avenging angel with the power to send me into the bowels of hell.

"He asked me why I didn't run away with the other boys. I thought about his question then said I didn't run because I hadn't done anything wrong. If I'd run, then it would've proved I was guilty of throwing the brick. He questioned the arresting officer, asking if he'd witnessed me throwing the brick, and when the officer said he hadn't, the judge dismissed my case with a stern warning that if I came before his court again he would have me locked up until I turned eighteen. My record was expunged and I'd been given a second chance."

"What did your parents say?"

"My father gave me the silent treatment for a week, while my mother acted as if she'd had two children instead of three. Meanwhile my younger brother, who was two years younger, wanted to know what it was liked to be locked up. When I told him it like being sent to hell he never asked me again. During the week I went to school and came home. On the weekends if I wasn't in our apartment, then I was in Ivan's studying. Occasionally we would meet Duncan in Manhattan and hang out together.

"Ivan and I graduated from George Washington High School. I went to John Jay College of Criminal Justice, Duncan went to Baruch College for business and Ivan was accepted into New York University's psychology department. I earned a B.S. in legal studies, then went on to Brooklyn Law. I spent three summers in Montgomery, Alabama, as an intern for the Southern Poverty Law Center. Meeting Morris Dees and Joe Levin, who founded the center, and Julian Bond, who was its first president, was and still is the most rewarding experience in my life."

"Are you a civil rights attorney?"

"Not really."

Ava sat up straighter. "What do you mean by 'not really'?"

"After I graduated and passed the bar I was recruited by a headhunter who represented a leading Park Avenue firm specializing in litigation. The money they offered me was mind-boggling."

"And you went for it?" Ava said perceptively.

"Yes. The starting salary was enough for me to pay off my student loans in three years instead of ten. But it came with a caveat. I was required to work at least sixty hours a week."

"Did you?"

Kyle nodded. "I did until I woke up one morning and couldn't force myself to get out of bed. I called Ivan and he told me that I was operating on one mental piston that was misfiring. He told me to get out before I burned out completely."

"Did you?" Ava asked again.

"Eventually I did. It was after I'd wrapped a very important case that I handed in my resignation. The partners called me in and asked if I wanted an increase in salary. Meanwhile I was pulling down close to seven figures, and one year I'd earned almost three million. That included bonuses. I told the partner it had nothing to do with money but survival. I was close to burnout and money was of no use to me if I wound up in a padded cell.

"I'd bought a house that I'd only used to sleep and change my clothes in. I was thirty-four years old, yet I felt twice that old and then some. My mother was disappointed that I'd decided to leave corporate America, but in the end she understood that I needed to protect my sanity.

"September eleventh changed this city and the entire country. Duncan lost his fiancée when the towers fell, Ivan's mental-health research firm lost its federal funding and I was out of work. I'd intended to take a year off and do absolutely nothing when my friends decided to buy a Harlem brownstone for their own business enterprises. And when they asked me if I wanted to invest in the building and set up a private practice I didn't hesitate. As they say, the rest is history."

Ava curbed the urge to applaud, and she couldn't stop the tears welling up in her eyes. "What a wonderful story."

"I couldn't have done it without my father's constant preaching or my mother's prayers."

"It was fate, Kyle. You were destined for success."

Reaching across the table, Kyle rose slightly and cradled the back of her head. He pressed a kiss to her forehead. "Thank you."

She wrinkled her nose. "You're welcome."

He winked at her. "Now it's your turn to tell me about Ava Warrick."

Ava stared at the backs of her hands. "My childhood wasn't quite as dramatic as yours. I was born in a D.C. suburb thirty-four years ago. My parents met in college. They dated and broke up so many times they had to know their relationship was unhealthy. But they did marry when my mom discovered she was pregnant months before they were to graduate. My father told my mother less than an hour after he'd married her that he thought she'd been sleeping with another student. It was only when my brother was born looking exactly like his father that Charles Warrick acknowledged that the child was his."

"If he thought she was sleeping around then why did he marry her?"

"His father put the fear of God in him. My grandfather was very controlling and unfortunately he passed the trait on to his son. My mother was trained to be a teacher, but my dad refused to let her work because he claimed he wanted her home to take care of his children. He wasn't that concerned with her neglecting her kids. It was that he didn't trust her. Unfortunately, Alice Warrick was so in love with Charles that she surrendered her will to him.

"I grew up watching the life go out of my mother each she time she celebrated another wedding anniversary."

An expression of shock froze Kyle's features. Although his mother had been a stay-at-home mother, his father's role was that of the wage earner and protector.

It was Frances Chatham who had the last word on anything that went on in her household. Whenever Elwin was away she was in charge and the disciplinarian. It was never "wait until your father gets home." When a crisis arose she took care of it.

"You told me your mother lives in D.C. and your dad in North Carolina, so I assume they're not together."

"They broke up ten years ago. I don't know where she got the courage or the strength to challenge my father, but the day after my youngest brother graduated high school Mom told Daddy she was done with being a housewife. She'd put her career on hold and stayed home with *his* children and now she was going to do what she wanted to do. She applied for a position with a child-care center in D.C. and got it.

"Daddy started up with her but it ended quickly when my brothers stepped in. It was the first time they'd ever challenged their father and Charles knew he either had to accept his wife becoming an independent woman or leave. In the end he chose to leave. When I asked Mom why she'd put up with his bullying tactics for so long, she said if she'd had three daughters she would've left him, but her sons needed a father in their lives."

"That's true, Ava. But not if the father is a negative influence. Some of the kids in my housing development had fathers who were alcoholics or abused their wives and sometimes their children."

"Daddy never hit us or raised his voice to my mother. It was just his asinine rule that she had to devote her whole existence to her children. I believe it was his way of making certain she wouldn't have a life outside the home. There is just so much cleaning and cooking someone can do without going completely mad. I resented the way my dad controlled my mother until I became a psychiatric social worker. Then I realized his passive aggression came from his childhood."

"Do you still interact with him?" Kyle asked.

"We are, as the kids say, pretty tight nowadays. We call each other all the time. If I go a week without calling him, then he calls me. He did apologize to my mother for stifling her, but it wasn't a big deal because she's moved on.

"I hardly recognize my mother nowadays. She sold the house and bought a condo not far from the convention center. She's teaching first grade in an excellent school district and she's dating a wonderful man who works at the Smithsonian."

Kyle's smile matched Ava's. He'd wondered if she was reluctant to marry because she believed her life would mirror her mother's, or if she'd had a similar experience with a man who'd tried to control her life.

"Good for her," he said.

Ava glanced at the clock on the microwave. "It's going to be a while before the potatoes are ready. Would you like a tour of the apartment now?"

"Sure."

They stood up and Ava led Kyle out of the kitchen and into the small bedroom where she'd slept the day she'd come home from the hospital. "This is what is referred to as the maid's room."

Kyle peered into a bedroom that was large enough for a twin-size bed, a dresser, a night table and a chair. "Do the Servinskys have a maid?"

"No. They have a cleaning service that comes once a week."

"Do they still come in even though they're not here?" he asked.

"Yes. This place is too big for me to keep clean."

"Who lets them in where you're at work?"

"Building management. They have keys to every apartment in the event of an emergency."

Kyle followed Ava as she showed him the first-floor master bedroom, guest bedroom and the third bedroom that doubled as a home office/library. Built-in bookshelves were packed from floor to ceiling with books on hospital and social-work administration, human behavior, research methods, welfare policy, clinical practices and micro- and macroeconomics.

"Which of the Servinskys was your professor?"

"Both. Dr. Servinsky was my undergraduate professor when I was an early-education major, and her husband was my professor in social-work school. I taught school for three years before deciding to become a social worker."

"Why did you switch careers?"

"I realized too late that I didn't have the temperament for a classroom filled with twenty rambunctious boys and girls. I'm much more effective counseling individuals and small groups."

Kyle followed Ava into the formal dining room where she'd set the table with two place settings. A bouquet of peach-colored roses in a crystal vase had become a centerpiece. They walked through the living room and up the staircase to the second floor. The new solarium created from two former bedrooms was the perfect place to begin or end the day.

A continuous wall of windows provided a panoramic view of the river and the George Washington Bridge. The sun was setting, casting a bright-orange glow over the calm surface of the Hudson River and the Palisades. A palette of white wicker chairs, seat cushions, sisal rugs, whimsically framed botanical prints and an abundance of flower arrangements and potted topiaries brought the outdoors in. Closing the distance between them, Kyle stood behind Ava at the windows.

"What are you doing?" she asked, when he touched her hair.

"Feeling your hair. How did you get it to curl so tightly?"

Ava smiled, but didn't turn around. "It's my natural hair. I usually flat-iron it then bump the ends."

Kyle tugged on a curl. "You don't relax it?"

"I have it relaxed when I let it grow because it takes too long to blow or flat-iron."

"It smells like flowers and coconut."

"My shampoo is…" Her words trailed off when a chiming echoed throughout the apartment. "Excuse me," she said, rushing over to the intercom on the wall outside the solarium. Ava pushed a button. "Yes," she said into the speaker.

"Miss Warrick, this is Roberto in the lobby. Miss Nelson and Miss Vargas are asking to see you. Should I send them up?"

"Yes, Roberto." She released the button and found Kyle staring at her.

"Should I leave?" he asked.

"Please don't," Ava insisted.

She hadn't realized how much she enjoyed seeing and talking with Kyle until today. At first she'd thought him pompous, arrogant, but she'd changed her assessment of him after listening to him talk about his brush with the juvenile justice system, and not wanting to disappoint his parents. She had clients with children who had begun their young lives as repeat juvenile offenders and who were now convicted criminals.

"Are you sure, Ava?"

She smiled. "Yes, Kyle, I'm very sure."

Chapter 5

Ava opened the door to find her agency's receptionist and a social-work intern flashing Cheshire-cat grins. Both were holding covered aluminum pans from which wafted the most delicious smells.

"Surprise!" they chorused.

"Come in," Ava urged, stepping back as they made their way into the spacious foyer. She'd gotten calls from some of her colleagues asking how she was feeling or if she needed anything, but she hadn't expected any of them to show up at her apartment.

Debra Nelson, the older of the two, had been with the New Lincoln Family Center for more than a decade, since it had opened its doors to provide mental-health counseling services to low-income Upper West Side residents.

Debra's dark brown eyes narrowed as she stared at Ava. Her equally dark brown smooth face was framed by a profusion of salt-and-pepper twists. "Damn, girl, you look as if you ran into a fist."

"It was an air bag."

Maribel Vargas, one of two bilingual social-work interns on staff from Fordham University's School of Social Welfare, shook her head while sucking her teeth. "You need to sue that car company. We took up a collection in the office and instead of buying flowers we decided food was a better choice. I called *mi tío,* who owns the best Dominican restaurant in Washington Heights, and told him to fix *un poco algo* for you."

"You didn't have to do that," Ava insisted, smiling. First Kyle, now her coworkers wanted to make certain she had enough to eat.

"Yes, we did," Debra countered.

Ava reached for Debra's tray. "Let me help you with that."

Debra slapped at her hand. "Leave it be. You're not supposed to do anything strenuous, and this is a little heavy."

"Let me take it," said a deep voice behind them.

Ava turned to find Kyle standing only a few feet away. She turned back to the two women. "This is my friend, Kyle Chatham. Kyle, these are my coworkers, Debra Nelson and Maribel Vargas."

Kyle took the trays of food. "It's nice meeting you, ladies."

"Same here," Maribel and Debra chorused, staring openly at Kyle.

He winked at Ava. "I'll put them in the kitchen."

"Thank you. Debra, Mari, please come sit down. I hope you're going to stay long enough to eat." She led them into the living room and waited until they sat on a tufted leather sofa before taking a matching loveseat.

"I can't stay too long," Debra said. "I usually give myself a facial on Monday nights."

"I can only hang out for a little while because I have to go home and hit the books," Maribel said. "I decided to take one course this summer," she added when Ava gave her a questioning look.

"Didn't you tell me you were going to take the summer off?" Ava asked Maribel.

"That was before I decided to break up with my boyfriend. He was taking up way too much of my time. Speaking of boyfriends," Maribel said sotto voce, "where did you find Señor Delicioso?"

It took Ava a few seconds to realize Maribel was talking about Kyle. "He's not my boyfriend."

Debra leaned forward. "Is he single?" she whispered.

Ava went completely still. Debra's query made her aware that she knew very little about Kyle Chatham. He'd told her he was thirty-eight, an attorney and lived in Harlem. She didn't know whether Kyle was single, married or engaged. He'd mentioned she was very different from a lot of other women he'd met, but that didn't translate into he was available.

"I don't know," she admitted. "As I told you, we're just friends."

"Do you want me to ask him?" Maribel questioned.

Ava stared at the graduate student. Maribel was strikingly attractive, with a mop of curly raven-black hair, rich olive coloring, delicate features and a pair of large hazel eyes that sparkled like precious jewels.

"Don't you dare!"

Debra slapped at Maribel's knee. "Behave yourself."

"I…." Maribel's response died on her lips and her eyes widened appreciably when Kyle walked into the living room. To say Kyle Chatham was drop-dead gorgeous was an understatement. When introduced to him, his intense, deep-set, warm-brown eyes seemed to look not at her but through her.

Maribel gestured to Ava to look behind her.

Ava shifted to find Kyle wearing his suit jacket. "Excuse me, ladies."

Rising to her feet, she walked over to Kyle and took his arm. "What's up?" she asked in a quiet voice.

"I'm leaving now."

"But I thought we were going to share dinner?"

He dipped his head. "We'll do it tomorrow. I put the steak away and turned off the oven. The potatoes will finish baking."

Ava stared up at the man who'd promised to come to see her the following night even though she didn't know whether he was committed to another woman. And if he was, then he was no different than the first man to whom she'd given her love *and* her innocence.

Reaching for his hand, she led him into the foyer. "I need to ask you something before I can agree to you coming back tomorrow."

Kyle looked down at Ava, his gaze meeting and fusing with hers. "You want to know if I'm married, don't you?"

A rush of heat stung Ava's face as she averted her gaze. "Yes."

His free arm going around her waist, Kyle pulled her closer, pressing his mouth to her ear. "I'm not married and I've never been married."

She smiled. "Engaged?"

"No. Now do I have your permission to come back tomorrow?"

"Yes, Kyle."

"Good." He released her, then leaned down to brush a kiss over her parted lips. "I'll see you tomorrow."

Ava watched as he turned, opened the door, then closed it behind him. She had an answer to Maribel's question. Kyle Chatham was a single man. No, she mused. At thirty-eight he wasn't just a single man but a bachelor—a confirmed bachelor.

She returned to the living room. "There's no way I'm going to be able to eat all that food, so either you stay and eat some or I'll make a couple of doggie bags."

Maribel popped up. "I'll stay long enough to eat some *plátanos maduros* and baked chicken."

Debra pushed to her feet. "I love me some sweet plantains. I'll stay, too."

Ava smiled. "Follow me, ladies." She wasn't going to tell them about asking Kyle whether he was married because she'd always managed to keep her private life private. No one knew she'd been living with a man until after she'd moved out and he began leaving harassing telephone calls on the agency's voice mail. That had ended when the medical director notified the police, who took the necessary action and the calls stopped altogether.

Ninety minutes later Ava closed the door behind her coworkers. She'd eaten Caribbean cuisine many times since moving to New York but none had surpassed the food Maribel's uncle had prepared. The baked chicken was flavorful and tender, the yellow rice with pigeon peas fluffy and savory and the fried plantains sweet with crisp edges. She'd packed takeout containers for Debra and Maribel because there was no way she would be able to eat half of the trays of food before it spoiled.

Walking across the living room, she climbed the staircase to the second floor. She went into the solarium instead of her bedroom. Whenever she wasn't eating or sleeping Ava could be found reclining on the chaise in the solarium, listening to music, reading or just staring out the window at the bucolic views of the river. She didn't want to think of the time when the Servinskys returned from their two-year assignment and she would have to look for another place to live.

She'd lived downtown, worked in midtown, and she now lived uptown. It was becoming more expensive to live in Manhattan, which meant living in one of the other four boroughs was becoming more of a consideration. Her first choice was Brooklyn, then the Bronx. Staten Island and Queens would be her last choices because they meant crossing a bridge or a two-fare zone to come into Manhattan.

A dull pain reminded Ava of her head injury as she closed her eyes. When she'd gotten up in the middle of the night she'd had to take two Tylenol within minutes of her feet touching the floor. After a breakfast of tea with a slice of buttered raisin toast, she'd gotten back into bed and slept until Kyle called her. It was more than twelve hours now since she'd last taken the pain medication and she was loath to swallow more.

Her high-school perfect-attendance award wasn't because she'd never gotten sick, but rather that she'd refused to acknowledge when she wasn't feeling well. She'd attended classes with sniffles, coughs, menstrual cramps and the occasional low-grade fever.

The swelling and bruising were fading rapidly but Ava knew it would take time for her headaches and dizziness to subside so she could resume her day-to-day routine.

Lines of frustration marred Kyle's forehead as he studied four photographs taken by a closed-circuit camera. He'd spent a quarter of an hour staring at the same images of Rashaun Hayden pointing a gun, another of him hitting the store clerk with a gun, a third of his client jumping over the counter and a fourth of Rashaun with a fistful of money.

Setting aside three of the photos, he picked up the one with Rashaun with the handgun. Swiveling on his chair, he stood up and walked over to the window. His eyes narrowed as he perused the photograph. Rashaun had worn a hoodie during the robbery, yet it hadn't concealed all of his face in three of the four photos. Enough of his features were visible to make him recognizable. However, it was the one with the gun where his features were hidden from the camera and it was Rashaun's hand that garnered Kyle's complete concentration.

"Kyle, there's a Jordan Wainwright on the line asking to speak to you. Do you want me to take a message?"

He turned away from the window and returned to his desk, activating the speaker feature on the telephone console. "Yes, Cherise. I'll talk to him." The last time he'd spoken to Jordan, Kyle had told his former colleague to get back to him in two weeks for an answer to whether he would hire him. He'd given the notion of bringing Jordan on as a partner a great deal of thought. The country had changed dramatically now that it had an African-American as president, the racial demographics of Harlem were changing every day, and if his practice was to achieve success then his staff had to reflect the neighborhood's demographics.

"Good morning, Chat."

Kyle smiled. Most of the staff at Trilling, Carlyle and Browne had shortened his last name from Chatham to Chat. "How are you doing, buddy?"

"I'm good, Chat."

"When would you like to sit down and discuss joining the firm?"

There was a swollen silence before Jordan said, "How about tonight?"

Kyle remembered he'd promised Ava they'd eat together. "Tomorrow is better for me."

"Name the time and place."

"I'm open, Jordan."

"Do you like Japanese food?"

"Yes," Kyle said, smiling.

"I'll make reservations at Hasaki for seven. It's on East Ninth Street near—"

"I know where it is," Kyle said quietly, interrupting Jordan. "I'll see you tomorrow at seven."

He ended the call and returned his attention to the photograph. Then it hit him! Rashaun was wearing a ring on his right hand in one photograph, but it was missing in the others. Punching the intercom, Kyle buzzed his legal secretary.

"Cherise, please call Mrs. Hayden and have her get back to me ASAP." He drummed his fingers on the top of the desk while waiting for Cherise to connect him with the teenager's mother.

"Hold on, Kyle. I'm putting Mrs. Hayden through."

"Mrs. Hayden, I'd like to ask you whether your son wears a ring?" he asked Rashaun's mother.

"No. His father and I won't let him wear any jewelry. Why?"

"In one of the photographs Rashaun is wearing a ring fashioned into a lion's head."

There came a beat. "I know for certain that Rashaun doesn't own a ring like that, but I know who does."

"Who, Mrs. Hayden?"

There was another pause. "He's a boy I warned Rashaun not to hang out with."

"What's his name, Mrs. Hayden?"

"I don't know his real name, but Rashaun calls him Boots."

"Does Boots have a last name?"

"I—I don't know it."

Mrs. Hayden couldn't give him a name but Kyle knew someone who could. He'd defended a young man charged with petty larceny and had convinced the judge to give him probation rather than jail time. His former client was familiar with enough neighborhood petty thugs to fill a book.

"I'll call my son and ask him."

"Don't do that," Kyle urged.

"Have you found something that will get my son off?"

"Mrs. Hayden, I'm going to be truthful with you. I believe Rashaun knows who robbed and beat that storekeeper."

"But, he swore to me he doesn't know who did it."

Kyle heard the desperation in his client's mother's voice. He didn't want to tell the woman he believed Rashaun was lying to her *and* had lied to him. "I know you want to believe your son, Mrs. Hayden, but as his attorney I don't believe him."

"What are you going to do, Mr. Chatham?"

"I'm going to do what I have to do to prove Rashaun's innocence."

"I've just about worn out my knees praying for Rashaun *and* praying for you, too."

"Thank you, Mrs. Hayden."

Kyle clenched his teeth in frustration after ending the call. He couldn't do what he actually wanted to do: get in Rashaun's face and tell him flat-out that he knew he was lying, that he knew he was covering for someone, that he knew he didn't want to snitch because he feared retaliation against himself or even family members.

Reaching for the telephone, he dialed the number to the cell phone he'd given his informant. It took less than a minute for Kyle to tell him what he wanted. He made another call, this one to the A.D.A. handling the Hayden case. The day before he'd asked for photos and today he wanted a copy of the tape from the closed-circuit camera.

"Look, Chatham, you got the pictures. The tape is going to show the same thing," the assistant district attorney said.

"I want the tape, A.D.A. Clarkson."

"Lighten up, Chatham. Rashaun Hayden is nothing but

a wannabe thug who should be taken off the street so he can't hurt law-abiding citizens trying to eke out a living."

"Save the summation for the courtroom," Kyle shot back. "I'll send a messenger to pick up the tape." He slammed the receiver on its cradle in frustration. NY vs. Hayden would mark the fourth time Kyle was scheduled to face the arrogant, condescending assistant district attorney.

Kyle and Skyler Clarkson had attended the same law school, were in some of the same classes, and as the son and grandson of judges, Skyler had perfected an air of entitlement that irked those who worked with him.

He made one more telephone call to Cherise to tell her to contact a messenger service to pick up the video tape from the Manhattan D.A.'s office. He pushed the Do Not Disturb feature on the phone, then walked into a smaller inner office he'd set up as his inner sanctum. It was where, when he was working around the clock, he took power naps on a sofa that converted into a queen-size bed, and it was where he retreated when he wanted to be alone to think and clear his head.

Reclining on the sofa, his head resting on one arm while his long legs hung over the other, Kyle's thoughts drifted to Ava Warrick when he should've been trying to identify a loophole in the D.A.'s case.

The assistant district attorney thought of Rashaun Hayden as a street thug while Kyle saw him as a gullible young man who'd chosen the wrong friends. Mr. Hayden had confided that once the trial was over he was relocating to his family's ancestral home outside Charleston, South Carolina. James Hayden, a carrier with the postal service, had put in for a transfer and his clinical-dietitian wife had already secured a position with a skilled nursing facility.

A smile softened the lines around Kyle's mouth when his thoughts drifted back to Ava. He hadn't wanted to leave her apartment the night before, yet he hadn't wanted to intrude on her time with her friends. Although she still bore some bruising and swelling from the accident, he'd found her beauty ravishingly refreshing because she'd made no attempt to camouflage her injury with makeup. There were women he knew who wouldn't permit him to see them without their makeup. They slept and woke with foundation, eyeliner and mascara. One had even gone so far as to have a plastic surgeon apply permanent lashes and eyeliner.

Kyle hadn't realized he'd dozed off until Cherise shook him gently. He opened his eyes. "What is it?"

"The tape is here. I thought you'd want to see it."

Swinging his legs over the sofa, he stood. "I do." He followed the legal secretary out of his office and into the conference room where she'd placed the tape into a video player.

Sitting on a chair, Kyle stared at the tape, his racing heart beating a tattoo against his ribs. Viewing the images on the large flat monitor revealed things that weren't apparent in the photographs. Rising, he stopped the tape and ejected it. He'd seen enough. The tape gave him what he needed to prove Rashaun Hayden hadn't committed the robbery or assaulted the storeowner.

He returned to his office to find Ivan Campbell sitting in the chair beside his desk. "To what do I owe the honor of your presence, Dr. Campbell?"

Ivan glanced over his shoulder. "I came to ask you about this coming weekend's get-together. Duncan told me you wanted to throw something at your place."

Kyle sat down behind the desk and placed the tape in a drawer. He stared at his friend. Ivan, at five-eleven, was the shortest of the three. He worked out every day in his in-home gym to keep his muscular body in top condition. His brooding expression kept most women at a distance until he smiled. The flash of white teeth in his mocha-hued face was dazzling *and* mesmerizing. He'd earned the reputation of a love-them-and-leave-them brother, because whenever he found a woman getting too close he'd smoothly extricate himself from the relationship.

Lacing his fingers together, Kyle gave Ivan a direct stare, noticing for the first time that the psychoanalyst was attempting to grow a mustache and goatee. "I'm going to be straight with you, Ivan. I can't eat your food."

"You're shittin' me, aren't you?" Ivan asked, deadpan.

Kyle leaned forward. "I wish I was. The last time I ate one of your burgers I thought I was going to have to have my stomach pumped. I downed so much of the pink stuff that my eyes turned pink."

"You know you *ain't* right, Kyle."

"It's just not me, Ivan. Duncan feels the same as I do."

A scowl twisted Ivan's mouth. "Damn. I thought the two of you were my brothers."

"We are," Kyle countered softly. "You and Duncan are closer to me than I am with my biological brother. If I didn't love you I wouldn't be up front with you. You grill sirloin burgers until they're hard as hockey pucks and gourmet steaks until they can be used as saddles for small dogs. It's criminal the way you abuse good meat."

"So, you think you grill better than I do?"

Kyle was hard-pressed not to laugh when he saw Ivan's crestfallen expression. "I *know* I grill better than you do."

"What am I going to do with all of the meat and food I ordered?"

"Bring it to my place. I'll pay you for it."

"I don't want your money, Kyle."

"What if we compromise? We can have the cookout at your place and I'll step in as grill-meister? Come on, man," he continued when Ivan opened his mouth. "You know I'm a better cook because of my dad. Whenever my father was home you found every excuse known to man to eat with us because your mother was less than proficient in the kitchen."

Ivan shook his head. "Now, why do you want to snap on my mother's cooking?"

"Weren't you the one who said she couldn't cook?"

"Only I can say it," Ivan retorted defensively.

"Sorry."

A beat passed. "Apology accepted. You can cook at my place."

"I'll tell my staff that the location's been changed."

Ivan nodded, smiling. "Are you bringing Tracey?"

"No," Kyle said quickly. "I stopped seeing Tracey some time ago."

"What happened, Kyle? I thought she was going to be the one who would make you pop the question."

"I thought so, too, until she started playing games." He wasn't one to kiss and tell, so Kyle didn't tell Ivan that the woman with whom he'd been sleeping had confronted him every couple of months with the possibility that she might be pregnant. He knew it wasn't probable, because he always used protection.

"Are you seeing anyone?" Ivan asked.

"No," he said truthfully. Having dinner with Ava at her apartment didn't translate into them seeing each other.

"Are you coming alone?"

"I'm not certain." Again Kyle had spoken truthfully. "There is someone I'm thinking of asking. Why?"

"I'm keeping a head count so I know how much food to have on hand."

"I don't mind kicking in for my people, Ivan."

Ivan dismissed Kyle's offer with a wave of his hand. "Don't bother. I've got it."

"What if I bring the beverages: soda, beer, water and wine?"

Ivan waved his hand again. "Bring whatever you want."

"I'm sorry to cut this short, but I'm going to have to

ask you to leave because I have to call someone about a client." Kyle needed a computer expert to validate his suspicions that the videotape had been edited.

Ivan pushed to his feet. "Tonight is my late night for seeing clients. How about dinner?"

"I'm sorry, but I have a prior engagement." First Jordan and now Ivan wanted him to eat with them.

"Even though you're coming over Saturday I doubt we'll get a chance to talk."

"What's going on, Ivan?"

"Nothing's going on. Don't you think it's odd that we got together more often when we didn't have our businesses under the same roof?"

"That's because we made the time to hang out together. And because we're in business for ourselves we have to concern ourselves with a mortgage, payroll and every once in a while do a little hustling to realize a year-end project."

Ivan smiled. "Preach, brother."

Kyle's smile matched Ivan's. "Get out of here so I can do what I have to do to keep a young man out of prison."

"Good luck," Ivan said over his shoulder as he walked out of the office.

Waiting until the door closed behind his friend, Kyle picked up the telephone. The person on the other end answered on the second ring. "I need you to check a tape for me."

"When do you need it?"

"Like yesterday. Can you come by and pick it up?"

"I'm sorry, Kyle, but I'm working on another project. If you drop it by I'll try and take a look at it. How long is it?"

"I haven't watched the entire tape, but I doubt it's more than five minutes."

"Bring it by my place and I'll look at it in between my other jobs."

Glancing at a wall clock, Kyle emitted an audible sigh. "I'll be there in an hour."

Chapter 6

Ava opened the door to find Kyle dressed in jeans, a T-shirt and running shoes. "What did you do, play hooky?"

"Why would you say that?"

"It's three o'clock in the afternoon and I doubt if you went into your office wearing jeans and sneakers."

Cradling Ava's chin in his hand, Kyle studied her face. There was only a hint of swelling along her cheekbone, while the bruises were still evident. She appeared refreshingly young and innocent with her fresh-scrubbed face and wearing a floral-print sundress with spaghetti straps that displayed an expanse of flawless brown skin, and tan ballet-type shoes. The curls in her hair were missing, replaced by the smooth, sleek hairdo she'd worn the night of the accident.

"I had to run an errand." Kyle had returned home, changed out of his suit and taken a taxi down to Alphabet City to drop off the videotape. Instead of taking a taxi back uptown, he taken the subway. It'd been a while since he taken public transportation, and it felt good to mingle with the mass of humanity that made New York City so unique. "How are your headaches?"

"They come and go."

"No more fainting?"

"No, doctor," she teased.

Kyle's eyebrows shot up. "Speaking of doctors, have you made an appointment to see one?"

"Yes, counselor."

He stared at her and then burst out laughing. "You must be feeling better because you're rather sassy today."

Ava flashed a sensual moue. "I haven't had to take any pain medication today."

"Good for you."

"I'm feeling better and I'm also experiencing cabin fever."

Kyle reached for her hand. "Would you like to go for a walk?"

The ringing of the telephone preempted Ava's reply. Easing her hand from his grip, she said, "I'll be right back."

Kyle walked into the living room and stood at the expanse of windows. He didn't think he would ever get used to the view of the river. He'd tried imagining living in the apartment and watching the seasons change. His family had lived on the fifth floor in their housing complex, while Ivan's family had lived on the four-teenth floor. He'd liked hanging out at Ivan's apartment because of the views.

Whenever classes were cancelled because of a blizzard he'd take the elevator to Ivan's apartment and spend the day looking out the windows at the neighborhood below. The coating of white covering up the dirt, grime and litter had turned the Harlem neighborhood into a winter wonderland. A highlight of the winter season after weeks of below-freezing temperatures was walking across town to Riverside Drive to see the blocks of ice on the surface of the Hudson River.

"Kyle."

The sound of Ava's soft drawling voice penetrated his musings. Turning, he saw her standing with a cordless phone in her hand. In the seconds it took to blink, Kyle was suddenly cognizant of why he'd followed the am-bulance to the hospital, and why he continued to see Ava when he should've walked away from her the night of the accident. The display of spunk and independence in no way compromised her femininity. He'd found himself involved with two types of women: the strong ones who exhibited more masculine traits than he, and those who feigned a helplessness that set his teeth on edge.

Kyle hadn't had so many women in his past that he'd forgotten their names or faces, but interacting with Ava Warrick made him aware that he'd had to date those women for him to become conscious of what he really had been looking for. He didn't have a laundry list of criteria for women he'd date like some men he knew. They wanted certain body and hair types, levels of education and ethnicities, unlike himself, who'd dated women from every ethnic and racial grouping. The only thing he required was intelligence, because he didn't want to spend time having to explain everything he said. If he'd wanted a daughter, then he would've had children.

"Yes, Ava?"

She approached him, extending her hand with the phone. "It's the insurance adjustor. He needs the name and address of the body shop where my car was taken."

Kyle took the phone, giving the adjustor the information on his cousin's body shop. He'd spoken to his second cousin, whom everyone in the family referred to as Junior, telling him of the dent in the Jag's rear bumper. Junior had personally come to look at the damage, stating the damage was minimal and that he would be able to repair it without replacing the bumper.

After he hung up, his gaze lingered on Ava's bare shapely legs as she walked out of the living room. For the first time he was glad he hadn't bowed to family pressure to get married. An aunt had asked whether he liked women, because when a man in his thirties was still single that made folks "wonder about his sexual proclivity." Kyle had kissed his mother's sister and reassured her that he *did* like women, but that he wasn't ready to marry and start a family. His mother had ended the discussion when she'd said she preferred a bachelor son to one who was a baby daddy.

He was standing in the same spot when Ava returned with a pair of oversized sunglasses perched on the bridge of her nose. The beginnings of a smile tilted the corners of his mouth. "You look as if you should be on the Italian or French Riviera."

"I wish I was," Ava said, smiling.

Closing the distance between them, Kyle extended his hand. "Are you ready for your walk?"

"Yes."

He opened the door and waited for Ava to lock it behind them and pocket the keys. They took the elevator to the lobby and out into the bright afternoon sunlight. "Do you want to walk uptown or downtown?"

"Let's head uptown."

Ava lost count of the number of times she'd walked the Morningside Heights neighborhood as an under-graduate Columbia University student. She'd shared a two-bedroom apartment on Morningside Avenue with another Columbia student who'd come from Iowa, and whenever she didn't have classes Ava could be found either in Harlem or the East or West Village. After graduating and securing a teaching position she'd met William Marshall; they'd moved into a miniscule East Village apartment, hosting cocktail parties on average twice each month. But it had all ended when their rela-tionship had changed gradually from live-in lovers to that of jailer and inmate.

It was then that she realized Will was having a problem separating from his role as a corrections officer whenever he was at home. He'd begun leaving his handgun in plain sight instead of locking it in a safe, and he'd wake up in the middle of the night screaming for inmates to get back in their cells.

She recognized impending burnout, and when she'd broached the subject with Will he went ballistic, threatening to kill her. That's when Ava realized if she didn't leave him then she never would leave alive. She carefully planned her escape, moving her personal possessions when he went to work, leaving the keys with the building superintendent. Will had called her cell until she was forced to change her number.

"Why do you continue to come see me?" Ava asked Kyle after a comfortable silence.

The seconds ticked off as Kyle pondered her question. He'd asked himself time and again why he found himself thinking about Ava, why he couldn't stay away from her, and at no time had he been able to come up with a plausible answer.

"I like you." The three words summed up his true feelings.

"You like me," Ava said slowly. "How, Kyle?"

Slowing, Kyle stopped. "I can't explain it."

Tilting her chin, Ava smiled up at him. "Come now. I thought most lawyers were blessed with a gift for gab."

He smiled. "True, but in this instance I find it somewhat difficult to explain myself. However, as a social worker I'm certain you're able to analyze body language and nonverbal communication."

"Most times I am."

"Then, what do you say to this?"

Kyle didn't give Ava a chance to react when he lowered his head and slanted his mouth over hers in a kiss that stole the breath from her lungs, leaving her stunned and struggling to keep her balance.

He reached out, holding on to her shoulders as she swayed slightly. "What say you, Miss Warrick?"

Her smile matched his. "I get the message loud and clear."

"And that is?"

"I think you like me, Mr. Chatham."

Dropping his hands, Kyle wound an arm around her waist. "There's nothing to think about, Ava. The fact is that I like you—a lot. You're beautiful, intelligent and straightforward. You call a spade a spade."

Ava gave Kyle a sidelong glance as they waited for the light to change before crossing the street. "That should be a warning to you that I'll let you know when you don't come correct."

"Ouch. You really know how to hurt a brother, don't you?"

"I thought you like my straightforwardness?"

"I do, but can't you try and soften it a bit?"

"You can't have it both ways, Kyle. I deal with black and white, not shades of gray."

His hold tightening on her waist, Kyle pulled Ava closer to his length. "I concede. I'll be your way."

A slight frown found its way between Ava's eyes as she opened her mouth to come back at Kyle but then changed her mind. She didn't want to spend their time together debating personality traits. He liked her and she liked him. The difference was she had yet to tell Kyle how she felt.

"Will you come with me to a cookout this coming weekend?"

"That all depends?"

"On what, Ava?"

"If my sister doesn't have her baby."

"If she doesn't have her baby, then will you come with me?"

"Where is the cookout, Kyle?"

"Harlem."

She smiled, nodding. "I'll go with you."

Dropping his arm, Kyle took her hand and gave her fingers a gentle squeeze. "Thank you."

"You're welcome."

They walked in silence until they were in front of the Low Library, then turned and retraced their steps.

"How would you like to eat in the solarium?" Ava asked Kyle once they returned to the apartment.

His sensual smile spoke volumes. "Now you're talking. Where are you going?" he asked when she walked into the living room.

She smiled at him over her shoulder. "I'm going upstairs to set the table."

Climbing the staircase, Ava removed the plants from a round rattan table, which she covered with a tablecloth and set it with china, silver and crystal from the second-story kitchen. She filled the dozen votives lining the windowsill with tea lights and lit them, then repeated the action with a quartet of white vanilla-scented pillars that doubled as a centerpiece.

When she returned to the kitchen on the first floor she found Kyle had prepared the dressing for the Greek salad and sliced the potatoes, which he had tossed with olive oil and herbs and left roasting in the oven. The most delicious aroma came from the steaks in a heavy skillet as he tested them for doneness.

Moving closer, Ava joined Kyle at the range, her arm going around his waist as if it were something she'd done before. "Are you cooking with the brandy or drinking it?" She pointed to the bottle of brandy.

"I'm going to cook with it."

She watched intently as he removed the skillet from the heat, added about half a cup of brandy, then returned the pan to the high heat until the liquid was reduced by half. He waited a couple of minutes, removed the steaks to a cutting board, added heavy cream and butter to the pan until the cream was reduced to a thick sauce, and then put the steaks, along with the accumulated juices, into the skillet to warm them through.

Dipping his head, Kyle dropped a kiss on Ava's hair.

"Please get the wine from the fridge. I'll bring the plates upstairs."

"What about the potatoes?"

"I'll bring them, too."

Five minutes later they were seated in the darkened solarium with the rays of the setting sun coming in through the wall of glass and flickering candlelight providing the only illumination as soft music issued from a satellite radio station.

Ava swallowed a piece of butter-soft steak with the savory sauce and then took a sip of fragrant merlot. "Have you thought of moonlighting as a chef?"

Kyle stared across the table at Ava over the rim of his wineglass. "No."

"Why not?"

"Because I barely have time to cook for myself."

She took another sip of wine. "How often do you cook for yourself?"

"Unfortunately, not enough. I usually spend so much time at my office that I end up ordering from a local deli."

Ava set down her glass. "I used to order out until I had an incident with a deli in the neighborhood where I work."

"What kind of incident?" Kyle asked, leaning forward.

"I'd ordered a salad plate with tuna, potato and hard-boiled eggs. Later that evening I wound up with stomach cramps that kept me up all night. When I told the owner what had happened he became very defensive, denying I'd gotten sick from something he'd prepared."

"What do you do now?"

"After that I started bringing my own lunch. I cook on Sundays for the entire week. The only thing I have to do when I come home is either to prepare a fresh salad or steam vegetables."

Kyle stared at Ava for several seconds. "Have you stopped eating at restaurants because of a single incident?"

"No. It's just that I refuse to eat anything that is pre-packaged or not cooked to order."

"That's good to know."

"Why's that, Kyle?"

"It would prove problematic if I wanted to take you out to dinner at a restaurant."

Ava's eyebrows lifted. "Who said I was going out with you?"

"You did."

"No, I didn't."

"Yes, you did, Ava. Didn't you say you were interested in me?"

Her mouth opened and closed several times. "You must have had a super-size portion of arrogance and cockiness for breakfast and lunch."

Kyle threw back his head and laughed, the rich, deep sound coming from his chest. "You were the one who wanted to know about me, not the reverse, Miss Warrick. When I told you there wasn't much to tell, you said you wanted to hear it anyway. You said, and I quote, 'Because I'm interested in you,' end quote."

Ava wrinkled her nose. "I *was* curious, Kyle."

"Curious enough to let me take you out?"

She knew she was caught in a trap of her own making. There was no way she would be able to spar verbally with Kyle Chatham and win every time they engaged in a debate.

"I'm no longer curious, but I will agree to let you take me out."

Why, Kyle thought, did Ava make it sound as if she were doing him a favor? But then again, she was, because no woman was obligated to date him. That was something he'd learned years ago. The first time he'd asked a girl to go to the movies with him and she refused, he'd sulked for days before realizing he wasn't exempt from rejection.

Placing his right hand over his heart, he inclined his head. "You honor me, milady, with your kindness."

It was Ava's turn to laugh at his theatrics. "What do we have here? You're a chef *and* an actor. What's next?"

Kyle sobered quickly. "That's it."

"Are you a good attorney?"

"I'm adequate. Why? Do you want me to sue the deli owner for you?"

"No!"

"You said his food made you sick."

"But I don't want to sue the man."

"Bringing a suit may save other people from the same fate."

"I don't want him to lose his business, Kyle."

"If the health department cites him for too many violations, then he'll be forced to close down."

Ava glared at her dining partner. "I don't have much faith in the criminal justice system." Her expression and voice communicated disdain.

A swollen silence ensued, only the sounds coming from the radio and their measured breathing audible. Kyle felt as if she'd personally attacked his vocation. It was obvious Ava had little or no respect for *shyster* lawyers or the criminal justice system.

"Why would you say that, Ava?"

"I've been involved with cases where judges have dozed off through the entire proceedings, then woken up to render the wrong decision. I've had mothers who should have never had their children placed in foster care, and then those whose children were returned to them as mandated by the court only to be taken away again."

"The law isn't perfect, Ava, especially when it's being interpreted by mere mortals."

A slight smile parted her lips. "Yours truly included?"

Kyle smiled and nodded. "Yours truly included."

The conversation changed from law to politics. "Where were you and what were you doing when the news came down that Barak Obama had won the election?" Ava asked.

Kyle winked at Ava. It was the same question he'd asked his parents and siblings after the historic event. "I was working late, but had the television on. As polls closed in several States I started keeping a tally. After a while I gave up all pretense of trying to read a brief. My buddies Duncan and Ivan were also working late, so we all got together in the kitchen to watch the returns. Duncan ordered takeout and once we cracked open a few beers it was on. The three of us polished off a twelve-pack before eleven o'clock, so when the announcement came that Barak had won we were less than sober or steady. All I can say was that it was a sorry sight to see three grown men literally crying in their beer."

She gave him a pointed look. "You weren't really crying, were you?"

"Yes," he confirmed. "It was a mixture of relief, joy and much too much beer. Where were you?"

"I was on the phone with my college roommate who'd flown back to Iowa that Sunday so she could vote. We talked for hours and when Iowa went blue both of us were bawling and babbling like idiots. We ended the marathon call when President-elect Obama made his victory speech. I was so pumped up that I couldn't sleep that night."

The negative vibes Ava gave off whenever she didn't want to be bothered, or when she felt herself liking a man a little too much, never reared their ugly head as she and Kyle discussed the events of President Obama's long and grueling campaign, the Democrats' electrifying convention and the night that changed America and Americans forever. The warning not to discuss religion or politics was for naught, because it was politics where she and Kyle found common ground.

"How long did you stand in line before getting into your polling place?" Kyle asked as he peered at Ava over the rim of his wineglass.

"Not quite two hours."

Kyle whistled softly. "You had me beat by an hour."

"What time did you get up?" she asked.

"I was in line a little before five, and the line was still down the block and around the corner."

Ava gave him a pointed look. "No wonder you waited only an hour. I got to my polling place at eight." The topic smoothly segued from politics to sports as the sun moved lower in the horizon and the candles flickered until they burned out one by one.

"Please, don't get up," Kyle ordered softly when Ava reached for a plate to clear the table.

"I'm not an invalid."

"I know you're not, but I've got this." He stacked plates and flatware with the agility of an experienced waiter.

Waiting until he'd taken everything to the downstairs kitchen, Ava removed the tablecloth, turned on a table lamp to its lowest setting and blew out the remaining candles. Kyle had stacked the dishes, serving pieces and pots in the dishwasher when she walked into the kitchen.

"You'd make some woman a wonderful husband."

Shifting slightly, he smiled at her over his shoulder. "Haven't you ever had a man cook for you?"

"Not really."

"Is that a yes or a no?"

Ava met his gaze. Will couldn't cook, so that meant she'd done all of the cooking. The exception was when they either went out or ordered takeout. "That's a no."

"That's going to change."

Vertical lines appeared between her eyes. "What are you talking about?"

"Whenever we get together I'll do the cooking."

She closed the distance between them until they were less than a foot apart. "Are you that certain we're going to get together *that* often?"

Running his forefinger over her injured cheek, Kyle dipped his head as his mouth replaced his finger. "Call it wishful thinking," he whispered.

Smiling, Ava lowered her chin. "Do you want me to grant your wish?"

"Yes, I do." Kyle's teeth closed gently on her earlobe.

The seconds ticked off before Ava whispered, "Wish granted."

Wrapping his arms around her shoulders, Kyle pulled Ava to his chest. "Thank you."

She nodded rather than replying. Interacting with Kyle Chatham was so different than what she'd experienced with the other men she'd known. He was arrogant, but instead of it becoming a turn-off, she understood it.

Kyle was good-looking, intelligent, charming and despite being single he wasn't a baby daddy. She'd found herself drawn to William Marshall because he hadn't any baby-mama drama. Maintaining a normal relationship with a man was challenging enough without having to deal with either a woman or women in his past. And if children were involved, then they usually put more stress on a relationship.

Man-sharing and/or playing stepmother was something she sought to avoid. However, if she did find herself totally in love with a man, then she was willing to make concessions. Her sister said she was unrealistic because Ava had set her standards much too high, but she was quick to remind Aisha that she also didn't date men with children because of an incident where a deranged woman had begun stalking her, claiming Aisha had come between her ex and his children.

She'd met men who refused to date single mothers, although they were single fathers. She would go out with Kyle, enjoy his companionship and if and when it ended she planned not to have to look back or wallow in regret.

"You're welcome."

Easing back, Kyle stared at Ava. "I'll call and let you know when I'm going to pick you up for the cookout."

Going on tiptoe, Ava kissed his cheek. "Good night, Kyle."

He returned the kiss on the uninjured side of her face. "Good night, Ava."

She walked him to the door and opened and closed it behind him. A hint of a smile tilted the corners of her mouth upward. "I like him." The admission had slipped between her lips. She was still smiling when she retreated to the kitchen to start the dishwasher.

Chapter 7

Kyle picked up a portion of sashimi with a pair of chop-sticks, staring intently at it before putting it into his mouth.

"If you're going to examine every morsel, then I would've suggested eating some place where the food isn't as exotic."

Kyle's head came up and he stared across the table at his dining partner. Jordan Wainwright's features were as patrician as his old-money lineage. Tall and slender, he exuded elegance, breeding, and his large hazel eyes, close-cropped black curly hair and deeply tanned face attracted both men and women. Heir to a real-estate empire second only to Prudential Douglas Elliman, the largest real-estate conglomerate in the east, Jordan's decision not to work for Wainwright Developers Group had caused an irreparable rift between grandfather and grandson.

"I'm sorry, Jordan, but my mind is elsewhere."

"Who is she?"

Kyle affected an impassive expression. "What makes you think it's a woman?"

Jordan's sweeping black eyebrows shot up. "I worked with you long enough to know that it's not a case you've been working on, because you were always the most focused one on our team. That's why the partners always made you lead counsel."

A slow smile crinkled the skin around his eyes. "You think you know me that well?" Kyle asked Jordan.

"Well enough, Chat."

"What else do you know?"

"I also know that you want me to work with you. If you didn't, then you would've told me that on the phone."

"You think you're slick, don't you?"

Jordan smiled, flashing a mouth of perfect white teeth his parents had spent a small fortune straightening.

"If I am, then I learned it from the best."

Kyle sobered quickly. "Why do you want to work for me, Jordan, when you can have any position you want with Wainwright Developers Group?"

A slight frown appeared between Jordan's eyes as he stared at the back of his hand resting next to his plate. "Working for my family's real-estate company isn't challenging. That's the reason I went to work for TCB. They may have worked us like pack mules, but in the end we became expert litigators and trial attorneys."

"That's true, but what makes you think working for a small law firm in Harlem is going to be challenging?"

"It doesn't have to be challenging, Chat, as long as I don't have to spend my time defending fat cats who cook their books then bail out with golden parachutes, leaving their shareholders with nothing."

Kyle gave Jordan a long, penetrating stare. "So, you think slumming in Harlem is going to be more challenging than defending white-collar criminals or working for your grandfather?"

A flush suffused the younger attorney's face under a deep summer tan he'd perfected hanging out at the Wainwright summer compound at Chesapeake Ranch Estates in Maryland. "You think I want to work in Harlem because I suddenly had an epiphany that defending the disadvantaged and underserved will absolve me of the guilt of defending crooks whose greed destroys lives and erodes this country's economy?"

"I can't help you do battle with your conscience, Jordan," Kyle said, deadpan, "but what I can do is let you work with me on a trial basis. I can't pay you six figures, but your salary will be comparable to a law..." His voice trailed off when Jordan opened his mouth. "Let me finish. I know you're going to tell me you'll work for nothing, but trust fund or no trust fund I'll pay you. My clients are no different from the ones who came to TCB. They may not have the same earning power but they, too, are looking for someone to help them with their legal problems.

"The indictments differ in that our defendants are charged with burglary, petty assault, possession with the intent to sell, solicitation, resisting arrest and armed robbery." Kyle paused, giving Jordan a chance to think about what he'd told him. "However, I do have a landlord-tenant case that should interest you."

Jordan sat up straighter. "Who's the landlord?"

There came a beat. "It took a lot of digging, but my paralegal discovered it is a Wainwright Developers Group holding company."

A pair of brown eyes with flecks of greenish-gray met and fused with a pair in warm honey-brown. "Now I know why you were reluctant to bring me on board."

Kyle shook his head. "You're wrong, Jordan. It has nothing to do with me going after your family's company."

A muscle twitched in Jordan's lean jaw. "Then what is it?"

"I wasn't sure whether you'd be able to talk the talk and walk the walk."

"People are people regardless of where they live, Kyle."

Kyle knew Jordan was angry because he hadn't called him Chat. "That's where you are wrong, Wainwright. Yes, Harlem is changing, becoming gentrified, but there are still some residents who live well below the poverty line who need more than an overworked public defender to solve their legal problems. Since I hung out my shingle I've had to set up a sliding scale for legal fees. You've heard of department-store layaway. Well, Kyle E. Chatham, Esquire, has legal layaway. Some of my clients are highly educated, while others can barely sign their names, but they're all treated with the same respect and dignity afforded those at TCB. If you want to work with me, then be prepared for whatever I'll throw at you. And that includes suing your family's real-estate empire."

Jordan lowered his gaze and a sweep of thick black lashes touched his cheekbones. "Are you saying you need money, Chat?"

Kyle went completely still. His friend and former colleague just didn't get it. "This is not about money."

"Then, what is it about? It can't be about your clients because you seem to be taking care of business, otherwise you wouldn't have a practice."

"I didn't say I have a cash flow problem. I've never had a problem covering payroll or monthly operational overhead."

"What about profits?" Jordan asked.

"I didn't go into private practice to concern myself with bottom-line profit margins."

A hint of a smile parted Jordan's firm lips. "How many employees do you have?"

"Four. Three are full-time and one part-time."

"What are their positions?"

"What are you getting at, Jordan?"

"Please answer the question, Chat."

"I have a full-time legal secretary, office manager and

paralegal. I also have a part-time paralegal for evening hours. I share a receptionist and cleaning service with two friends who each own a third of the building."

"How would you like to hire a full-time legal researcher and law clerk?"

Kyle shook his head. Carrying two mortgages—one on his home and the other on his business—had taken a sizeable bite out of his savings. "I'd love to, but it would strain my budget."

Jordan leaned closer. "Make me partner, Chat, and I'll cover business expenses for the next two years. If you want I'll make it three."

Crossing his arms over his chest, Kyle studied the thirty-two-year-old attorney who'd come to him asking to be a partner when he could've set up his own law firm. "What's this all about, Jordan? Why me and not some other firm? Better yet, why don't you set up your own firm? Who are you pissed at?" he asked when Jordan compressed his lips into a thin, hard line.

Pushing back his chair, Jordan reached into the pocket of his suit trousers and threw a large bill on the table. "Thanks for meeting with me."

"Sit down!" The two words came out with the impact of the crack of a whip. The younger man complied. "What are you doing, Jordan?" Kyle's voice was lower, softer. "You graduate Harvard Law, and instead of joining your family business you go to work for TCB. You leave them, then come to me for a position. What gives? Who are you trying to punish?"

Jordan's expression grew hard and resentful as his long, slender, groomed fingers curled into tight fists. "My grandfather," he said after a pregnant pause.

"Does it have anything to do with African-Amercans?" he asked perceptively.

"Yes."

Kyle was hard-pressed not to laugh. "You're pissed off with your grandfather, so to punish him you leave a plum position with Trilling, Carlyle and Browne, where last I heard you were rumored to become a junior partner, to come uptown to work with a struggling law firm whose focus is to protect the legal rights of the disenfranchised and underserved people of color?"

"I didn't have to come to you."

"But you did," Kyle argued softly. "I don't want to know why you're at odds with your grandfather, but if you're serious about working for me then you're hired. However, I'm not going to make you partner until you prove yourself. I'm going to give you the landlord-tenant case. Use whatever resources you need to make your granddad and the holding company's bastard slumlord pay for what they've done to the eighty families who live in their hovel."

"When do you want me to start?" The warmth of Jordan's smile echoed in his voice.

"I'm closing the office on Monday to give the employees a four-day weekend, so it will have to be Tuesday. What are you doing this coming weekend?"

"My mother asked me to come down to Maryland for the holiday. Why?"

"My friend is hosting a cookout at his place on Saturday. If you decide to come, then you'll get to meet the people you'll be working with in a more relaxed setting."

"I'd love to come, but my mother is hosting a fifty-fifth birthday celebration for my dad at our summer place."

Every Fourth of July weekend Christiane Wainwright closed up the Fifth Avenue maisonette and relocated her household, including the household staff, to the family compound at Chesapeake Ranch Estates, Maryland. When she'd called him to tell him about the family gathering, Jordan's first impulse was to decline because Wyatt Wainwright would also be there. But then, his mother was not to blame for her father-in-law's treachery. Taking on and winning the landlord-tenant case would do little to affect Wainwright Developers Group's bottom line, but the negative publicity attendant on a family member suing the conglomerate on behalf of low-income tenants would be publicly embarrassing to a man who'd spent more than half a century building and maintaining the real-estate giant.

Kyle smiled. "Hopefully you'll be available for the next one."

Jordan returned the smile. "I'll make certain to be available."

The two men reminisced about the cases they'd taken to trial, ninety-eight percent of which they'd won. Lingering over entrées of grilled salmon with miso basil, *yasai soba* with vegetables in a hot broth, tempura shrimp and vegetables and sake, Kyle and Jordan lapsed into the familiarity that had been apparent when they'd worked together as litigators.

Kyle picked up the tab, and Jordan left to hail a taxi to take them uptown. Jordan exited the cab on Fifth Avenue at Ninety-Eighth Street while Kyle continued on to West One Hundred Thirty-Ninth Street.

Walking into his kitchen, he checked his voice mail. There was one message from his sister, another from his mother asking if she was going to see him over the holiday weekend. Kyle called his mother, promising to drive up to Tarrytown to spend Monday with her.

Jordan had accused him of daydreaming about a woman, and his newest employee was right. When he least expected it, Kyle's thoughts drifted to Ava, her bruised face, soft curly hair, beautifully modulated voice and her lush, womanly body.

Whenever he met a woman it was never his intent to think of her as an object of sex. If he wanted sex, then he could always pick up a stranger and go at it. Although he'd dated a lot of women, he hadn't slept with a lot of women. Sleeping with a woman went beyond a physical commitment—it was also an emotional commitment.

There was something about Ava Warrick that made him want to commit to her, emotionally and physically. What Kyle liked about her was that she wasn't *easy.* He'd learned from experience that if a woman opened her legs to him within days of their meeting, then she would open her legs to any man who gave her attention or offered her a compliment. Any woman willing to jump into bed with him after their first, second or even third date, he walked away from. Although he enjoyed being a bachelor and what the status offered, Kyle unconsciously viewed every woman as a potential wife.

He'd told Ava that he would call her once the details for the cookout were confirmed, but decided to text her instead. Retrieving his cell phone, he typed in the time he would pick her up on Saturday. Ivan had asked everyone to arrive around two in the afternoon, but Kyle knew he had to get there earlier to fire up the grill and make certain he had what he needed to make the outdoor gathering a success.

An hour later, he sat in his den watching the Yankees play the Seattle Mariners. Whenever his dad was home from the railroad, he'd made it a practice to take Kyle and Kenneth to Yankee Stadium. Kyle had become a rabid sports fan when he'd added football and basketball as spectator sports. He, Ivan and Duncan usually reserved Sundays and Monday nights during football season for hanging out at one another's homes to view the games.

Kyle hadn't realized he'd dozed off until the chiming of the phone startled him into awareness. Reaching for the cordless instrument, he mumbled a sleepy greeting.

"What are you wearing, handsome?"

He sat straighter. "Who's this?"

"I'll give you one guess."

"Ava?"

"Yes, it's Ava. Do you have so many women calling your home that you don't recognize my voice?"

Now Kyle was fully alert. "No, but you're the only one with a southern accent. And I don't have that many women calling to ask what I'm wearing, because the ones who do are usually sleeping with me."

"I don't have an accent."

He noticed she hadn't responded to the possibility that they could possibly share a bed. "Yeah, you do. You say y'all instead of you all."

"Everyone says y'all."

"I don't."

"That's because you're unique, Mr. Chatham."

He smiled. "You think so?"

"No, you think so," she teased, laughing softly. "I'm calling you to respond to your text. I'll be ready at twelve. Do you want me to bring anything?"

"No."

"What about dessert?"

Kyle's smile grew wider, although Ava couldn't see it. "What are you suggesting?"

Her soft laugh came through the earpiece. "Don't tell me you have a sweet tooth."

"I have more than one sweet tooth. It's more like thirty-two."

"Have you ever had red-velvet whoopie pies?"

"No. What are they?"

"Whoopie pies are two fluffy cookies with a cream filling."

Kyle smiled. "Oh, now I know what they are."

"I was thinking of making some, but instead of a chocolate cookie I'll make a red-velvet version with a cream-cheese filling."

"It sounds yummy. How many do you plan to make?"

"That all depends on how many people are coming to the cookout."

"I don't think there will be more than thirty."

"Good," Ava said. "I'll make enough so each person can get at least two."

"How large will they be?"

"I'll make them about an inch in diameter."

"No, you didn't say an inch. I could eat at least a dozen by myself."

"A dozen will give you more than half your daily caloric intake."

He laughed. "That means I'll just have to work out more often."

"How do you keep so slim?" Ava asked him.

"I usually walk to work. There's also a gym on the street level of the building where I have my office."

"That's nice."

"It is," Kyle confirmed. "When I pick you up on Saturday I'll give you a tour. It's two blocks from Ivan's house."

"Getting back to the cookies, I'll make a special

batch for you and if you complain about an expanding waistline or cavities I'm not going to entertain it."

"Won't matter," he drawled, "because I have an excellent dental plan."

"On that note I'm going to hang up. Good night, Kyle."

He held the receiver to his ear, then said, "Good night, Ava."

The distinct click indicated she'd hung up. Depressing a button, Kyle replaced the phone in the cradle. Reaching for the television remote, he turned the TV off. Ava had shocked him when she'd asked what he was wearing and in doing so had revealed another facet of her complex personality.

Ava Warrick was a tease—a beautiful, sexy tease.

Ava opened the door and waited for Kyle to exit the elevator. A bright smile curved her mouth when she saw him. It'd been four days since they'd been together and she noticed things about him that weren't so apparent before. Despite the elegant cut of his suits, she preferred seeing him dressed down. A stark-white golf shirt and faded jeans displayed his toned, slim body to its best advantage. A faded denim baseball cap with a New York Yankees' logo covered his head.

Kyle approached Ava, arms extended, and he wasn't disappointed when she went willingly into his embrace. "Hey, you," he crooned in her ear.

Raising her chin, Ava smiled up at him. "Hey, you, back."

Cradling her chin in his hand, he stared at her face. There was no sign of bruising or swelling. She'd applied a light cover of makeup to her flawless complexion. "You look beautiful."

A rush of heat stung Ava's cheeks. "Thank you."

"Where are the cookies?"

"I'm on to you, Kyle Chatham. You tell me I'm beautiful to soften me up then ask about cookies in the same breath."

Kyle tightened his hold on her body as he pulled her gently into the apartment and closed the door. He pressed her back to the door. "I could've asked what you are wearing under that very cute dress." She'd selected a sunny-yellow, jungle-print sundress that exposed her arms, shoulders and back. Spaghetti straps crisscrossing her back revealed she wasn't wearing a bra, and he averted his gaze so as not to stare at the soft swell of breasts rising and falling above the V-neck bodice.

Ava flashed a sensual pout. "I'll give you one guess."

"That's not fair. I'd allow you more than one guess."

Going on tiptoe, she brushed a kiss over his smooth jaw. "That's where we differ, Kyle. One guess, one chance."

"Hey," he crooned softly, "what happened to the Ava who's sensitive, compassionate and benevolent?"

"That Ava is for clients, and you're not one of my clients."

"What do I have to do to become a client?" Kyle asked, pressing his groin to hers.

She gasped audibly. "Don't do that."

"Do what, sweetheart?"

"Don't call me sweetheart."

"I just called you sweetheart." Kyle pressed even closer as the flesh between his legs stirred restlessly.

"What are you doing, Kyle?"

Cradling her face between his hands, he held her immobile. "As a social worker I'm certain you're familiar with nonverbal communication."

A slight smile softened her full lips. "I am, but what is it we're doing?"

Kyle wiggled his eyebrows. "We are, as the kids say, *con-va-sate-in.*"

Throwing back her head, Ava laughed until tears filled her eyes and ran down her cheeks. "You are really crazy."

He wanted to tell Ava he was indeed a little crazy, and about her. He'd known her for a week, and already he felt closer to her than he had with other women with whom he'd had extended relationships. Kyle knew he couldn't continue to press his body to Ava's without dire consequences. Taking a step back, he released her.

"We'd better leave now if I'm going to give you a tour of the office before we head over to Ivan's place."

Closing her eyes, Ava breathed in and out steadily, hoping to slow down her runaway pulse. Although Kyle had put some distance between them, she still could feel his heat, the solid wall of his chest and thighs. Everything about the man who'd unexpectedly come into her life was shockingly memorable. Even when they were apart she still remembered everything about him: the way he held his head when deep in thought, the shape of his large, well-groomed hands, the lingering scent of his very masculine cologne that was the perfect complement to his body's natural scent, and his voice—low and sensuously hypnotic. Pushing off the door, she walked to the kitchen to retrieve a large airtight container with the whoopie pies.

"The doctor cleared me to return to work," she told Kyle, who stood at the sink with a glass of water.

"He said you're okay?"

"Yes. He took another scan with a state-of-the-art imaging machine and he said there's no evidence of an aneurysm. I was so relieved that I went to the market to shop for the ingredients I needed for the cookies."

"How many did you make?"

She wrinkled her nose. "I think about twelve dozen."

Kyle raised his eyebrows. "You think?"

"Give or take a few."

She'd been so excited about getting a clean bill of health that she'd spent hours baking dozens of cookies, then filling them with softened cream cheese and marshmallow cream. A call from her local pharmacy had wakened her Friday morning with a reminder to pick up her three-month supply of contraceptives. Despite not being sexually active, Ava took the low-dose birth control pill to control a heavier than normal flow.

She'd got out of bed, showered and left the house before nine for the first time in days, stopping to pick up her prescription, eating a leisurely breakfast in her favorite neighborhood coffee shop and riding the bus downtown to purchase yarn and a supply of fat quarters for quilting from a craft boutique she'd discovered by accident when strolling along the Upper East Side.

Ava returned to the apartment to find that the cleaning service had left everything immaculate, and she settled down to piece together a pram pillow for her unborn niece. Aisha had declared vehemently she didn't want to know her baby's sex, but had changed her mind when Ava promised to knit or crochet blankets, sweaters, hats, and piece a handmade quilt for her niece or nephew.

Aisha, the consummate style diva, wanted only the best for her baby and that included having her color-coordinated. Ava knitted and crocheted the requisite pink for girls, but the quilted crib and pram blankets were soft shades reminiscent of cantaloupe and honeydew.

Kyle set the glass on the countertop. "How many did you make for me?"

"Not too many." She pointed to a small black-and-white shopping bag on the countertop next to the sink. "That's yours."

He peered into the bag and smiled. A clear plastic container tied with a black satin bow was filled with round, red cream-filled cookies. "You are something else. Thank you."

Ava inclined her head. "You're welcome." Turning, she opened the refrigerator. "You're going to have to carry this one."

Kyle removed the large container, decorated with a striped red-white-and-blue ribbon, from the refrigerator, setting it down on the table. "How did you lift this?"

"It's not that heavy."

"It's heavy enough, especially for a woman."

Ava rolled her eyes upward. "Maybe it's too heavy for someone who's anorexic, but not for yours truly."

"You think you're fat?" Kyle asked, surprised.

"No," she replied, "but I'm not skin and bones, either."

He closed the distance between them. "I think I can speak for most men when I say that no man wants a woman with bones sticking out all over her body. I like your body just the way it is. I also like your face, the color of your skin and your hair. In other words, I like you, Ava Warrick."

Ava felt a shiver go through her when she looked into the slanting, catlike, warm brown eyes, searching for a hint of guile. Men had told her things they thought she wanted to hear because they wanted her in their beds, or they wanted to take advantage of her vulnerability whenever she told them she'd just gotten out of a less-than-healthy relationship.

She'd met Kyle exactly one week ago, and he'd been the consummate gentleman. He hadn't made an off-color remark or attempted to touch her inappropriately. He was perfect in every way, which made her wonder why some woman hadn't taken him off the market. Was he, she mused, commitment-shy? Or did he like being a bachelor so much that he hadn't found the need to change his marital status? After all, he didn't have to marry a woman to have sex with her, so he enjoyed the best of both worlds.

"And I like you, too, Kyle."

He gave her a sexy smile. "Thank you. Are you ready to leave?"

"I have one more thing to get, then we can leave."

"What is it?"

Ava opened a cabinet and removed a decanter bottle filled with pale-green olive oil and a profusion of herbs. "I put together a house gift for the host."

Kyle shook his head in astonishment. "You didn't have to do that."

"Yes, I did, Kyle Chatham. I never go empty-handed to someone's house the first time."

"Yes, but—"

"Please, Kyle," Ava interrupted, "let's not fight. I feel great and I want to enjoy spending time with you and your friends."

Smiling, he pulled her into his arms, lowered his head and kissed her with a passion that was as foreign to him as the emotions that he was beginning to feel for a woman who'd come out of the night and into his life.

Deepening the kiss, Kyle waited for Ava to exhale to slide his tongue between her parted lips. Her taste and smell became a permanent tattoo on his tongue. It took Herculean strength for him not to pick up Ava and carry her upstairs to her bedroom.

Reluctantly, he tore his mouth from hers, eyes wild

with a passion he was helpless to control. "Let's go before I do something I have no right to do."

Ava nodded numbly. She didn't trust herself to speak, for if she did then it would be to beg Kyle to take her to bed. It was a good thing they were going out, because each time she saw him it became more and more difficult to hide her feelings for a man who made her want him, despite her vow that she would never again let herself get involved with another man.

Chapter 8

Kyle unlocked the passenger side of the Jag, waiting until Ava was seated before storing the cookies and the olive oil in the trunk. He rounded the car and slipped in beside her.

They hadn't exchanged a word since leaving the apartment, and he feared that he'd gone too far, moved much too quickly when he kissed her. Ava was very different from other women he'd known. Firstly, most them of were less than reticent about wanting to know more about him, or even about getting together. He'd lost track of the number of women who'd asked him out first. Kyle found that a complete turn-off, because he always wanted to do the pursuing. There was no fun in the chase if the prey refused to run.

It had taken him a while to realize he was more conservative than most of his contemporaries. Even if women threw their panties at him he refused to bite. His rule was, if she was easy with him, then she would be easy with any other man. After all, she wouldn't know if he was a serial rapist or, even worse, a serial killer, until it was too late. He was shocked that more parents didn't warn their daughters about the wolves in sheep's clothing.

He started up the car, shifted into gear and pulled away from the curb in a smooth burst of speed. "Do you know when you're going to get your car back?" Kyle asked when he'd stopped at a red light.

"Your cousin called yesterday to tell me he'd ordered the bumper, and it would probably be in Tuesday or Wednesday."

"If you need a car before yours is ready, then you can borrow mine."

Ava stared at Kyle's distinctive profile. "That won't be necessary. I take the subway to and from work."

"Do you park on the street?"

"No. I have space in a garage." She parked her car in a garage that belonged to Mrs. Servinsky's brother-in-law for a fraction of the exorbitant yearly fee. The college professors had become her guardian angels. She would live in their apartment for two years rent-free and the slashed-to-the-bone fee to garage her car permitted Ava to save a lot of money for when it came time for her to get her own apartment.

"Why do you have a car if you don't use it every

day? Wouldn't it be more economical to rent one when you need it?"

"I could ask you the same question.'

Kyle gave Ava a quick sidelong glance before returning his gaze to the road. "The difference is I don't have to pay to garage my car."

"Where do you park it?"

"My house has an attached carriage house I use as a garage. Speaking of cars, will I be able to leave my cookies in the trunk for an extended length of time?"

"No. They should be refrigerated because of the cream cheese."

"If that's the case, then we'll stop by my place first."

Ava knew she was gaping, but she couldn't conceal her shock when Kyle escorted her into his kitchen. Black granite countertops and stainless-steel appliances provided the perfect backdrop for off-white cabinetry and black-and-white vinyl flooring.

"Would you like a quick tour?" Kyle asked after he placed his cookies in the refrigerator.

She glanced at the clock on the built-in microwave. It was almost one o'clock. "Do we have time?"

Kyle nodded, smiling. "We have plenty of time. We'll drop the food off at Ivan's, and from there walk over to the office." He held out his hand and he wasn't disappointed when Ava placed her smaller hand in his.

He'd gotten up earlier that morning to marinate meat and then drop it off at Ivan's place. His friend was quick to inform him that several cases of beer and wine had been delivered just before he'd arrived. When the psychotherapist complained that he had enough beverages on hand for a fraternity party, Kyle had unceremoniously dismissed him with a wave of the hand and walked away. There were times when he found Ivan as anal as some of his clients.

"We'll start upstairs, then work our way down. I thought about putting in an elevator, but changed my mind because walking stairs is a good form of exercise."

"How many rooms do you have?"

"There are six bedrooms and six bathrooms, and that includes a downstairs one-bedroom duplex."

Ava slowed as she climbed the staircase. Riding elevators had spoiled her. "Do you live here alone?"

Kyle also slowed his pace. "Yes. I thought about renting out the duplex, but changed my mind. I like my privacy."

Ava met his eyes, "But there's enough space here that you wouldn't have to run into the other tenant if they're occupying the lower floor. If I'd grown up in a place like this and if family dynamics had been different I don't think I would've ever left home."

Kyle stopped on the second-floor landing, cradling Ava to his chest. "If you hadn't left, then I would've never met you."

Tilting her chin, she stared up at him. "Would that have been so profound?"

He gave her a tender smile. "It would've been very profound."

"Are you saying that because you think it's what I want to hear?"

Kyle sobered as a scowl clouded his handsome features. "You think I said that to placate you, to stroke your ego?"

"I don't know what to think, Kyle. I haven't had a good track record with men."

"Maybe it's because you've been dealing with losers?"

"They were beyond losers. They were more like socio- and psychopaths. And you'd think I would've recognized all the signs early on, but I suppose at that time in my life I didn't want to be alone. It's amazing, but there are as many reasons why women don't leave men as there are why they never should've hooked up in the first place.

"I've counseled women who dumb themselves down because they don't want their men to feel insecure. Then there are the ones who are so grateful to have a husband that they overlook all of his wrongs. I have a client who has chosen to ignore her husband's mental abuse because he married her when she found herself pregnant. She doesn't love her husband, yet talks about being grateful that he saved her."

"Not all men are you like your father."

Ava forced a smile. "I know that."

"And not all men are like your ex-boyfriends."

"I realize that now. You're nothing like Will."

"Was he your ex?"

There was only the sound of measured breathing as Ava and Kyle stared at each other. "Yes. He was a Jekyll and Hyde. I waited until he left for work to move out, and eventually I had to get a restraining order keep him away from my job."

"How long has it been since you last saw him?"

"Almost two years."

"Let me know if he ever bothers you again. I know people who could put him away for a very long time."

"He wouldn't have to go very far to be locked up."

The seconds ticked off before Kyle's expression mirrored realization. "He's in corrections?"

"Bingo!"

"Talk about flipping the script. He probably wouldn't last a week in the general population."

Curving her arms under Kyle's shoulders, Ava went on tiptoe and pressed her mouth to his. "I don't want to talk about him."

"Then we won't."

Kyle escorted her up the curving staircase, and she admired the massive banister and newel posts made of Honduran mahogany. On the third floor there were three bedrooms with working fireplaces and two full bathrooms. The two smaller bedrooms had areas with tables that doubled as desks.

"Whenever I have guests they stay up here," he explained, retracing their steps.

Ava walked in and out of rooms with furnishings carefully chosen for the utmost comfort and relaxation. The suede-leather-and-iron headboards and footboards, oversized club chairs with matching ottomans and silk drapes at tall casement windows beckoned one to linger to enjoy the elegant solitude.

"Where's your bedroom?" Ava asked.

Kyle tightened his hold on her fingers. "It's on the second floor. It has a balcony overlooking the backyard and an additional bedroom I use as a den."

Ava learned a lot about the man with whom she'd found herself drawn to when she walked into his bedroom. A California-king, Asian-inspired bed with a massive pale-gray suede headboard was the space's focal point. Soft eggshell-white walls, recessed lights, gleaming wood floors and a marble fireplace gave the room a spare look. The den contained a large wall-mounted television, a dark gray leather chaise and loveseat and floor-to-ceiling bookcases packed with books, CDs and DVDs. A home theater system rested on a table below the television. Walk-in closets took up another wall in the master bedroom.

She walked to the French doors that led to the balcony. "How often do you get to sit out on your deck?"

Kyle came up behind her, wrapping both arms around her middle. "Not often enough. But I plan to change that."

Peering up over her shoulder, Ava smiled. "How?"

"I want you to come for a sleepover. You can pick any of the upstairs bedrooms. And when you get up we'll have breakfast on the deck."

"You have it all figured out, don't you?"

"Again, it's wishful thinking."

An Important Message from the Publisher

Dear Reader,

Because you've chosen to read one of our fine novels, I'd like to say "thank you"! And, as a special way to say thank you, I'm offering to send you two more Kimani™ Romance novels and two surprise gifts – absolutely FREE! These books will keep it real with true-to-life African American characters that turn up the heat and sizzle with passion.

Please enjoy the free books and gifts with our compliments...

Linda Gill

Publisher, Kimani Press

off Seal and
Place Inside...

Two Kimani™ Romance Novels
Two exciting surprise gifts

PLACE
FREE GIFTS
SEAL
HERE

168 XDL EVGW   368 XDL EVJ9

FIRST NAME   LAST NAME

ADDRESS

APT.#   CITY

STATE / PROV.   ZIP / POSTAL CODE

Thank You!

BUSINESS REPLY MAIL

FIRST-CLASS MAIL   PERMIT NO. 717   BUFFALO, NY

POSTAGE WILL BE PAID BY ADDRESSEE

**THE READER SERVICE
3010 WALDEN AVE
PO BOX 1867
BUFFALO NY 14240-9952**

NO POSTAGE
NECESSARY
IF MAILED
IN THE
UNITED STATES

Turning in his embrace, she flashed a pout. "Try not to use up all of your wishes too soon."

"How much time and how many wishes are you going to grant me?"

"Three months, ten wishes."

Kyle frowned. "Why are you so stingy with the wishes?"

"I could've said ten wishes in ten days."

"That would leave me only eight wishes for the next three days."

"The choice is yours, counselor."

Kyle knew when he'd been bested although he considered himself a winner because Ava had agreed to go out with him for the next three months. "I accept."

Ava patted his chest. "I thought you would."

Bending slightly, he scooped Ava up in his arms and carried her down the staircase to the first floor. "You can see the rest of the house when you stay over. We better take the cookies over to Ivan's before the filling spoils."

Kyle was fortunate to find parking only doors from Ivan's brownstone. It was a summer weekend and many city residents were either on vacation or had abandoned the city for eastern Long Island or the New Jersey shore. He carried the container with the baked goods, while Ava cradled the bag with the flavored oil.

"I love Harlem," she said reverently, staring at the brownstones, most of which had been restored to their original magnificence.

"So do I," Kyle concurred. "I wouldn't think of living anywhere else."

Ava knew why Kyle had chosen to live in Harlem rather than in other trendy neighborhoods populated by young professionals. As a Columbia student she'd discovered the historic neighborhood was much more than tenements. It had brownstones, townhouses and mansions, condominiums and co-ops—one of which she hoped she would one day call her own.

She followed Kyle through the open wrought-iron gate and down three steps to the street-level entrance. He rang the bell and within seconds the door opened. Ava found herself mesmerized by a man with a sensually brooding expression reminiscent of a taciturn actor in a Jane Austen film. Like Kyle, he was also dressed casually. A brightly colored, short-sleeved Hawaiian shirt and jeans did little to conceal his rock-hard muscular body. His dark brown gaze shifted from Kyle to her. A slow smile spread across his face and Ava hadn't realized she was holding her breath until she felt the band of constriction across her chest.

Ivan's smile grew wider as he stepped back. "I'm forgetting my manners. Please come in."

Kyle handed his friend the plastic container, then wrapped an arm around Ava's shoulders. "That needs to be refrigerated. But first let me introduce you to Ava Warrick. Ava, this is Ivan Campbell—friend and unofficial brother."

Ava offered her hand. "It's nice meeting you, Ivan." She

handed him the shopping bag with the flavored oil. "What's in the container is for your guests. *This* is for you."

Ivan took the shopping bag. "Thank you, Ava. What's in the container?"

"Red velvet—"

"No, you didn't say red velvet? Did Kyle tell you that my favorite cake is red velvet? I have Cake Man Raven on speed dial."

"Who is Cake Man Raven?" she asked.

Ivan and Kyle shared a look. "Why doesn't she know about Cake Man Raven?" The doorbell rang, preempting whatever Kyle was going to say. "Please get the door, Kyle, while I put this away. Ava, you can come with me."

She followed her host through an entryway and into a room that doubled as a parlor. They passed several rooms until she stood in the middle of a large kitchen with a long table filled with trays of food covered with colorful plastic wrap. The sound of music came in through a screened-in door that led to the backyard.

"How long have you known Kyle?"

Ava met Ivan's gaze as he opened the refrigerator. "Not very long."

"He's a good guy, Ava."

A slight frown formed between her eyes. "Why are you telling me what I already know?"

"I just want you to know what you have."

"Do you think I don't deserve to have a good guy?"

"No, Ava, please don't misconstrue what I'm saying."

"I'm not misconstruing anything, Ivan."

The two engaged in what could only become a stare-down stalemate. Ivan put the container in the refrigerator, closed the door and then turned to face Ava. "I'm sorry."

She smiled. "And I'm sorry I came off so defensive."

"Hey, doc, can you come out here?" shouted a man from the backyard.

"That sounds like my pain-in-the-butt brother-in-law. Come on out back with me and I'll introduce you to my family."

Ava stepped out of the kitchen and into an expansive backyard enclosed by a six-foot fence that provided absolute privacy from neighbors. A large white tent shielded those lounging on chairs and chaises from the harmful rays of the intense summer sun. A disc jockey, who'd set up his computer and speakers in a corner, was taking requests.

She exchanged polite greetings with the dozen or so men and women already gathered under the tent. Almost all of them were sipping from large cups that were either red, white or blue.

Kyle emerged from the house with Duncan and his aunt, his gaze sweeping over the small crowd for Ava. He found her with Ivan, who'd handed her a beverage. His gaze lingered on her slender ankles and narrow feet in a pair of black ballet-type shoes. The hem of the skirt on the colorful empire-waist dress ended mid-thigh. Each time she took a breath a soft swell of breasts rose and fell above the V-neckline.

A smile crinkled the skin around his eyes. Ava appeared relaxed, comfortable as she laughed at something Ivan had whispered in her ear. Yes, he thought, she was definitely a keeper. Ivan's mother's sister, his brother-in-law and his pubescent niece had arrived early, along with Ivan's personal secretary and her three children. Knowing he didn't have to keep Ava entertained, Kyle walked over to the outdoor stove to fire up the gas grill.

"Who's the beauty with Ivan?"

Kyle shifted to see Duncan staring at Ava. "She's my date."

Duncan's head came around, his expression registering complete shock. "Your date?"

"Yes, DG. She's my date."

"When did all of this happen?"

"I said she's my date, not my fiancée."

Duncan's clear gold-brown eyes widened. "Are you saying she's available?"

"Hell no, she's not available."

"Just checking," Duncan drawled, patting Kyle's back. "I'm going to get something to drink. Can I get you something?"

"Get me anything that's non-alcoholic and carbonated. Never mind. I'll go with you *and* I'll introduce you to my date." Dropping an arm over Duncan's shoulder, he steered him over to Ava and Ivan.

Ava caught the scent of Kyle's cologne even before she turned around. "Hey," she said, smiling.

Dipping his head, he dropped a kiss on her expertly coiffed hair. "I want to introduce you to Duncan."

Ava purposefully averted her gaze from the incredibly beautiful man staring at her as if she were a frothy confection. She'd heard women talk about "pretty brothers" and Duncan was exactly that and then some.

She extended her hand. "Ava Warrick."

Duncan took her hand, squeezing it gently. "Duncan Gilmore."

Kyle splayed his hand over her back in a proprietary gesture that wasn't lost on his two friends. "Are you ready to eat?"

"What's on the menu?" Ava asked.

"We're going to start with the ubiquitous hamburgers and franks, then later on I'm going to broil some steaks."

She smiled up at Kyle. "I'll have a cheeseburger."

"Do you want the cheese on or in the burger?"

"We have a choice?" Ivan asked.

Kyle gave his non-grilling friend a pointed look. "Of course you have a choice. Why kind of cheese do you want, sweetheart?"

"I'll have blue cheese," Ivan said quickly.

"I wasn't talking to you, Ivan," Kyle growled between clenched teeth. "And there's no way in hell you could ever be my sweetheart. Especially not with that stubble on your face."

Ava laughed along with the three friends. They shared a camaraderie that made them as close as or closer than brothers. "I'll also have one with blue cheese, darling."

Kyle brandished a fist at his friends. "If either one of you answers to that I'm going to knock you out."

"There's no need for hostility, my brother," Ivan crooned.

"Preach, my brother," Duncan intoned in an exaggerated baritone.

Their antics set the stage for an afternoon and evening of frivolity. People crowded into the backyard to eat, drink, trade stories and listen to music. Kyle demonstrated his culinary skills when he grilled burgers and steaks to order. Ava marveled that he knew exactly how much time it took to cook a burger to rare, medium-rare and well-done perfection though flipping each only once.

Trays of potato salad, coleslaw and deviled eggs, and platters of fresh fruit and vegetable salads were devoured quickly, and what wasn't eaten was packed in takeout containers. Ava's red velvet cookies were a big hit, along with slices of Cake Man Raven's carrot cake.

It was close to nine when she found a chaise, collapsing into its softness. The DJ had lowered the music and the repertoire of slow jams lulled her into a state of total relaxation. She'd just dozed off when she felt the crush of a hard body next to her.

"Kyle?"

"Yes, sweetheart."

"I don't think I can move."

"Why?"

"I ate and drank too much."

"What were you drinking?" he whispered close to her ear.

"Whiskey sours."

"That's a frou-frou drink. It goes down like Kool-Aid."

She smiled. "A very potent Kool-Aid."

"How many did you have?"

"Three."

"Three drinks over eight hours shouldn't have you out of sorts."

"I'm a cheap drunk, Kyle."

He chuckled softly. "I'll remember when I attempt to seduce you."

Ava opened her eyes. "You don't have to get me drunk to seduce me."

Kyle raised his head, meeting her resolute gaze in the glow of spotlights ringing the property. "I'll remember that, too."

"I'm ready to go home whenever you are."

Lowering his head, Kyle nuzzled the side of her neck. "Do you want to come for a sleepover tonight?"

Ava hesitated because she didn't want her time with Kyle to end, yet she knew that staying over would lead to things she wasn't ready for. She wasn't a prude but she knew jumping into bed too soon was the number-one mistake most women make. She wanted to wait, because she wanted to know if what she felt for Kyle was more than infatuation—gonads calling out to each other.

"Not tonight."

Kyle kissed her ear. "I'll take you home now."

"You're not upset?"

A slight frown creased his smooth forehead. "Of course not. If you don't feel comfortable sleeping at my place, then that's something I'm going to have to accept."

Wrapping her arms around his neck, Ava pulled his head down. "I am really getting to like you, Kyle Chatham. I suppose I shouldn't say things like that or you'll get a swelled head."

"Which head are you talking about, sweetheart?"

Ava gasped. "Oh! You are so nasty!"

"And you're not?" he teased.

"Not as nasty as you."

"That's debatable, Ava."

"Take me home before you say something unforgivable."

Kyle pantomimed zipping his lips. Sitting up, he swung his legs over the chaise, then extended his hand to pull her up. They said their goodbyes to Ivan and Duncan who were in deep conversation with several women who lived in a neighboring brownstone.

The ride across town was accomplished in complete silence and when Ava closed the door behind Kyle she knew he truly was special.

Chapter 9

Ava was sitting in her office, reading through a week of correspondence when the telephone rang. She picked up the receiver after the second ring. "Miss Warrick."

"Miss Warrick, this is Mrs. Walcott."

She put aside the minutes from last month's staff meeting to give her client her undivided attention. "How are you today?"

"I don't know, Miss Warrick." A sob came through the earpiece. "I know I'm not scheduled to meet with you until Thursday, but can you see me today?"

Doreen Walcott had come to the New Lincoln Family Center after her husband ended their eight-year marriage to move in with his secretary, leaving Doreen to care for their three young children. Although her ex-husband provided financial support for his sons, he'd waived his rights for visitation. After she'd been evaluated, Doreen was scheduled for two individual and two group sessions each month.

Ava checked her planner. "I wouldn't be able to see you until four."

"But I have to pick the children up from school."

"Can't you let your housekeeper pick up the children?"

"My babies look for me to pick them up, not my maid."

"You can't have it both ways, Ms. Walcott."

"It's Mrs. Walcott, not Ms."

"Do you want to see me at four, or do you want to wait until Thursday?"

"I'll see you at four."

Ava smiled. "Please try not to be late."

The former high-school homecoming queen had been spoiled and pampered by her father, and her husband had continued the practice until he tired of her whining and immature behavior. His constant plea for her to grow up had fallen on deaf ears until one day he'd had enough and had begun coming home later and later until he stopped coming home altogether. Ava had assigned Doreen to a parenting group because of her inability to cope with being a single parent. She ended the call and went back to reading.

She'd slept late on Sunday, and when she woke with a headache Ava knew the cause: the whiskey sours. When she finally got her bearings, she called her sister, mother and father. Aisha complained that she felt and looked like a beached whale, and that she refused to look at a mirror even when styling her hair.

Ava looked forward to spoiling her niece, and had offered to babysit whenever her sister and brother-in-law wanted to take time to be alone together. Aisha told her if she had her own child then she wouldn't have time to come from New York to Maryland to babysit. What Ava found odd was that at thirty-four she still hadn't felt the pull of motherhood. Perhaps it had something to do with her past relationships with men. However, she wouldn't think about babies, whether they were hers biologically or adopted, until she felt the time was right. And if it was never right then she would become one of millions of other women who'd elected not to bear a child.

A soft knock on the door garnered her attention and she glanced up to find the medical director's secretary in the doorway. "Yes, Tina?"

"Dr. Mitchell would like to see you in her office."

Ava didn't understand why the psychiatrist sent her secretary instead of picking up the telephone to call her herself. "I'll be there in a few minutes."

Tina blushed. "She wants me to bring you."

She wanted to tell the timid woman that she knew the way to Dr. Laura Mitchell's office, but didn't want to put Tina on the spot. "Here goes nothing," Ava mumbled as she pushed back her chair and came to her feet.

"*¿Qué pasó?*" Maribel whispered as Ava passed her desk.

"I don't know," she answered, sotto voce.

Any time someone was summoned by the medical director it usually boded ill for that individual, and Ava couldn't think of anything that could've had the irritating woman's nose out of joint except that she didn't like that she'd been away from the office for a week.

Schooling her expression not to reveal what she was feeling, Ava walked into the large sun-filled office and sat down.

"You wanted to see me?"

Laura Mitchell, who'd been standing staring out the window, turned slowly. A natural blonde, she wore her thick hair in a tight matronly bun. Large gray eyes in a ghostly pale face reminded Ava of pieces of chipped ice. No one in the agency knew anything about the doctor's personal life. There was a betting pool as to how old she was and the consensus was that she was somewhere between thirty-five and forty.

Slipping her hands into the pockets of her white lab coat, Laura Mitchell stared at the social worker she'd been unable to subjugate or intimidate. "How are you feeling?"

The query caught Ava completely off guard. "Much better. Thank you for asking."

Laura sat on the edge of the desk and stared at her Ferragamo pump. "I suppose you're wondering why I asked to see you."

"I can't begin to fathom why you would want to see me."

Dots of red appeared on the doctor's pale face. "Do you like working here, Ava?"

Heat pricked Ava's cheeks, but thankfully her darker complexion concealed her reaction to the question. "Of course. If I didn't, then I wouldn't have stayed."

"I know we haven't seen eye-to-eye on how to run this agency, but I'm a psychiatrist and you're a psychiatric social worker trained in administration."

"Where are you going with this, Dr. Mitchell?"

"I've heard the grumblings and rather than lose staff I've decided to make a few management changes. Effective today you'll be New Lincoln Family Center's executive director."

The seconds ticked off as Ava stared at the woman who'd seemed intent on making her life a living hell until she confronted her. And it hadn't been an idle threat when she'd told Dr. Mitchell she would walk out *and* sue her personally if she continued with her unwarranted harassment. The friction between them had begun after Will started leaving threatening messages on the agency's voice mail.

"What about you?" Ava asked when she recovered.

"I'll remain on staff as medical director, but on a part-time basis. My responsibilities at the hospital have become somewhat overwhelming and my husband gave me an ultimatum. It's impossible to hold down two full-time positions and maintain a healthy marriage."

So, she is married, Ava mused. "How often will you come in?"

"No more than twelve hours a week. At that time I'll go over the evaluations and review medical records on the clients who are on medication. I want you to move into this office and I'll take yours. Of course, more responsibility means you'll have to be compensated. I met with the agency's board last week and they've agreed to give you an increase in salary that translates into about eighteen percent. You're going to have to reorganize your caseload, because of the added administrative responsibility."

Ava nodded numbly. She would still see clients, but now she was responsible for staff supervision, monthly reports and direct contact with the agency's board of directors. "This means I'm going to increase Maribel and the other intern's caseload."

"Do whatever you feel you have to do to keep the agency running smoothly and our clients served. Pack up what you want to bring over and I'll have Tina move my files to your office."

Ava's eyes narrowed slightly as she stared at the woman who had become more of an anomaly than she'd been when she'd taken over as medical director two years before. "Thank you for recommending me for the position."

"I didn't recommend you because I like you, Ava. I did it because you're more than qualified for the position. There are going to be some rumblings because the social workers who've been here longer than you may feel they should get the position by virtue of longevity. They know social-work practice but lack leadership skill. You're the only one who has and probably will continue to challenge me. I don't like it but I have to respect you for it."

Ava inclined her head in acknowledgment. She'd never been insubordinate yet she hadn't been as malleable as some of the staff. She'd always been straightforward without appearing confrontational.

"Should I tell the staff of the changes or will you do it?"

"I'll leave that up to you."

Ava nodded again. "I'll tell Tina to type up a memo informing everyone of a twelve-thirty staff meeting in the conference room, and that lunch will be provided. We should have enough money in the sunshine fund to cover the cost of food."

Dr. Laura Mitchell did something no one at the agency had ever seen her do: she smiled. "I'll see you in the conference room at twelve-thirty."

Ava left the office, stopped at the desk of the woman who was now her administrative secretary and told her what to put into a memo for immediate distribution. She also instructed Tina to take the interns with her to pick up lunch at the Whole Foods Market located in the Time Warner Center at Columbus Circle.

When she'd been summoned to see Laura Mitchell, Ava never would've suspected the turn of events that would change her life. When she'd left teaching to return to school for a social-work career, her focus had been on casework. However, when a faculty advisor had suggested administration because the field still had too few females in administration, she'd decided to redirect her course concentration. Now, fortified with undergraduate degrees in early childhood education and behavioral sciences and an M.S.W., and as a certified social worker, she was firmly on solid ground with her professional career.

Tina appeared as surprised as Ava had been at the announcement that Ava would be moving into Dr. Mitchell's office and that the medical director would take her old office. "I'll make sure to clean out Dr. Mitchell's office before the end of the day."

Ava smiled at the petite, hyperactive woman whom everyone teased relentlessly because of her name. Although only forty, Tina Turner had been married and divorced three times. She confessed to ending her marriages because her husbands were slobs and she was tired of picking up after them. The truth was they couldn't put up with her constant need to keep everything in its rightful place. Tina knew she had OCD and was seeing an outside therapist to address her disorder.

Always dressed to the nines, today Tina wore a periwinkle-blue silk-wrapped tunic top over an off-white pencil skirt, and because she had a sample shoe size her closet was filled with the most incredible designer footwear.

"Thank you, Tina."

"Are you going to be my new boss?" Tina whispered.

"Yes, I am."

Tina's blue eyes rolled upward as she appeared to whisper a prayer. "It's been a long time coming, but my prayers have been answered. I didn't know how much more I was going to be able to take from Dr. Mort."

Ava bit back a smile. Most of the staff had begun referring to Dr. Mitchell as Dr. Mort within days of her coming on board and the name had stuck. There was no doubt that with the decrease in her workweek from thirty-five to twelve hours, the staff's morale would increase.

Ava returned to her office and closed the door. Clenching her teeth tightly, she cut a step as she celebrated in private. Opening a drawer in her desk, she reached into her handbag and took out her cell phone. Her joy was so great that she had to tell someone before the staff meeting.

Ava called her mother and sister, but hung up when she heard their voice-mail messages. She knew she wouldn't be able to reach her father and she never called her brother at the prison. She thought of calling Karen, her former college roommate, but then remembered she'd gone back to Omaha for her brother's wedding. Scrolling through the cell's directory she saw Kyle's name and numbers.

She remembered him telling her that he'd closed his office on Monday to give him employees a long weekend. Punching in the number to his cell, she drummed her fingers on the stack of letters, memos and reports that still needed to be read and disseminated.

"Hello."

Ava sat up straighter upon hearing his silken baritone greeting. "Hello, Kyle. Did I catch you at a bad time?"

"For you there is never a bad time."

"What if you were in court?"

"I turn my cell off whenever I'm in court. Now, what did I do to have the honor of hearing your sexy voice this morning?"

"You picked the right profession, because you surely have the gift of gab, counselor."

A deep chuckle came through the tiny earpiece. "You don't think your voice is sexy?"

"I never gave it a thought."

"Think about it, Ava, because it is."

Ava wanted to tell Kyle that he was the one with the X-rated voice. "I called to share some good news."

"What is it?"

She told him about her meeting with the medical director. "I was seriously thinking about looking for another position but I decided to hold off until after I bought a co-op."

"Congratulations! We're going to have to celebrate your promotion. What are you doing tonight?"

"I'll probably go home and do the happy dance."

"What do you think about doing the happy dance at my place? We can cook outdoors and dance under the stars."

"I like the sound of that. Would you mind if we have a sleepover?"

"Now you're talking! What time should I pick you up?"

"Is seven too late?"

"No, it's perfect. I'll see you at seven."

"Seven it is." Ava disconnected the call, stunned that she'd asked Kyle if she could sleep at his house.

As she aged she'd become more assertive and her attitude was more in-your-face. The truth was she liked Kyle Chatham—liked everything about him, and she didn't want a sleepover as much as she wanted to sleep with him. She'd dated Will for several months before she'd shared his bed, and it had proven absolutely nothing. Things she should've noticed when they were dating she'd ignored until it was too late. She didn't blame Will as much as she blamed herself because, as a trained therapist, she should've been aware of the nuances that clearly demonstrated her ex-lover's emotional instability.

She would date Kyle, sleep over at his house and, if their relationship became more intimate, then she intended to enjoy it until either of them decided it was over. Ava wasn't looking for marriage and neither was Kyle, so it would be a win-win for both.

Tina, who'd forwarded all agency calls to the answering service, stood at the door to the conference room handing each staff member an updated table of organization. After she'd typed the memo and given it to Ava to check for wording, she was instructed to update the organizational chart with the new positions and titles. Her title had been changed from secretary to the medical director to executive assistant.

Ava nodded to Tina when the last employee filed into the room and spotted the buffet table set with trays of fresh fruit, freshly baked breads, sushi, cheese and various salads. She met the medical director's gaze before smiling at those seated around the table.

"I called this meeting to apprise everyone of several administrative changes. Effective immediately I will assume the title and responsibility of executive director and Debra Nelson will become social-work supervisor. Our interns will take on an increased caseload with a commensurate stipend.

"Dr. Mitchell's hospital affiliation will not permit her to give New Lincoln Family Center as many hours as she would like, so she will be available only twelve hours each week. For those who have clients on meds Debra will meet with you to schedule a time to meet with Dr. Mitchell for follow-ups.

"Dr. Mitchell asked the board to reapportion her salary to staff, so that translates into seeing a bit more in your biweekly paychecks. I will carry a smaller caseload, and I'm going to need your utmost cooperation when dealing with our funding sources. Both city and state are threatening to cut our funding, so I'm going to have to devise ways to do some fundraising. I've never been very good at begging, which means I'm going to have to step up to the plate and learn to put pride aside and ask. If anyone has any suggestions, please let me know. As in the past, my door is always open. Are there any questions?"

"Will you still be on the on-call schedule?" asked the agency's only male social worker.

Ava shook her head. "No. If anyone would like to

earn a little more comp time, then let me know." The agency couldn't afford to pay overtime, but offered compensatory time instead at time and a half.

Debra raised her hand. "I don't mind being on-call."

"Any one else want to come off the on-call schedule?" Ava asked. No hands went up. "I guess that settles it. Tina will give everyone a revised on-call list. Dr. Mitchell, would you like to say something to the staff?"

All eyes were trained on the medical director. "No, thank you. You've said it all."

Ava smiled. "I have one more thing to say: let's eat!"

When Kyle stepped out of the elevator he found Ava standing outside her apartment waiting for him. After sharing the morning and afternoon with his parents, he had stopped along Tarrytown's business district to buy something to commemorate her promotion. He had gone from store to store until he stopped in a jewelry shop to buy a gold wishbone necklace. It was personal, but a heart pendant would've been too personal at this time in their relationship.

"What are you hiding behind your back?" she asked with his approach.

Kyle extended his right hand. "Congratulations."

Ava's smile was dazzling. "They're beautiful." He'd given her a bouquet of snowy white roses, tulips and lilies. It was the second time Kyle had given her flowers. "We can leave as soon as I put these in water."

"Bring them with you."

"But I can't enjoy them if they're at your house."

Kyle angled his head, kissing the end of her nose. "Then you'll just have to come over every day to see them."

"Sleeping at your house every day is tantamount to living together, and that's something I've promised myself that I'll never do again."

His eyebrows drew together in a frown. "Sharing a bed is living together. Have I asked you to share my bed, Ava?"

"No."

His frown disappeared as quickly as it had formed. "Do you want us to sleep together?"

Her jaw dropped. "What kind of question is that?"

"It's a very direct question. Do you or don't you?"

Ava stomped her foot as she'd done as a child when things didn't go her way. "Why are you putting me on the spot?"

Kyle cradled her face in his hands. "I'm not putting you on the spot, darling. I just need answers from you. You've granted me ten wishes, and I want every wish to be the same."

She blinked once. "What wish is that?"

The skin around Kyle's eyes crinkled attractively when he gave her that smile that made her heart do a flip-flop. "I want to make love to you again and again, over and over."

"Why me, Kyle?"

"Why *not* you, Ava?"

"Please don't answer my question with another question."

"I want to make love to you because you are beautiful *and* crazy sexy. I don't think you realize just how sexy you are."

"There are a lot of sexy women in the world," Ava argued softly.

"That's true, but they don't appeal to me."

"And I do?"

"Yes, baby. Yes, you do."

"What if I won't sleep with you? Would you still want to see me?"

Kyle inhaled, held his breath for as long as he could before exhaling. He silently cursed the men in her past who had made her so distrustful. "I would continue to see you even if you never let me make love to you."

"Won't that make you a little frustrated?"

He gave her the smile parents usually reserved for their children. "I'm certain I'd be more than a little frustrated, but there are ways to get rid of the frustration other than sleeping with a woman."

"You wouldn't do *that*."

"Hell, yeah, I would. And it wouldn't be the first time, Ava."

Ava drew in a breath and closed her eyes. "I thought my life was wonderful until you came along. If you'd left me on that corner I wouldn't be going through what I'm feeling now."

"And what is that, Ava?"

She opened her eyes as a hint of a smile flitted over her lips. "I want you, Kyle, and it doesn't matter that over a week ago I didn't know you existed. Every time we're together a certain area of my body goes completely haywire."

Kyle took a step. "Which area?" he whispered in her ear.

"The one between my legs," she whispered back.

Reaching for her free hand, he placed it on his groin. The hardness and heat under the denim roared like the heat from a furnace. "It's the same with me."

Ava groaned aloud. "Don't tease me, Kyle."

He increased the pressure on her wrist. "What do you want?"

"Do you really want to know?" she teased.

"Yes, baby, I want to know."

Going on tiptoe, she pressed her mouth to his ear. "Make love to me."

Chapter 10

Bending slightly, Kyle swept Ava up into his arms. He knew her agreeing to sleep with him was a decision that hadn't come easily for her. What she'd said was true. A little over a week ago neither had known the other one existed, but time meant nothing because he would've felt the same if they'd been together a month, a year.

Despite her outward bravado, Kyle detected a vulnerability in Ava that surfaced when he least expected it. And he suspected it'd begun with her overbearing, controlling father. The first man in her life should've been the one to nurture and protect her and her mother. Then there was the corrections officer who'd made her an unofficial prisoner, forcing her to concoct a plan to escape him.

Kyle didn't know if he was in love with Ava, but whatever he was feeling, it came very close to that peculiar emotion. He'd always told himself that he would consider marrying a woman if she complemented him. Ava Warrick complemented him.

"I have protection on me."

"I'm on the pill."

Kyle and Ava, who'd spoken in unison, shared a smile.

"I'm not carrying any STDs," Kyle said.

Ava flashed a smile. "Neither am I."

He dropped a kiss on her hair. "That means we should have a good ol' time sleeping together."

I hope you're right, she mused. It'd been a long time since she'd had sex, and she was looking forward to experiencing why she'd been born female. Kyle carried her through the foyer and into the living room, where she placed the bouquet of flowers on a side table next to the staircase.

Her arms tightened around his strong neck as he carried her up the stairs and down the hall to her bedroom. She'd drawn the drapes at the windows, and there was still enough light coming through the sheers to create the perfect mood for what was to come.

Kyle walked to the bed, lowering Ava onto the crisp floral sheets. His body followed hers down. He sat on the side of the mattress and removed her sandals. His gaze never wavered when he lowered the zipper on her jeans. Sliding a hand under her buttocks, he eased the pants off and down her hips. The heat and the scent of her perfumed skin wafted into his nostrils.

Lowering his head, he pressed his mouth to her flat belly over the waistband of a rose-pink bikini panty. The skin on her belly was the same color and as flawless as her face.

"Nice," he crooned, placing tiny kisses around her belly button. "Nice, sweet and very, very sexy."

Even if she'd never felt sexy, Ava did at that moment. She felt sexy *and* desirable. Nothing mattered except the man in her bed. Just when she'd given up trying to meet someone with whom she could have a normal relationship, she'd run into Kyle Chatham. What she found so ironic was that she had literally run into him.

Since her breakup with Will she'd found herself alienated from the friends they'd cultivated as a couple. When she'd left D.C. to attend school in New York, she'd left her childhood friends, and when she broke up with Will she'd left her new friends without a trace because she couldn't count on them not to tell Will where she lived. The only person she could now call *friend* was Karen Anderson.

After they'd graduated, Karen had moved in with one of her professors. The brilliant man was twice her age and had come from old money. They lived together for years, then, without warning, he asked her to marry him. They married quietly, and less than year later he passed away, leaving her everything, including a collection of art pieces that were currently on loan to the Metropolitan Museum of Art.

Ava exhaled audibly when Kyle's fingers went to the buttons on her shirt. One by one he undid the buttons, baring her chest to his rapacious gaze. "Do you always wear matching bras and panties?"

Her chocolate-brown lace demi-bra trimmed in rose-pink lace matched her panties. "I usually buy them as sets. Don't your undershirts match your boxers?"

"No. All of my undershirts are white and my boxer briefs are different colors."

Her hands slipped under the hem of his shirt, searching under the waistband to his jeans. "What color boxer briefs are you wearing tonight?"

Kyle's hands were equally busy as he divested Ava of her blouse, then reached around her back to unhook her bra. "You're going to find out in a few…" His words trailed off when he stared, complete surprise freezing his features, at her breasts. A lump rose in his throat, making swallowing painful.

Ava saw his stunned expression. "What's the matter?" Her query was a whisper. When he didn't answer she followed the direction of his gaze. "Yes, Kyle, they are mine."

Her clothes artfully disguised her full breasts. Even when wearing a revealing neckline she made certain to buy garments with built-in bras. Her chest and hips had been as slim as a boy's for years until she began taking contraceptives. Not only had the pill offset her menstrual dilemma, but its properties had helped to fill out her body.

"They are perfect. You are perfect," he said reverently. Kyle found Ava's body as perfect as the rest of her. What he hadn't known when her car collided with his was that he had to date a lot of women in order to find the right one. His hands trailed up her inner thighs, and within seconds her panties joined her bra, jeans and blouse at the foot of the bed.

Kyle's eyes darkened as he moved over her, and Ava felt the pressing need of his hardness against her. He wanted her and she needed him with an intensity that took her beyond herself and all that was real. If Kyle found her different from the other women he'd known, then it was the same with her.

Pushing into a sitting position, she undid the buttons on Kyle's shirt, baring a smooth, dark brown, broad chest and rock-hard abs. She heard him catch his breath when she unsnapped his jeans. Going on her knees, she pressed light kisses over his pectorals and lower. "They're black," Ava whispered. Her hands were as busy as her mouth when they slipped into his boxer briefs to find him fully erect. "Is this all you?" she whispered again. His erection was enormous.

Kyle chuckled softly. "Yes."

Ava took her time undressing her soon-to-be lover until he lay as naked as she. At last she went into his embrace, the curves of her body fitting into the hard contours of his like puzzle pieces. Resting her leg over Kyle's thigh, she tilted her chin as his head came down.

A deep feeling of peace seeped into her as she savored the velvet warmth of his kiss. Parting her lips, Ava swallowed his breath. She felt the pulsing length of his heavy penis against her thigh, the rapid beating of his heart against her breasts, the slow, drugging kisses that left her shaking like a fragile leaf in the wind.

It'd been years since she'd shared her bed, and although she wanted Kyle inside her she was willing to wait. There was a dreamy intimacy to their kisses and touching that was as satisfying as penetration.

Kyle pulled Ava closer as he took full possession of her mouth. He wanted her so badly that he forced himself to go slowly. He wanted to kiss her—all over. He wanted to taste every inch of her body from head to toe in an attempt to imprint her in his heart and brain. And if he were truly honest with himself he would've acknowledged that he was falling in love with Ava Warrick.

Splaying his hand over her thigh, he caressed her hip in a slow up-and-down motion. Skin to skin, heart to heart, they'd become one. He hadn't entered Ava, yet he felt the sweet satisfaction that followed a climax.

"Kyle?"

"Yes, baby?" He felt her trembling under his sensual ministration. Ava's answer was to grasp his hand and place it between her thighs, coating his fingers with the moisture from her rising desire.

Ava felt hot, cold, then hot again. She'd been celibate too long for any prolonged period of foreplay. "I can't wait any longer."

Kyle heard *and* felt her desperation, her plea overlapping groans of erotic pleasure. He had wanted to take her within minutes of seeing her naked, fast, hard, deep but he was mindful of how long it'd been since a man had made love to her.

Pressing her down to the mattress, he eased her legs apart with his knee and entered her slowly, pushing into her hot wetness and praying he wouldn't spill his passion on the sheet before he was fully sheathed inside her.

For what seemed to be minutes, yet in reality was seconds, Ava held her breath. She was aware each time Kyle pushed, pulled back and then pushed again, his erection disappearing inch by delicious inch inside her until she felt him touch her womb. He set a rhythm she followed easily. Then, without warning, it changed, slowing, stopping before starting up again. Each time she felt the familiar flutters signal that she was going to climax, Kyle pulled her back. He did it again and again.

And when he didn't pull her back, when he let her go over the precipice, she bared her throat and screamed his name, rising to meet him in uncontrolled passion that surged through her body and left her gasping and trembling. The warmth of Kyle's body, the clean scent of his skin, had become an aphrodisiac with the power to pull Ava into an undertow of pure ecstasy.

Kyle's hands explored her thighs, hips and the firm roundness of her breasts. He tried concentrating on everything else to keep from releasing his passion because he wanted it to go on and on until he collapsed from sheer exhaustion. Ava's body was hot, tight and he fitted so snugly inside her it was as if they'd been created for each other. The ache of his sexual hunger for her surprised him in its intensity; his whole being was flooded with love and desire for the woman writhing under him.

Ava's legs circled his waist and he cupped her hips to bring her even closer. Holding her captive, he quickened his thrusts as her breath came in long, surrendering moans of satisfaction. Burying his face on the pillow under her head, he bellowed out his own release. He lay motionless, savoring the pulsing aftermath of his climax as Ava's rapidly pumping heart kept tempo with his own.

Although Kyle had made love to her, he'd held back. He wanted Ava to get used to their sleeping together before introducing her to other positions guaranteed to bring both of them the most exquisite erotic pleasure.

Reluctantly, he withdrew and gathered her close. They'd made plans to go to his place to have dinner and dance under the stars. That would have to wait for another time. After all, Ava had promised to give him the next three months of her life, and Kyle intended to make the most of their time together.

Ava awoke totally disoriented. She was in bed, but not alone. As soon as she attempted to move her legs she realized what had happened. Shifting, she tried to get into a more comfortable position, but one of Kyle's legs made that impossible. She whispered his name, and the only response she got was a grunt.

She pushed against his solid shoulder. "Kyle, you have to move off me."

"What…what!" he sputtered, sitting up and looking around.

"It's all right, darling. I just needed you to take your leg off mine."

Kyle ran a hand over his head. "Did I hurt you?"

"No," Ava said. "Now, go back to sleep."

Kyle gathered Ava to his chest, smiling when she pressed her buttocks to his groin. "What time is it?"

She glanced at the small clock on the table on her side of the bed. "It's one-forty."

"Are you hungry?"

Ava giggled. "No. Why?"

"I'm hungry enough to eat a whole pig."

"Didn't you eat today?"

"I ate *yesterday*. I had brunch with my parents around eleven, but didn't eat anything after that because I thought I was going to have dinner with my girlfriend."

Ava smiled when he called her his girlfriend. "We would've had dinner if you hadn't made love to me."

Kyle's teeth nipped her shoulder. "We would've had dinner if you hadn't begged me to take you to bed."

Ava went completely still. "I didn't beg you, Kyle Chatham. I remember asking you to make love to me. Don't forget you could've refused."

"You've got to be kidding. The only time I'd refuse not to make love to you would be if I couldn't get it up."

"Remember there are pills for men with ED."

"What's with you and ED issues?"

She giggled like a little girl. "You were the one who mentioned not being able to get it up, not me."

His hand caressed her breasts. "Thankfully I can still get it up."

"I'm thankful, too."

His hand stilled. "What are we going to do?"

"What are you talking about?"

"Are we going to get up and get something to eat or are we going to make love again?"

"I need to take a shower before I do anything. I'm sweaty *and* sticky."

Kyle nuzzled the nape of her neck. "We can take a shower together. Is there a restaurant around here that stays open late?"

"There are a few within walking distance."

"What do they serve?"

"Everything. Why?"

"I'm not sure what I want to eat."

Shifting to face him, Ava kissed his throat. "We don't have to go out. There is food in the refrigerator."

"Do you have the ingredients for an omelet?"

"I think I do. How often do you eat in the middle of the night?" Ava asked.

"Hardly ever," Kyle admitted as he sat up and swung his legs over the side of the bed. He turned on the lamp on his side of the bed, then came around the bed and scooped Ava up into his arms, smiling when she rested her head on his shoulder. "I forgot to give you something."

Her head came up. "What on earth are you talking about?"

He carried her back to the bed. "Reach inside the back pocket of my jeans."

Ava reached down, picked up his jeans and found a small, square, silver-foil-wrapped package with a miniscule black bow. "What is it?"

"Open it and see."

"Put me down, Kyle."

He complied, placing her on the rumpled sheets. Smiling, Kyle watched Ava remove the bow as if it were fragile porcelain. The seconds ticked as she took off the paper. He didn't think he would ever forget the look on her face when she removed the top.

Ava's eyes were bright with unshed tears when she looked up at Kyle. He'd given her a diamond wishbone necklace suspended on a yellow gold chain. "It's beautiful. Thank you, darling."

He winked at her. "You're welcome, darling."

She handed him the necklace. "Please put it on."

It took several attempts, but he finally fastened the clasp, the pendant resting on her breastbone. The gold glowed against her rich brown skin. "It looks nice."

Ava rose to her feet. "I guess I'll have to increase your allotment of wishes."

"How many more am I going to get?"

She winkled her nose. "Five."

"Why so stingy?"

"All right, I'll give you ten more wishes and another month."

Kyle's smile was dazzling. "I'll take it." He extended his hand. "Let's take that shower so I can put some food into my belly before I faint on you."

Ava patted his belly. "We can't have that, because if you're too weak then I can take advantage of you."

"What would you do?" Going on tiptoe Ava whispered what she would do to him. "Oh, please, baby, can we do it in the shower?"

"No!"

"What if I make it one of my wishes?"

"Then I'd have to grant it."

Staring at Ava under lowered lids, Kyle focused on her mouth. "I want you to take advantage of me."

"Your wish is my command."

Tightening his grip on her hand, he led her out of the bedroom and into the bathroom. Kyle came to regret his wish when, under the fall of lukewarm water, Ava took him into her hot mouth and made love to him in the most intimate way conceivable. It ended when he made love to her again and this coupling was vastly different from the first as he took her from behind. It ended with them collapsing to the floor of the shower stall where they lay facing each other in a fetal position.

Kyle stared at the moisture curling Ava's hair and spiking her lashes. It was only now that he knew what Micah Sanborn had meant when he said he'd fallen in

Man of Fate

love with Tessa Whitfield within a week of meeting her for the first time. It was no different for Kyle. He'd fallen totally and inexorably in love with Ava Warrick.

Kyle stood off to one side to allow Jordan Wainwright to enter the office that had been set up for him. He knew most of his staff was curious about the tall, well-dressed man who'd greeted their boss with a rough hug and a slap on the back. Kyle decided to wait until later to introduce them to his new associate.

"The door on the left is your private bathroom and the one on the right is a closet. A carpenter will be in at the end of the week to install bookshelves. If there's anything else you need just let me know."

Jordan shook his head, his luminous hazel eyes aglow with excitement. "It's great, Chat. I'd rather look out on trees and flowers than concrete and steel. This place is exquisite."

Kyle nodded in acknowledgment. He'd spent a small fortune reconfiguring the bedrooms into offices. "There's a kitchen, dining room and games room on the street level for building employees. And there's no need for you to work out at your high-ass sports club because we also have a gym with showers on the first floor."

"Who else occupies this building with you?"

"Duncan, he's the financial planner, has his offices on the first floor and Ivan, who's a psychotherapist, is on the third floor. Everyone who comes to the building has to identify themselves before they're buzzed in. The place is wired with closed-circuit monitors and cameras, and the security system is wired directly to the local precinct."

"Have you ever had any problems?"

Kyle wondered if Jordan was concerned about someone assaulting him. "No. Not only is Mount Morris a National Historic District, but the residents also engage in a neighborhood watch. Not much can go on without someone reporting it. And I don't know if you noticed when you came down the block that many of brownstones are equipped with cameras similar to those in banks. So, rich boy, you don't have to worry about someone running upside your head."

Jordan blushed to the roots of his raven-black hair. "If I was *that* concerned about my safety then I never would've considered working in Harlem."

"And if I thought you were some Fifth Avenue stuffed shirt, you wouldn't be standing here," Kyle retorted. "I'd wanted to have your name up on the door when you got here, but there wasn't enough time because of the holiday weekend."

"I appreciate it, but having my name on a door isn't as important as me getting back to practicing law."

"How long has it been since you left TCB?"

"It'll be a year at the end of August."

"What have you been doing?"

"Not much. I was seeing a girl who lived and worked in D.C. I'd asked her to come live with me in New York, but she didn't want leave her position as a legislative assistant. I knew I didn't want to live in D.C., so we split up."

"Don't tell me you can't find a woman in New York?"

Sitting on the edge of his desk, Jordan gave Kyle a direct stare. "I do all right until I open my mouth to introduce myself. The minute they hear the name *Wainwright* they sit up and take notice as if shocked by a jolt of electricity. I'm so tired of hearing 'Are you one of those Wainwrights?' that I'm ready to change my name legally to Jordan Jones. It's like hearing the name *Trump* and people assume you're related to Donald Trump."

Kyle smiled. "My heart bleeds for you, Jordan," he drawled facetiously.

Jordan Wainwright was born not with a silver but a golden spoon in his mouth. He'd told Kyle about his family one night after he'd had a little too much to drink. His grandfather, a descendant of working-class European immigrants, was rumored to have had been involved in clandestine criminal activities until he caught the eye of a young woman from a French-Canadian family who'd made their fortune in fur-trapping.

Wyatt had fathered three daughters before his wife gave him his only son, who had disappointed his father when he refused to join Wyatt's rapidly expanding real-estate business after graduating from college. Their relationship had changed when Edward, also called Teddy, married beautiful social-climbing Christiane Johnston. She'd convinced her husband to reconcile with his father when he presented Wyatt with his first grandchild, Jordan Wyatt Wainwright.

It would be a decade before Wyatt celebrated the

birth of another grandson. Jordan was ten when Noah was born. Two years later, Rhett, named for Rhett Butler from *Gone with the Wind,* slept in the nursery in the Wainwright's Fifth Avenue maisonette. Christiane and Edward Wainwright welcomed their first daughter, Chanel, named for the famed fashion designer Coco Chanel, the year Jordan celebrated his sixteenth birthday.

Again, a rush of color darkened Jordan's deeply tanned face, making his eyes appear lighter than they actually were. "Maybe you should change places with me for a week, Chat, and then you'd know what I have had to go through."

"No, thank you, buddy. I like who I am."

And he did like Kyle Chatham—a lot. There was never a time when Kyle wanted to be anyone else but Kyle. He'd learned not to repeat mistakes and felt genuine pride when he turned failure into success.

Jordan flashed a brittle smile. "Maybe one of these days I'll tell you about my family feud. When do you want to me start working on the landlord-tenant case?" he asked, deftly changing the topic.

"Cherise will give you the file after the staff meeting. Staff meetings are held on Mondays before ten. We review cases and catch one another up on progress or lack thereof on the status of each case. We're very informal with one other except when clients are present. Then, we go into überprofessional mode. We have strict rules about eating at one's desk. If you don't feel like going downstairs to the dining room, then you can use the conference room, providing it's not in use.

"I've instituted an open-door policy. The exception is personal or private telephone calls, or if you're seeing a client. I'll see that you get a set of keys and the code to the security system that is monitored 24/7. Tuesdays, Wednesdays and Thursdays are our late nights for clients who can't come during the day. Ivan, Duncan and I share the day and evening receptionists and the cleaning service. The part-time paralegal comes in for our evening clients. Fortunately, everyone works well together. Last year was the first time I was able to offer year-end bonuses."

"How does it look for this year?" Jordan asked.

"It looks good, too. Now, if you win our landlord-tenant case, it will be more than good."

A sardonic smile twisted Jordan's sensual mouth. "How much do you want to soak the bastards for?"

"The cost of all the repairs and add twenty-five percent on top of that for depraved indifference and insufferable arrogance."

Crossing his arms over his chest, Jordan angled his head. "Would it bother you if I added a dose of humiliation?"

"Do whatever you have to do to win the case."

Jordan's teeth flashed whitely in his face as he exhibited a Cheshire-cat grin. "You're really feeling generous, aren't you?"

"Why would you say that?" Kyle asked Jordan.

Jordan sobered. "You've changed, Kyle. In the past you've gone strictly by the book."

"I'll probably say the same thing about you a year from now. I didn't leave Trilling, Carlyle and Browne because of some blood feud, but because I wanted to defend the little guy and not the designer-suited crook who paid a firm millions to buy his freedom. Do I sound idealistic? Maybe," Kyle said, answering his own question. "But at least when I put my head on a pillow at night I can sleep with a clear conscience."

"That means we're not all that different," Jordan stated emphatically.

Kyle wanted to tell Jordan being male attorneys did not make them similar. There were too many other variables that had come into play. But he would let the younger man believe what he wanted to believe. His only focus was achieving a positive outcome for the clients he represented, and making certain Ava would not only become a part of his life but also his future.

Chapter 11

Kyle's head came up when he heard the soft knock on his office door. "Yes, Cherise?"

"I...I don't know how to say this."

"What is it?" he asked his secretary.

"May I come in and close the door?"

He waved a hand. "Come in."

Cherise Robinson registered the note of impatience in her boss's voice. For the past two weeks she'd found him distant, and the one time she forgot to give him a message that Miss Warrick had called he'd practically bitten her head off.

She walked into the sun-filled office and closed the door. The furnishings in the executive suite reflected the personality of the man sitting behind the solid mahogany desk. A matching credenza held a variety of paperweights in various sizes and shapes. Framed and laminated diplomas covered a wall facing shelves packed with law books and journals. Cherise found it odd that Kyle's office didn't claim one photograph, which translated into his ability to completely separate his professional life from his personal life.

Kyle stared at spots of bright color on Cherise's cheeks. He opened his mouth to ask her whether she wore a hat when outdoors, then stopped himself. Cherise should know that with her fair complexion she was more susceptible to the damaging rays of the sun than her darker sisters.

"What is it, Cherise?"

"There's been a slight problem since Jordan Wainwright joined the firm."

Lacing his fingers together, Kyle leaned forward. "What kind of problem, Cherise?"

"I don't know how to say this."

Kyle frowned. "That's the second time you've said that. If something's bothering you, then spit it out."

"It's the girls from Ivan's and Duncan's offices."

"What about them, Cherise?"

Kyle was close to losing what was left of his patience. His dark mood had begun when Ava had called to tell him that she was going to Maryland to be with her sister who'd delivered a baby girl. He hadn't realized how much he missed her until he heard her drawling, sultry voice. One night she'd called just before he went to bed and he spent the entire night tossing and turning restlessly. He called her the next day and asked that she call him at his office. At least at work he had enough distractions to keep him from thinking about her.

"They find every excuse in the world to come into the office, hoping to see Jordan."

"Can't they see him in the dining room?"

"He doesn't eat in the dining room."

Kyle paused. "Where is he eating lunch?"

"He goes out for lunch. The few times he ate in the dining room they kinda bum-rushed him. The poor man couldn't even finish eating because they were all up in his face. I would've told Tanya to handle it, but she's on vacation until the end of the month."

Sighing and blowing out his breath, Kyle reached for the telephone. If his office manager hadn't gone on vacation he never would've heard about the piddling annoyance. Punching in an extension, he asked the receptionist to connect him to Duncan, and then punched the speaker feature.

"DG, I'm having a problem with your staff of the female persuasion."

"What's going on, Kyle?"

"It appears that some of them find every excuse in the world to drift up here to make moon eyes at my associate. It's gotten so bad that the man goes out for lunch rather than be set upon in the dining room."

"Are you sure about this?" Duncan asked.

"I'm only telling you what Cherise told me. Apparently it's getting so bad that it's disrupting my staff. And you know I can't have that."

"Don't worry, Kyle, I'll take care of it."

"Thanks, buddy."

"No problem."

Kyle ended the call. "One down and one to go," he said under his breath. He had the receptionist patch him through to Ivan, but was told that Ivan was in session. "Please leave a message for him to call me. It's rather important."

Cherise's eyes sparkled like polished copper pennies. "Thank you, Kyle."

"No problem. If Jordan's in his office, please ask him to see me."

Pushing to her feet, Cherise left the office. Two minutes later Jordan walked in. He'd loosened his tie and rolled back his shirt cuffs. Kyle gestured to the chair Cherise had just vacated.

"Please sit down. Why didn't you tell me the women from the other offices were annoying you?"

Jordan focused on a spot over Kyle's shoulder. He'd noticed something about his friend and boss that wasn't apparent when they'd gotten together for drinks earlier that year. Kyle Chatham was only thirty-eight, but he was graying at an alarming rate.

"They don't annoy me. I suppose all of the attention makes me a little uncomfortable."

"Why didn't you say something, Jordan?"

"I didn't want to make trouble."

"It's not about making trouble," Kyle countered, "it's about maintaining a comfortable work environment. I won't stand for someone outside this firm disturbing our peace any more than I'd permit our employees to cross the line to disrupt Ivan's or Duncan's. You're a helluva lawyer, but if you hope to make partner you're going to have to assume more of a take-charge stance. My secretary shouldn't have had to come to me on your behalf."

Jordan nodded. "You're right. I'll step up next time."

Kyle smiled. "Good. Now, are you ready for your tenants' meeting tonight?" Jordan was scheduled to meet with the tenants' association bringing the suit against his grandfather's company.

A sinister smile marred Jordan's good looks. "I've never been more ready for anything in my life."

"Be careful, Jordan. Motivation fueled by revenge can force you to take unnecessary risks," Kyle warned softly.

Jordan's expression was a mask of stone. "It's a risk I don't mind taking." He exhaled a breath. "I'd like you to come with me tonight."

"Why? I thought you have everything under control."

"I do, but I'd like you there as an observer."

"I'm not going to be much of an observer if the tenants recognize me," Kyle countered.

"If you look as if you're going to a ball game they'd never recognize the always sartorially resplendent Kyle Chatham, Esquire."

"Speak for yourself, Wainwright. I'm willing to bet you've never bought a suit off the rack."

"Why should I when I can use my father's tailor?"

Kyle knew arguing with Jordan about his wardrobe would end in a stalemate. The young attorney, always impeccably attired, had set the bar for the other attorneys at Trilling, Carlyle and Browne. Even the senior partners and associates rethought their fashion choices after Jordan joined the firm. He was never seen without his solid-gold, scales-of-justice cufflinks—gift from his father to commemorate his son's law-school graduation.

"Do you really want me to tag along?"

Jordan nodded. "I need you there to evaluate if I'm able not only to walk the walk but also talk the talk." He'd set up a meeting with the rent-strike leaders in a small eatery on Adam Clayton Powell Boulevard.

"Okay, Jordan. I'll come. But I don't intend to get involved."

"I don't want you to get involved. I've spent countless hours on this case and I don't intend to deviate from the script."

"What time do you want me to show up?"

"Get there about seven-fifteen." Jordan stood. "I'll see you later."

Kyle stared at the departing figure of the man who, in two weeks, had turned his firm upside down with his A-list fashion-model looks. His staff had buzzed about the new attorney, but within hours had settled down to their assigned tasks. However, it appeared that the period of adjustment for the women who worked for Ivan and Duncan hadn't come as easily.

His phone rang. It was Ivan. It took Kyle less than a minute to inform his friend about his employees' inappropriateness. There came a pregnant pause, then Ivan said he would address the problem.

He'd just hung up when his private extension rang. Glancing at the display, Kyle saw Ava's name and cell number. Smiling, he picked up the receiver. "Hello, auntie. How are you?"

"I'm good, thank you. I'm calling to let you know that I'm coming home tomorrow."

"That's the best news I've heard in two weeks. I've missed you so much, baby."

There came a beat. "And I've missed you, too, Kyle."

He picked up a pencil and made interlocking circles on a piece of scrap paper. "How's your sister doing?"

Ava had gotten the call her sister had gone into labor, but after sixteen hours had been unable to deliver her baby. When doctors decided to perform a C-section, Ava had made arrangements to fly, rather than drive, to Maryland.

"She's getting around pretty good now."

"How's the baby?"

"Omigosh, Kyle. You have to see her! She's more beautiful every day."

"She must look like her auntie."

Ava laughed. "No, she looks like her paternal grandmother. She's such a good baby. After Aisha feeds her she goes right to sleep. The only time she cries is when she wants to be changed or fed."

"What time are you coming in?"

"Why?"

"I'll come and pick you up."

"You don't have to do that, Kyle. I'll take a cab."

"What time does your flight come in?"

"It's scheduled to touch down at three-twenty."

Kyle scribbled her name over the circles. "I'll meet you. Are still coming into LaGuardia?"

"Yes, and don't forget to call the airport before you head out."

"You worry too much, Miss Warrick," he teased.

"I just don't want you to waste your time, Kyle."

"Waiting for you is hardly wasting time, Ava. I've waited thirty-eight years. A few more hours will not make a difference."

"Goodbye, Kyle."

"Why are you hanging up?"

"I have to go, Kyle."

"No, you don't. Isn't this what you social workers call avoidance? Are you trying to avoid the inevitable?"

There came a pregnant pause before Ava said, "What is the inevitable?"

Kyle stopped doodling. "That it is fate that brought us together."

"I'm a realist, therefore I don't believe in fate, Kyle."

"Perhaps I'm going to have to change your mind."

"You can try, but I doubt you'll be successful."

He smiled. "We'll see, won't we?"

"Yes, we will. Goodbye, Kyle."

"Goodbye, darling."

Kyle's smile was still in place when he began putting his desk in order. He'd planned to work late, but had promised Jordan he would come to his meeting—incognito. Walking out of the office, he stopped to tell Cherise he was leaving and to call his cell if she needed to reach him.

He took the stairs to the first floor and left the building, walking out into the oppressive mid-July heat and humidity.

When Kyle got out of the taxi and walked in the direction of Adam Clayton Powell Boulevard he noticed a small crowd had gathered on the north side of the street. A news van from a prime-time network was parked along the curb. Vehicular traffic, including buses, slowed as drivers and passengers craned their necks in an attempt to see what was happening. Taking advantage of the lull in the flow of traffic, he jogged across the avenue, weaving between cars.

The scene that greeted Kyle was one he would remember for years to come. Jordan, who'd gathered the members of the rent-strike committee, was holding a press conference on the street like an elected official. Grinning, the skin around his eyes shielded by a pair of sunglasses, he moved closer to hear what Jordan was saying.

Jordan spied Kyle standing off to the side of the

swelling crowd. He doubted if the tenants' committee recognized him in a loose-fitting T-shirt, baggy jeans, running shoes, a cap and shades. With a barely perceptible nod, he turned his attention to the cameraman who held up his hand before lowering a finger one-by-one. It was his signal to begin the interview.

A recognizable investigative reporter in a business suit turned to face the cameraman. "We're live in Harlem to call attention to the plight of a group of citizens who have taken on a Goliath named Wainwright Developers, the second-largest real-estate company in the east. What makes this lawsuit so unique is the man who has offered to represent them. His name is Jordan Wainwright, grandson of the company's president and CEO." Shifting slightly, she held the microphone closer to Jordan. "Mr. Wainwright, what made you decide to bring a suit against your family's company on behalf of the One Hundred-Fourteenth Street Tenants' Association?"

"I didn't bring the suit. The association did. I'm their legal representative."

"Are you saying they came to you even though they know you have ties with Wainwright Developers?"

Jordan's eyes narrowed slightly as he gave the reporter a penetrating stare. "I don't have ties with Wainwright Developers. I work for K. E. Chatham Legal Services. When the case came across my desk I accepted it as I would any other case. The tenants have not brought a frivolous suit. It's been six months since they have had hot water. They heat water to bathe and wash dishes and use their ovens to heat their apartments during the winter months."

He held up enlarged photographs of the interiors of some of the apartments. "What you see here is unconscionable. These pictures show missing tiles and holes in the floors of bathrooms where one is able to look into the apartment below. Window sashes are so rotted that tenants can't raise them to put in window air-conditioning units. Walls are covered with mold and insect and rodent infestation is rampant, and yet building management demands they pay rent to live in such squalor. They've called 3-1-1, filed complaints and, aside from a few minor repairs, none of the major problems has been corrected."

Jordan looked directly into camera. "I'm ashamed to be a Wainwright when I see people living in conditions not fit for human habitation. I promised these tenants that I'm going open my wallet to pay for new windows and air-conditioning units for each apartment. I'm also going to underwrite the cost of a new heating system for the two apartment buildings so they can stop heating water on their stoves. I will spend whatever it takes to make the eighty units habitable. Meanwhile I'm going to sue the hell out of Wainwright Developers Group. I've always respected my grandfather, but this is one time I have to say—shame on you, Wyatt Wainwright."

He turned his back, huddled with the tenants, then, en masse, they walked into the restaurant to rousing applause from the spectators. The TV reporter had to shout her name and station call letters to be heard over the escalating noise.

Kyle laughed so hard his sides hurt. Jordan Wainwright had missed his calling. Instead of practicing law he should've gone into acting. There was no shame in his game. He's used his name and his wealth to embarrass not only the holding company, but the parent company. Reaching for his cell phone, he hit speed dial for Jordan's cell.

Jordan answered after the third ring. "Did you see it?"

"I saw *and* heard it," Kyle confirmed.

"What did you think?"

"I think I'm going to start calling you *gangsta.*"

"Wait a minute, Chat. Let me move where there's not so much noise. Kat said the segment should air before the end of the week."

Kyle noticed Jordan had referred to Katrina Nichols as Kat. "How well do you know *Kat?*"

"We went out a few times, then decided we got along better as friends."

"What about the fallout from your grandfather?"

"I welcome it, Chat. One thing he can't stand is negative publicity. He prides himself on his philanthropy and to be labeled a slumlord is certain to tarnish his image. When I went into some of those apartments I couldn't believe people were forced to live in such horrific conditions."

"Welcome to the real world, Jordan."

"Even if Wyatt wasn't my grandfather, he's still going down. Are you going to come in and join us?

"No, thanks. This is your moment. Enjoy it." Kyle punched a button on the tiny phone and pushed it into his jeans. Jordan's method may have been a little unorthodox, but it was certain to gain the attention of Wyatt and the city officials.

Ava sat up in bed reading, her back supported by several pillows. It was the last night she would sleep in her sister's Silver Spring, Maryland, home and she hadn't realized until she spoke to Kyle earlier that afternoon how much she had missed him.

It had taken two days—less than forty-eight hours— of sleeping with Kyle to become addicted to his lovemaking. He'd given her the go-ahead to take advantage of him and she had. Her brazen shower exhibition had not only taken Kyle by surprise, but also herself, and each time she recalled what they'd done to each other, her body reacted. Coming to Maryland to help her sister had put some distance between her and her lover, but had done little to quell her desire for him.

"Ava, are you up?"

She set aside the magazine. "Yes. Come on in."

Aisha Warrick-Davis opened the door and walked slowly into the bedroom and crawled into bed with her sister as she'd done when they were children. "I can't believe two weeks have come and gone so quickly."

Ava tugged on Aisha's thick braids. "It did go quickly. Is Crystal asleep?" Her sister was a younger version of Alice Warrick. She'd inherited their mother's café-au-lait coloring, large brown eyes and delicate features. And, like Alice, she was a teacher.

"Yes. Raymond just put her to bed."

"You guys are lucky she's a good baby."

Aisha rested her head on Ava's shoulder. "I'm blessed that you came to be with me."

"I told you I would come down when you had the baby."

"You'd planned to hang out and bond with your niece, not cook and do housework."

"Stop, Ai," Ava said softly. "And you hadn't planned on having a C-section. Besides, I cook once a week and I don't do housework."

She'd promised her sister that she would take two weeks of her annual four-week vacation to come and help her out after she gave birth. Raymond Davis had wanted to hire a private-duty nurse for his wife, but Aisha complained about having strangers in her home.

"That's true," Aisha concurred. "Mama just called to say she got approval to take a week off, so she'll be here Friday night." Alice Warrick had come from Washington, D.C., to spend the weekends with her daughters and grandchild, but had had to return to work every Monday morning.

"I probably won't get a chance to visit again until the Labor Day weekend."

Aisha shifted into a more comfortable position. "Raymond and I talked about coming up to New York for Labor Day. By that time Crystal will have had her shots, and she can hang out big-time with her auntie."

"Auntie Ava's going to spoil her rotten."

"What Auntie Ava needs is a baby of her own to spoil rotten."

Ava shook her head. "I don't think so. A lot of things have to happen before I think about becoming a mother. Remember, I'm going to have to move when the Servinskys return. I have to contact a real-estate agent for listings of co-ops before the end of the summer."

"Have you thought about renting?"

"I don't want to rent."

"You don't want to rent, you don't want a baby and you probably don't even want a man."

"I never said I didn't want a man." Ava knew she sounded defensive, but she was past caring. Whenever she and Aisha disagreed, it was always about a man. Her sister believed she wouldn't be complete unless she had a man in her life.

"Do you have a man, Ava?"

"Yes, I do." The admission was out before she could censor herself.

"I hope he's nothing like that last loser you hooked up with."

"He's the complete opposite."

"How did you meet him?"

Ava told her sister how she'd run into Kyle's classic car. She was forthcoming about everything that had happened between them with the exception of their sleeping together. They talked until Aisha's eyelids grew heavy. She kissed her sister, left the room and entered her own bedroom, where her husband waited in bed for her.

Chapter 12

Kyle tore open the package with the videotape he'd dropped off to the computer geek. His heart rate accelerated, beating a rapid tattoo against his ribs. The typed report verified his suspicions. The tape had been edited.

He pumped his fist in the air. "Yes! Yes! Yes!" His shouting had Cherise and Jordan racing into his office; they stared at him as if he'd lost his mind. Kyle hoisted the video in the air. "I got the evidence I need to prove Rashaun Hayden's innocence."

Cherise rolled her eyes while shaking her head. "I thought something was really wrong," she mumbled under her breath as she walked away.

Kyle beckoned Jordan closer. "Come take a look at this."

Jordan's gaze shifted from the tape to the typed report. He was still on a natural high from his staged television interview. "How did the D.A. get this tape?"

"The store owner gave it to the police, who in turn handed it over to the D.A.'s office."

"Somebody messed up—big-time. What are you going to do, Chat?"

Crossing his arms over the front of his stark-white shirt, Kyle narrowed his gaze. "I'm not certain. If we go to trial there's no doubt the case will be dismissed for lack of evidence. If I call Clarkson at the D.A.'s and tell him I know the tape has been doctored, then it would be up to him to uncover the culprit—providing someone at his office isn't culpable. Then, we need to find out if someone had it in for Rashaun and wanted to set him up. I have someone looking for a guy known as Boots, but Mr. Boots seems to have disappeared."

"What's up with this Boots person?"

"He's known to wear a ring with a lion's head."

"What if you can locate Boots?" Jordan asked.

Kyle lowered his arms. "I think it's time I have another talk with Rashaun and let him know it was Boots who robbed that bodega and see how he reacts."

Excitement fired the green in Jordan's eyes. "I would like to be present when you talk to him."

"I don't see that as a problem." Slipping the tape and report into the mailer and locking it in a drawer of his desk, Kyle pocketed the key. "I have to leave to pick up someone from the airport. That means you're in charge."

A wave of apprehension gnawed at Jordan. His ego had gotten the better of him when he'd asked Kyle to make him partner when in reality he didn't know enough about the firm's client population to assume the responsibility of handling everything that came across his desk. He knew the law but nothing about the clandestine web of street informants. He was still in the same spot when Kyle slipped into his suit jacket and walked out of the office.

Welcome to the real world, Jordan. Kyle's words taunted him. Growing up rich and protected definitely had *not* prepared him for the real world.

Kyle spied Ava as soon as she walked into the baggage-claim area. He wanted to go to her but his legs refused to move. Overhead light reflected off the brilliance of the diamonds in the wishbone pendant around her neck. If he hadn't changed outwardly in two weeks, she had. Her hair was longer and her face thinner. His gaze lingered on the long-sleeved white T-shirt she wore over a pair of dark blue cropped pants before easing down her bare legs and feet slipped into a pair of leather sandals. He closed the distance between them as she glanced up at the monitor for the carousel where she would retrieve her luggage.

"Are you Miss Warrick?" he whispered close to her ear.

With wide eyes, Ava turned to find Kyle standing behind her. "How long have you been waiting?"

"Not long." He'd called the carrier and the recording had said that Ava's flight had been delayed in Baltimore. Angling his head, he brushed a kiss over her mouth. "Welcome home, darling."

A rush of heat stung Ava's cheeks with the public display of affection. "Thank you. I'm glad to be back."

"Are you?"

"Very." She hadn't lied to Kyle. She *was* glad to be home and even more delighted to see him again.

A loud buzzing sound signaled the start of the conveyer. "How many bags do you have?" Kyle asked.

"I have only one."

"I'll get your bag and then I want you to wait at the curbside while I go and get the car."

Ava was too exhausted to argue. Her flight had been delayed a couple of hours when a passenger complained of chest pains. Eventually a doctor was summoned and the elderly woman was removed from the cabin.

Ava's bag was one of the first off the belt. Kyle carried it outside the terminal to an area for passenger pickup. "Don't run away," he teased.

Kyle returned and stored her luggage in the trunk while Ava settled down in the leather seat. Her two-week vacation had been anything but a vacation. She'd gotten up early every day to make breakfast. It had been three days before Aisha was able to get out of bed and bathe the baby. Between cooking three meals a day, putting up laundry, shopping, dusting, vacuuming and cleaning, she collapsed into bed every night, sleeping soundly only to wake up and begin again. She covered a yawn with her hand.

Kyle gave her a sidelong glance. "Sleepy?"

She flashed a tired smile. "A little. I did manage to nap during the flight, but as soon as I dozed off it was time to touch down."

Putting the car in gear, he pulled away from the curb. "When are you going back to work?"

Ava closed her eyes. "Not until Monday."

He smiled. "What are you going to do until Monday?"

"Relax."

Accelerating, he maneuvered onto the parkway leading to Manhattan. "Do you mind if we relax together?"

"Doing what and where?"

"We can relax at my place. Remember, we still haven't danced under the stars."

Ava opened her eyes to stare at the man who made her feel things she didn't want to feel, made her want him even when they were miles apart. This was a man who touched a part of her no man had been able to touch, a man who had turned her sane, comfortable world upside down.

"The night we were supposed to dance under the stars we were a little occupied doing other things."

"Was that the night you took advantage of me?"

"Kyle!"

"Was it, Miss Warrick?"

"You practically begged me to do it." Ava didn't

know why she sounded so defensive when she'd enjoyed making love to him in the most intimate manner.

Kyle rested his right hand over her knee. "You're right, darling. I'm sorry about teasing you."

She covered his hand on her knee. "Apology accepted, darling."

He moved her hand to the gearshift as he shifted into a higher gear. "Am I your darling, Ava?"

The slip-slap of rubber on the roadway filled the interior of the small car. "Yes, you are," she said in a voice so soft that Kyle had to strain his ears. "You're my darling and I want to spend the next three days with you dancing under the stars."

"Is there anything else you want from me?" he asked.

"No. Why?"

"Just asking," he said, deadpan. Kyle wanted to know because whatever she wanted—if it was within his power—he would give to her. "Is there anything you need to pick up at your place?"

Ava leaned over to rest her head on his shoulder. "Yes. I need to pick up my mail and some clothes. What about you, Kyle?"

"What about Kyle?"

"Don't you have to work?"

"Am I not entitled to take a few days off to hang out with my girlfriend? Besides, I haven't taken a day off this year. The exception is holidays."

Lifting her head, she kissed his cheek. "Yes, you are more than entitled."

"Thank you, boss."

Ava's expression stilled, becoming serious. "I'm not your boss."

"Yes, you are. Whatever you'd ask me to do I'd do."

Pulling her lip between her teeth, Ava pondered his statement. "If I ask you to marry me or get me pregnant, would you do it?"

Kyle gave Ava a quick glance. "No."

"No," she echoed. "Is it because you're afraid of commitment?"

"It has nothing to do with commitment, Ava. It has to do with you. You were the one who said you didn't want to marry *and* you also said you didn't want to be a baby mama."

"What if I change my mind?"

Silence swelled inside the car until it was deafening while a lump formed in Kyle's throat, making swallowing painful. Ava wasn't the first woman who'd mentioned marriage and babies, but she was the only one he would consider marrying.

"Ask me again when you really mean it."

"That's not going to happen, Kyle, because I'd never want to appear so desperate that I'd ask a man to marry me."

He smiled. "Here I thought you were a modern liberated woman."

"I am, but not *that* liberated. Some old-fashioned customs or traditions should never change."

"I agree with you."

As their gazes met and fused for a second, Ava felt an unexpected surge of warmth settle between her thighs. "What don't you want to change?"

Kyle returned his gaze to the road. "I believe if a man gets a woman pregnant that he should marry her."

"What if he doesn't love her? Or if she doesn't love him?"

"It's not so much about love, Ava, but about being responsible. There are couples who marry because they believe they're madly in love. Then they fall out of love and either separate or divorce."

"But that sounds like a shotgun marriage."

"How can it be a shotgun marriage when both agree to marry for the sake of their child? As a social worker you probably see children exhibit a myriad of problems because their fathers aren't in the home. You hear about athletes being role models for our youth. I don't want some baller being a role model for my son. I should be his role model and I can't be that if I'm not in his life every day, 24/7."

"What if you and your wife decide to end your marriage because it would be in the best interests of your children? What then, Kyle?"

"Divorce shouldn't translate into alienation or desertion."

"You're preaching to the choir, Kyle. As much as I resented the way my dad treated my mother, I never hated him, because after a while I realized his passive-aggressive behavior stemmed from his inability to control his own life. Even though he was a married man with children he was still controlled by my grandfather. When I read *The Color Purple,* I thought Alice Walker had eavesdropped on my family."

"The Chathams are hardly the Brady bunch. My dad didn't marry my mother until I'd celebrated my first birthday."

"Why?"

"Her father never liked my dad because he was a Vietnam vet and Gramps thought they were all a bunch of pot-smoking misfits."

"Did your grandfather ever change his mind?"

"Not initially. Dad had gotten a job with the railroad and there were times when my mother would take me with her whenever my father had the route that went from New York to Florida. It must have been fate, but the train broke down in Virginia, and while the passengers waited for another train, my parents found a justice of the peace who married them. When they returned to New York my dad showed his father-in-law the marriage license, then waited for Mom to pack her clothes and took her home with him."

Ava applauded like a small child. "What a wonderful story."

"My mother calls my dad her romance-novel hero."

Ava wanted to tell Kyle that he, too, was a romance-novel hero. He was *her* hero—the best of the best men.

Kyle spun Ava around, then dipped her, his mouth inches from hers. "Are you ready to go inside?"

Ava closed her eyes. She'd spent three hours reclining on a chaise on the deck at the rear of Kyle's house before he'd pulled her up to dance with him.

He'd driven her to her apartment to pick up her mail from the doorman, who'd stored it in a secured room where tenants' packages were held for them. She lingered long enough to fill a weekender with shorts and tank tops. Kyle had invited her to relax and that was what she planned to do.

"Can't we spend the night out here?" she mumbled.

Kyle pulled her closer to his body. "No, sweetheart. I can't have birds and squirrels sampling your goodies."

Smiling, she opened her eyes. Soft floodlights illuminated the space. "What goodies are you talking about?"

"Your fingers and toes, of course. What goodies did you think I meant?"

"The other goodies."

Kyle carried her up five steps and into the kitchen, setting her on her feet. "If you're talking about those goodies, then I'm going to make certain you don't share them with anything or anyone else."

Ava stared at Kyle's broad back when he turned to close and lock the door leading to the deck. "How are you going to do that?"

He returned to the kitchen, towering above her like an avenging angel. His toned body in a black tank top and matching loose-fitting drawstring lounging pants made it difficult for her to draw a normal breath. The first time she'd seen him completely naked, Ava hadn't wanted to believe that Kyle's business suit had concealed that slim, rock-hard body that had her practically salivating. And what lay under the pants never failed to make the area between her legs moist with desire.

Cradling her face between his palms, Kyle lowered his head and placed light, teasing kisses around her mouth. "I'm going to start by tasting your delicious lips," he crooned. He drew his tongue over her parted lips as if he were licking the cream off a frothy dessert.

His hands slipped under the straps of her top. "Then I'm going to sample your beautiful breasts." Dipping his head, he eased her back against a door of the refrigerator and suckled her breasts, alternating between nipping her nipples with his teeth and rolling his tongue around the swelling buds.

One hand moved lower, searching under the elastic band of her lounging pajamas. His fingers searched under her thong panty to find her wet and pulsing. Withdrawing his hand, his gaze fused with hers, he put his fingers to his mouth and sucked each one. "You taste as delicious as you smell."

Anchoring her arms under Kyle's thick shoulders, Ava pressed closer. She wanted him so badly it hurt. Biting on her lip, she drew in a breath. "Oh, baby."

Kyle pressed his groin to her middle, wanting Ava to feel how much he wanted to be inside her. "What is it, baby?"

"I need you," she gasped.

"I need you, too."

Desire swept over Ava as she clawed at the drawstring on his pants and pushed both hands down the cotton fabric to grasp his magnificent erection. The heaviness of his testicles and penis set her aflame and only Kyle Chatham could extinguish the out-of-control flames.

Kyle's pants settled around his feet and he stepped out of them, as he continued to suckle her breasts. Wrapping an arm around her waist, he pulled at her pants and panties at the same time.

Ava released Kyle's erection long enough to pull her top over her head and push her pants off her hips. Seconds later the thong joined her pants on the tiled floor. A soft groan escaped her when he cupped her hips in his hands, lifting her off her feet. Somewhere between sanity and insanity she wrapped her legs around his waist as he pushed inside her warm body in a single thrust of his hips.

They stood in the dimly lit kitchen, her back against the smooth, cool surface of the refrigerator door, mating. That was the only word Ava could come up with to describe their coupling.

A deep groan that came from Kyle's throat accompanied each thrust. The wetness coming from Ava trickled down his thighs as he tried to get even closer. The inferno that had begun in her was transferred to him and in a moment of madness he regretted that she was using birth control. It had taken thirty-eight years for him to feel the pull of fatherhood, and he wanted the woman in his arms to bear his children.

"Yes, yes, yes," Ava chanted over and over until it became a litany. The flutters began, softly at first, and she knew it wouldn't be long before she climaxed. But she didn't want to have an orgasm. She wanted this to go on and on and on.

Kyle felt Ava's vaginal muscles contract around his penis, squeezing and pulling him in before easing. The familiar tingling at the base of his spine signaled he was close to ejaculating when that was the last thing he wanted to happen.

But nature was not to be denied. He couldn't control his hips as they moved back and forth like a jackhammer. Tightening his grip on Ava's waist, he lifted her even higher for deeper penetration. Then it happened; Kyle felt as if the top of his head had exploded when semen shot from him with the velocity of a fired missile.

Kyle's deep growl of satisfaction made the hair stand up on the back of Ava's neck and within seconds her cries overlapped his as they climaxed simultaneously. She was still trembling when he lowered her legs.

"Shame on you, Kyle Chatham," she whispered in his ear.

"Why shame on me?"

"You have how many beds in this house and we make love in the kitchen."

Kyle eased his still-pulsing penis from her. "We could've used the table or countertops," he teased.

"Yuck! I will not make love where we have to prepare food."

"Stop being so parochial, Ava."

Easing back, she gave him a long, penetrating stare that mirrored disbelief. "How parochial can I be if I let you make love to me up against a refrigerator? And don't forget what happened in the…"

Her words died on her lips when he covered her mouth with his. "That is something I'll never forget as long as I live."

Neither will I, Ava thought when Kyle took her hand. They walked through the expansive living/dining room to the staircase.

There was nothing more to be said because their bodies had done the talking for them. The uninhibited, erotic coupling had cemented their relationship physically and emotionally.

Chapter 13

Ava stood in the doorway, waiting to greet her ten o'clock client. A bright smile lit up her eyes when she saw the woman wasn't wearing her usual attire of sweats and running shoes. Today she wore a classic man-tailored white blouse, black slacks and conservative black pumps.

"Good morning, Lisa. You look very nice."

Lisa Wilson flashed a shy smile. "Thank you, Miss Ava."

"Please come in and sit down."

Waiting until her client was seated, Ava closed the door then went over to sit behind her desk. Whenever she was in session she turned off the overhead light, leaving on a table lamp. The soft golden light created an atmosphere of calming peace.

She'd moved into the medical director's office and decorated it to reflect her own personality. A round table held a profusion of green and flowering plants in colorful pots. Her professional diplomas and social-work license were displayed on one wall while a facing wall had a quartet of pen and ink drawings she'd purchased from a Greenwich Village street vendor.

Ava focused on the framed photograph of her niece, taken minutes after her birth, then turned her attention to Lisa. The thirty-two-year-old woman was the single mother of four children, each from a different man. She would've had more children if she hadn't made the decision to have her tubes tied.

Each time Lisa delivered a child she'd suffered acute postpartum depression. The last bout had far exceeded the first three episodes, lasting more than six months. Ava, with the assistance of her social-services case-worker, had helped Lisa get job training after a vocational aptitude test had indicated her strength in secretarial studies.

"How are you today?"

Lisa patted her freshly relaxed hair cut into a becoming short style. Her smooth, full, dark brown face belied her age. "I have a job interview this afternoon," she announced proudly.

"Where is the interview?"

"It's in the garment district. It's only a part-time

position answering telephones and opening the mail, but it's a start, Miss Ava."

Ava smiled. "It's more than a start, Lisa. It is the beginning of the rest of your life."

"I want to be able to take care of my babies, because I want them to be proud of me."

"They are proud of you," Ava said softly, "because you love them. Don't ever let anyone tell you that you're not a good mother. They're always clean and well-fed."

"That's because I take care of them first then myself."

Ava laced her fingers together atop the desk. "That's all well and good, but if you don't take care of yourself you won't be able to take care of your children." An expression of confusion clouded Lisa's face. "Whenever you take an airplane you will hear the flight attendant say that in the event of a loss in air pressure, oxygen masks will drop from an overhead compartment. They caution adults flying with children to put the masks over their own faces first, then their children's."

"I see what you mean. I'm going to have to leave now, because I don't want to be late for the interview."

"What time is your interview?"

"Eleven."

"Why didn't you call and cancel if you had an interview at eleven?" She stood up. "Now, go and catch your bus or train."

Lisa rose to her feet, extended her arms and hugged Ava. "Thank you so much, Miss Ava, for everything. I couldn't have gotten this far without you."

"Yes, you would, Lisa. It just would've taken a little longer." She dropped her arms. "Call me and let me know how it went."

Lisa blinked back the moisture filling her eyes. "I will. Wish me luck."

Ava squeezed her hand. "You already have it." She walked Lisa to the door, watching her as she walked, her head held high.

The fifty-minute session had ended early and that left time for Ava to complete the session notes on her earlier clients. Her former caseload of eleven clients and two groups had dwindled to four and one group. She had never realized how much she enjoyed counseling until faced with the ever-increasing bureaucratic paperwork. It had also become her responsibility to schedule supervision with each counselor to review their caseloads.

Her respite came when she went home. Since returning from Maryland she'd begun spending weekends with Kyle. Although he'd asked to see her more often, she didn't want to get in over her head. Ava kept telling herself that she wasn't in love with Kyle Chatham, but each time they made love her body said differently.

The buzz of her intercom broke into her concentration as she reread her case notes. She pushed a button on her telephone console. "Yes, Tina?"

"Do you still want me to hold your calls?"

"No. Are there any messages?" She always transferred her calls to Tina's number whenever she was in session or supervision.

"There's a Mr. Chatham holding for you. Should I put him through?"

Ava's heart rate kicked into a higher gear. "Yes, please. Hey, you," she crooned when hearing his baritone greeting. "I thought you were to be in court this morning."

"It was adjourned until next week. I'm calling to ask if you would accompany me to a dinner party given by a friend. It's going to be the first time they're entertaining as husband and wife."

"Where do they live?"

"Brooklyn."

"Are you driving or should I drive?" She'd gotten her car back from the body shop and it looked as new as it had when she had driven it off the car dealer's lot.

"I'll drive," Kyle volunteered.

"What if we compromise, darling?" she whispered even though there was no one else in the office.

"How, sweetheart?"

"You drive my car."

"That sounds like a plan. You can drive to my place and we'll leave from there."

"That sounds like a very good plan. What day and time is the dinner party?"

"It's scheduled for Saturday at eight. And before you ask, dress is casual. Now that we've solved our weekend plans, what are you doing tonight?"

Ava glanced at the open planner on her desk. "I have an appointment to get my hair trimmed."

"What time do you expect to be finished with your hair?"

"Probably around six. Why, Kyle?"

"I want you to help me pick out an anniversary gift for my parents."

"How long have they been married?" Ava asked.

"This Saturday will be thirty-seven years."

Reaching for her mouse, Ava clicked on the online icon. "Do you have a few minutes while I go online to check on gift ideas?"

"Sure."

"What did you give them for their thirty-fifth?"

"My sister and I sent them on a cruise to Alaska and my brother sent them a generous check."

"It's hard to top that," Ava murmured as she scrolled through a site listing traditional and modern anniversary gifts. "There's nothing listed between thirty-five and forty, so you have a lot of options."

"What do you suggest?"

"It would depend on your parents' lifestyle."

"They're very active. They golf, bowl and Dad cooks several times a week at a local Salvation Army Center."

"What about a spa, Kyle? You can send them to a spa in Arizona where they can get in touch with their inner selves and nature. I heard Sedona is really beautiful."

"Ava, you're incredible! I love you. Thanks."

"You…you're welcome, Kyle."

"I'll talk to you later, baby."

Ava held the receiver long after she heard the

recorded message telling her to hang up and try her call again. She couldn't believe Kyle could be glib. How he could tell her he loved her then hang up.

Get a grip, Ava, she told herself. People said *I love you* all the time and it was quite different from being in love.

However, it was different with her because not only did she love Kyle Chatham, she was *in love* with him.

Kyle and Jordan sat in the reception area, their gazes fused to the flat-screen television. The piece about the tenants' strike was scheduled to air on the evening news.

Pressing his palms together, Jordan touched his chin. He'd spent weeks waiting for the segment to air. Kat had called to tell him that her producer didn't think it was newsworthy enough for immediate airing, so she had to wait for an opening in the investigative scheduling.

His hands came down. He leaned forward, resting his elbows on his knees. "It's about to begin, Chat."

Kyle, who'd assumed a similar pose, shook his head. "Get ready for the fireworks and the backlash."

Katrina Nichols appeared on the screen. The camera favored her because she looked prettier, softer than she did in person. When the camera panned over to Jordan, Kyle registered the soft gasps from the women in the reception area. It was apparent they recognized that the man sitting only feet from them was the same as the image on the screen. He was at the perfect angle for the sunlight to slant over his face. His eyes shimmered like multifaceted citrines and peridots. The inky darkness of his cropped hair and bronzed skin was mesmerizing.

The network aired Jordan's rant in its entirety, followed by Katrina's attempt to gain access to Wyatt Wainwright's office for feedback or a rebuttal.

Jordan straightened, his face a glowering mask of rage. "She didn't tell me she was going to *him* before the network aired the piece."

"Maybe she wanted to get your grandfather's side of the story at the same time."

"His side of the story!"

Kyle came to his feet. "Let's discuss this upstairs, Jordan." There was a slight edge in his voice that made the suggestion a command. He waited until they were seated in his office to round on his associate.

"I told you, motivation fueled by revenge is risky. You were ballsy when you decided to go to the press. Would I have done it? Probably not. But then, Wyatt Wainwright isn't my grandpa. You took a risk, Jordan. You put yourself out there, now you have to deal with the fallout. And you did a very noble thing when you promised to underwrite the costs for the repairs to their apartments, but it's also risky because your granddad could possibly play golf or poker with the judge who hears our case and we end up with nothing. Or he could have engineers rule that the building's structurally unsafe and should be condemned. You lose your money and the tenants lose their only home.

"A threatened man is a dangerous man. We've filed the papers for the suit, so I suggest you call your grandfather and set up a meeting. We can ask the officers of the tenants' association to come along. I'll chair the meeting so it doesn't get personal. And if your grandfather refuses to compromise, then we'll resort to non-violent tactics."

"What are you suggesting?"

"I'll pay someone to picket his home and his office building with signs outing him as a slumlord. He can't have the picketer arrested because they will be on city property. And because it will be a lone picketer there won't be any need to get a permit for assembly. If people see the picketer day after day it's bound to make an impact on Wyatt's so-called impeccable reputation. The man can't continue to give his money to his favorite charities while at the same time subjecting people to squalid living conditions."

Jordan inclined his head. "When do you want me to call him?"

"Now."

Removing the cell phone clipped to his waist, Jordan hit speed dial and the speaker. "May I please speak to Wyatt. This is Jordan."

"Hold on, Jordan. I'll see if he's available to speak to you." Jordan met Kyle's steady gaze as he waited for either his grandfather or the man's loyal secretary to come back on the line.

"What the hell do you want, Judas?" asked a booming voice pregnant with sarcasm.

Jordan's impassive expression did not change. "I need to talk to you."

"Haven't you done enough talking to the press, sonny boy?"

"I didn't say all that should've been said, that's why I want to set up a meeting to talk to you."

"There's nothing to talk about."

"Oh, yes, there is, Grandpa. It would be a good thing if we can resolve these issues before it winds up on a court calendar."

"It will never get that far. I know enough prosecutors and judges in this city who will make certain it will never hit any docket in this state."

"Careful, Grandpa. I could be taping this call."

"You traitorous little sonofabitch!"

"Don't even go there! You have exactly sixty seconds to give me an answer. Yes or no." The sweep hand on Jordan's watch made a full revolution.

"Okay. You'll get your meeting."

Jordan and Kyle each gestured a thumbs-up at the same time. "Call me tomorrow at my office and give me several time slots. My number is—"

"I know where you work." The call ended abruptly with Kyle and Jordan touching fists. They'd scaled the first hurdle.

"'I know where you work,'" Jordan said, mimicking his grandfather. "The old blowhard used to scare the hell out of me just by walking into the room."

"Intimidation only works when the one being intimi-dated exhibits fear. I want to remind you that Rashaun Hayden and his parents are coming in early Friday morning. After I talk with them, I'll decide whether we want to embarrass the D.A.'s office or the NYPD."

"If it were me I'd prefer ripping the D.A. a new one."

Kyle smiled. "Only time will tell who'll jump out of the trick bag first."

Ava looked at the mirror, not recognizing the eyes staring back at her as her own. She'd spent the past four hours in the hospital at the bedside of a former client who'd been beaten so severely that she'd lost her sight in one eye.

When she'd got the call from the hospital social worker telling her that her name and telephone number were listed as an emergency contact for a patient who'd been found unconscious near the Lincoln Tunnel, Ava knew who it would be even before being told her name.

Julie Douglas was only twenty-two, but after turning tricks for almost a decade she looked twice her age. Rain, as she was known on the streets, had come from Seattle to New York with an older cousin. The cousin had hired her out to men when he ran low on cash, and by the time Julie was fourteen she'd become a hardcore hooker with an off-and-on drug habit, earning a long rap sheet for soliciting and pandering. A sympathetic judge offered Julie an alternative to jail: counseling.

Ava had assisted Julie in getting a place to live and had helped her get into a job-training program, but the lure of drugs and the street had proved too powerful, and, after a year of staying clean and sober, Rain was back with prostitution. She'd come by the agency, heavily made up and scantily dressed in her "working" clothes, just to talk. Although she was no longer a client Ava gave her all the time she needed to vent and to perhaps consider changing her lifestyle.

She hadn't seen or heard from Julie in nearly a year, so Ava had hoped that she'd gone back to Seattle to reconcile with family. She refused to believe that something had happened to the young woman who'd occasionally come in with a black eye or bruises. Whenever Ava asked if her pimp had beaten her, Julie's response was that she was her own woman and there was no way she was going to lie on her back then turn her money over to a man.

When Ava asked her why she slept with men for money, Julie's response was that if men were willing to pay for her services then she was a fool if she didn't take their money. She said they felt sex was better if they paid for it.

As she sat staring at Julie's face, bruised and swollen beyond recognition, Ava wondered if, when she recovered enough to leave the hospital, Julie would return to the world's oldest profession.

Turning on the faucet, she splashed water on her face, then blotted the moisture with a paper towel. An announcement came through the speakers indicating visiting hours were over. Ava would go home, but once Julie was discharged where would she go? The address on the card in Julie's purse did not exist and the telephone number was a business listing. The only hint of truth was the business card Ava had given Julie years before.

She knew she wouldn't be able to talk to Julie until the doctors decreased the powerful sedative that helped her rest comfortably. Gathering her handbag, she walked out of the bathroom and headed for the exit.

Once outside the hospital she turned on her cell. She had two voice-mail messages. The first one was from Debra, who wanted to know about Julie Douglas. She called Debra, giving her an update on Julie's condition. When she called Kyle she couldn't hold back the emotions that had started building when she walked into a room to find her former patient hooked up to tubes and machines.

"Someone tried to kill her, Kyle. She's only twenty-two. She had her whole life ahead of her and now she's blind in one eye and may lose the other."

"Ava, where are you?"

"I'm outside St. Luke's-Roosevelt Hospital."

"Stay there. I'm coming to get you."

"Don't, Kyle. The subway's right here. I'll be home in a few stops."

"Do not get on the subway."

"Then I'll take the bus," Ava said.

"Ava! Listen to me. Stay where you are and I'll come pick you up. Now, tell me you'll wait."

She closed her eyes. "Don't yell at me, Kyle."

"I'm not yelling at you, baby."

"Then you were raising your voice."

"I'm sorry if I raised my voice. Go back into the hospital and sit. Give me about twenty minutes to half an hour. Okay?"

Ava opened her eyes. She was too emotionally drained to fight or argue with Kyle. "Okay."

Chapter 14

Kyle handed Ava a mug of steaming liquid. "I know it's hot, but it will help you to relax."

She wrapped her hands around the ceramic mug, the heat warming her chilled fingers. Nighttime temperatures were in the seventies and even with the cool air coming through the vents in Kyle's house it wasn't cold, but Ava was freezing. She glanced up at him over the rim. "What's in it?"

"Tea, honey, lemon and brandy."

She took a sip, then another until she drank all of the toddy. The soothing liquid slid down the back of her throat, settling and warming her chest. "It's good." She set the empty mug on a coaster on the bedside table.

Kyle got into bed next to Ava, pulling her to his chest. Instead of driving her back to her apartment he'd brought her home with him. She was monosyllabic when he filled the bathtub with water, gave her a bath and dried her without a word passing between them. He knew she was upset about a hospitalized client, yet he hadn't broached the subject because he didn't want her to relive the ordeal.

Leaning over, he turned out the lamp on his side of the bed, plunging the room into darkness. Diffused light from the solar lights in the backyard came through the sheers at the French doors.

"Remember, you don't have to go in to work until the afternoon, so don't jump up at six." Ava had told him that she'd stayed in the office until midnight working on reports the past two days and planned to work half days the rest of the week.

"I don't want to wake up," she slurred.

"Don't say that, Ava. You had a bad day, but come morning you'll see things differently."

"See, Kyle? I left a twenty-two-year-old who will never see out of one eye and may lose her sight in the other. Do you think she's going to want to wake up?"

"Yes, she will, because she'll be alive. No one, whether blind or sighted, wants to die. Her daily routine will change, but she will continue to live."

"What are the odds of a blind prostitute making enough money to support her drug habit?"

Kyle blew out a breath. "Very, very slim."

"How about nonexistent?"

He dropped a kiss on her hair. "Your work isn't much different than mine. Our clients come to us because they have either legal or emotional roadblocks that disrupt their lives. And it becomes our responsibility to advocate for them."

"Who's going to advocate for us when we need help?"

"I'll advocate for you and you can advocate for me."

Ava snuggled closer to Kyle, feeding on his warmth. "You will take...take care of me?" She was slurring her words.

"Yes, baby, I will take care of you."

A silence ensued. "Why, Kyle? Why do you want to take care of me?"

Kyle pondered Ava's questions. He'd asked himself over and over why he wanted to take care of her and the answer was always the same: because he was in love with her.

"Because you've become very special to me, Ava. You fill a void in my life no other woman has been able to do. I..." His voice trailed off when he heard the soft snores. Ava had fallen asleep.

Easing her down to the pillow, he pulled a light-weight blanket up and over her shoulders. He lay completely still, his mind awash with things he wanted to tell Ava. He wanted to tell her he loved her, loved her enough to propose marriage, loved her enough for her to bear his children and loved her enough to want to die in her arms.

* * *

Kyle sat on the side of the bed, leaned over and kissed Ava's forehead. "I left a set of keys for you on the countertop next to the coffeemaker."

Ava opened her eyes, peering blurrily at Kyle. He was dressed for work. "Do you want me to set the alarm?"

"Yes. Just set the On button and you'll have thirty seconds to close the door."

"Thank you, darling."

He smiled. "What are you thanking me for?"

"For knowing that I needed not to be alone last night."

"You don't ever have to be alone. Any time you want to move in just let me know."

"Kyle, I can't—"

"I know," he said, interrupting her. "You don't do well living with a man."

"You'd better get going if you want to get to your meeting on time."

"Are you trying to get rid of me?"

Ava patted his shoulder through his suit jacket. "I'm hoping to get a few more hours of sleep."

"On that note I'm leaving. I'll see you later."

"Later."

Ava held her expression of indifference until Kyle left the bedroom, and then she let the love she felt for him fill her from the inside out. It was becoming more and more difficult to hide her love for him. The only time she was able to let go was during lovemaking. It was then she surrendered all of herself, holding nothing back. If only he took the time to assess how different she was in and out of bed, he would see the truth.

Kyle waited for James Hayden to seat his wife before introducing everyone around the conference table. "Mr. and Mrs. Hayden, I'd like you to meet the firm's associate attorney Jordan Wainwright. Mr. Wainwright will answer any of your questions in regard to your son's case if I'm not available." The Haydens smiled at Jordan.

"Seated across from Mr. Wainwright is Ms. Dickson, who will record this morning's meeting." He'd asked his nighttime paralegal to come in early with the court stenographic machine. His gaze shifted, focusing on Rashaun, who sat slumped in his chair as if he didn't have a care in the world.

Kyle glanced down at the typed report in the NY vs. Hayden folder. "I've asked you to come in this morning because we've come up with some inconsistencies in the evidence gathered by the D.A.'s office."

James Hayden blinked slowly behind his glasses. "What inconsistencies are you talking about?"

Jordan glared at Rashaun, who sat up straighter. "We have a videotape that will prove Rashaun wasn't involved in the robbery."

Mrs. Hayden turned to look at her son. "But the police told us they have pictures of Rashaun with a gun."

As agreed upon beforehand, Kyle would address Mrs. Hayden's questions and Jordan James Hayden's. They'd decided to play good cop, bad cop in the hope that Rashaun would give up the name of the person pretending to be him.

"I had an expert go over the tape and he verified that it'd been edited." Kyle laid out five photographs. "This is the first shot. Note the time on the clock on the wall. It reads five-seventeen. In the next four photos the same clock is reading ten-twelve. There is a difference of five hours and five minutes between the onset of the robbery to when the perpetrator exits the bodega. The most obvious inconsistency is the hand holding the gun. In the first photograph the supposed Rashaun isn't wearing a ring and in the other photos he *is* wearing one."

Placing his elbows on the table, Jordan gave each Hayden a long stare. "We know who that rings belongs to, and it's not Rashaun. Someone who closely resembles your son knew he was having a problem with the owner of that bodega, so he decided to put on a hoodie like one that he knows Rashaun owns, and he goes back and holds up the clerk. But what he forgot to do was take off the ring."

"Who is Boots, Rashaun?" Kyle asked the seemingly shocked teenager.

"I don't know no Boots," he mumbled.

"Yes, you do," Kyle countered. "Correct me if I'm wrong, but don't you owe Boots for some weed you—"

"You doing drugs?" James shouted. The look in his eyes spelled trouble, serious trouble for his son.

Rashaun shook his head. "I ain't doing no drugs, Pop."

"Then what the hell were you doing with weed?"

Kyle knew he had to diffuse the situation or he would

have to defend James Hayden for assault. "Rashaun asked Boots for the drugs because he intended to sell it."

Mrs. Hayden shot up. "Sell it! You were going to sell drugs?"

Pushing back his chair, Kyle rose to his feet. "Mr. and Mrs. Hayden, please try to remain calm. I know this comes as a shock to you, but I need answers from your son as to why he's willing to take the fall for Boots."

Mrs. Hayden, her chest rising and falling heavily, sat down again, while her husband changed seats to put some distance between him and his son.

Kyle exhaled an audible breath. "I'm going to ask you this only one time and I expect you to tell me the truth. Why are you willing to do a bid for Boots?"

All eyes were trained on Rashaun as he stared at the surface of the conference table. He was medium height with clean-cut looks that would give him nerd status. There was something about him that reminded Kyle of himself when he'd run with the wrong crowd. He was willing to commit the crime, but just running with the other guys enhanced his street cred.

"I saw Boots pop someone," Rashaun mumbled. "He told me if I snitched then he would take care of me."

Kyle felt a chill snake its way down his spine. His informant had finally come through with the information that Boots was recruiting boys in the neighborhood to sell drugs. He started them out with weed, then crack, heroin and cocaine.

"Did he kill this person?" Rashaun nodded. "You're going to have to give me the name of the victim."

"What's going to happen to my son?" Mrs. Hayden asked, dabbing the corners of her eyes with a tissue.

"I'm going to talk to a friend who works out of the Brooklyn D.A.'s office. Even though Rashaun didn't commit the crime, he knows who did, and that means he withheld information. A.D.A. Clarkson knows about the edited tape. He's launched an internal investigation to see who is responsible. The case against your son is on hold indefinitely. That means if you want to leave the state you can."

Rashaun looked at his parents. "Where are we going?"

"Never you mind," his mother snapped angrily. "I don't know how many times I told you 'bout hanging out with those thugs, but you wouldn't listen. Now when your ass is in trouble I can't get you to leave the house."

Jordan pushed a pad and pencil at Rashaun. "I want you to write down the name of the person Boots shot."

Rashaun gripped the pencil and scrawled a name on the legal pad. In the uncomfortable silence that followed, Kyle shared a knowing look with his associate. They'd solved one crime but had opened another. Murders occurred much too frequently in the city, and the number of those that went unsolved was staggering.

Kyle tried to give Rashaun a reassuring smile. "If the information you just gave us leads to a conviction, then you're entitled to a reward under the Crime Stoppers program if Boots is convicted."

Rashaun chewed his lower lip. "Will I have to testify in court?"

"Not if Boots accepts a plea deal."

"How can you be sure he's going to cop a plea?"

"I'm not sure, Rashaun. But with him facing an armed robbery and assault charge, he would want to cop a plea with an additional manslaughter charge guaranteeing him a possible life sentence. A.D.A. Clarkson is out for blood, so I don't know how generous he'll be once they apprehend Boots."

"Are they looking for him now?" James asked.

Kyle nodded. "The police had issued a warrant for his arrest. Mr. and Mrs. Hayden, I would like to thank you for your cooperation."

James leaned over to shake Jordan's hand, then Kyle's. "We should be thanking you for keeping our son out of prison. I think he's learned his lesson."

Mrs. Hayden glared at her only child. "And if he hasn't learned his lesson then you'll have to defend me because as sure as I brought my son into this world I'll also take him out."

James put an arm around his wife's shoulders. "It's all right, baby. Rashaun isn't going to give us any more trouble. Are you, boy?"

"No."

"No what?"

"No, sir."

Kyle doubted whether Rashaun wanted to go one-on-one with his father; the man was built like brick wall. One blow from his ham-like fist could easily put someone on their back. "I have your numbers, so I'll be calling with an update. Good luck, Rashaun."

The teenager ducked his head. "Thank you, Mr. Chatham."

The paralegal took the tape from her machine and placed it into an envelope to transcribe it later. She nodded to Kyle and left the conference room, following the Haydens.

Kyle and Jordan smiled at each other. "The bluff worked."

Jordan shook his head in amazement. "I was beginning to believe you myself."

"Sometimes you have to twist a lie in order to get the truth. I'd like you to call Skyler Clarkson and give him what he'll need to close the books on a cold case."

"Are you certain you want me to call Clarkson?"

"Very certain, Jordan. The A.D.A. and I are like oil and fire. Whenever we come together there's an explosion. I think he took offense when I called him a racist bastard."

"Is he a racist bastard?"

"Hell, yeah, he is. And he doesn't bother to hide it."

"Thanks for the heads-up. What's with your comment about the Haydens leaving the state?"

Kyle told Jordan that James Hayden had put in a request to the postal service for a transfer to South Carolina. His transfer was approved, pending the early fall retirement of several carriers.

Jordan smiled. "In other words, he's trying to get his family the hell out of Dodge."

"It's either that or his son will end up in Boot Hill. You did good, Wainwright."

"I learn from the best."

"You're really lobbying for that partnership, aren't you?" Kyle teased.

Jordan sobered. "Making partner isn't that important anymore. Helping people like the Haydens or the tenants' committee has become my focus."

"Are you saying you don't want to be a partner?"

"I don't care one way or the other."

Kyle knew he would ask Jordan to become a partner. There was enough brashness in the young attorney that he was sure to make a name for himself in the Harlem community.

"Have you heard anything from your grandfather?"

"Not yet. But the longer he waits the more he'll have to pay, and the payment will not necessarily be monetary."

Kyle wasn't going to touch that because he didn't want to become embroiled in a family feud when it wasn't even his family. He sat down when Jordan left the room, flipping through the folder on NY vs. Hayden. The case wasn't closed but he knew it wouldn't be long before all the charges were dropped. He had to follow up to make certain everything to do with Rashaun's arrest was expunged.

Ava focused on Kyle as he motioned for her to come closer. She'd maneuvered into the carriage house next to the Jaguar and cut off the engine to her Maxima. Reaching for her weekender on the passenger seat, she got out.

Lifting her chin, she wasn't disappointed when Kyle brushed a kiss over her mouth. "Hi."

Kyle kissed her again as he reached for her bag. "How was your day?"

"It was good. I went back to the hospital to see Julie."

"How is she doing?"

"The doctor says she's the same. They have her in a drug-induced coma because of the swelling in her brain."

Holding Ava's hand, Kyle led her up the steps and into the kitchen. "What about her family?"

"What family she has is in Seattle. Even when she was my client she refused to talk about her family. Her street name was Rain because she said it reminded her of home."

Dropping her bag on the kitchen floor, Kyle pulled Ava to his length. "I'm glad you decided to come over tonight rather than tomorrow."

"I didn't want to stay home and think about Julie."

"Here I thought you wanted to see me."

Ava stared up at her lover. She noticed several new lines around his eyes that hadn't been there before. His cropped hair was perfect, as if he had it cut on a weekly basis. And despite the feathering of gray in his hair he projected a boyish look.

"I did want to see you."

"Not as much as I want to see you. I never get enough of you."

Ava buried her face between his neck and shoulder. "I think we'd better get out of this kitchen before we end up in a compromising position."

"You didn't like making love in the kitchen?"

"Of course I enjoyed making love with you. It's just that I'd never made love in the kitchen before."

Pulling back, Kyle smiled at Ava. "I'd like for us to make love in every room in the house."

"Your fantasies are getting the best of you."

"No, they're not. Let's try it."

"There's nothing wrong with your bed." Ava let out a shriek when Kyle swept her off her feet and carried her through the living room to the staircase leading to the upper floors. He didn't stop on the second floor. He continued to the third floor and stalked into the first guest room.

She wasn't given the opportunity to catch her breath before she found herself on her back with Kyle pressing her down to the mattress. His fingers were deliberate when he divested her of her clothes in under a minute.

Going to his knees, Kyle stared at Ava as he undressed. He didn't think he would ever get used to seeing her naked. Each time his gaze caressed her body it was a visual feast he longed to imprint on his brain.

He sat down, supporting his back against the headboard. Tonight he planned to get his wish. He would watch her as they made love. Reaching for her, he settled Ava to straddle his thighs, hardening quickly when her breasts brushed his chest.

Ava closed her eyes, gasping when she felt the erection pulsing against her belly. Kyle Chatham had become her drug of choice. The more they made love the more she wanted him. She leaned closer, rubbing her breasts back and forth over his solid pectorals.

"I don't want to wait," she whispered hoarsely.

Wrapping an arm around her waist, Kyle lifted Ava as he eased his blood-engorged penis into her. They both sighed in pleasure. Twin desires rose quickly, spiraling out of control.

Ava rose and fell over his erection, taking as much of him as she could before raising her hips to establish a rhythm that had every nerve in her body screaming.

Cradling her waist in his hands, Kyle tried to establish a slower cadence to delay the rush of passion rushing headlong through his body. He'd wanted a prolonged coupling, but it was not to be.

Pressing his head to the headboard, he closed his eyes, groaning as if in pain. The pleasure Ava offered him took him beyond sexual satisfaction. Her eager response to his lovemaking had become a raw act of possession. She was passion, desire and love.

The hysteria of delight seized Ava as gusts of ecstasy swept over her. She loved him, she loved him so much, and if her lips couldn't tell Kyle then her body would. Raising her hips slightly, she held on to the sack cradling his testicles and squeezed gently. She wanted to touch him—all over. She wanted to taste him—all over. Ava angled her head and suckled him as he'd suckled her.

Kyle bellowed as if he'd been branded by a heated iron. "No! Please!" He was pleading with Ava to stop, but she was relentless. Seeking respite from her exquisite torture, he flipped her on her back. He held her ankles and rested them on his shoulders. He entered her again, riding her like a man possessed.

It ended when Ava screamed his name as her flesh contracted around him, milking him at the same time as she melted all over him. He lowered her legs but didn't pull out. Kyle wanted to savor the oneness for as long as possible. They lay together, joined, legs entwined, heart to heart, skin to skin, man to woman.

Burying his face against the column of her scented neck, he breathed a kiss there. "I love you."

Ava froze, believing she'd imagined his declaration of love. "What?"

"You heard me, Ava Warrick. I love you."

"How? Why?"

Raising his head, he glared at her. "You're a very bright woman. Figure it out." Releasing her, he swung his legs over the bed and walked out of the bedroom.

Ava panicked, moving off the bed to follow him. He'd made it down to the second landing when she leaned over the banister. "Kyle." He stopped his descent, but wouldn't look up at her. "I love you, too."

Kyle turned slowly, retracing his steps as Ava came to meet him. No words were needed when he cradled her to his heart. He loved her and she loved him. For the first time in his life everything was right in his world.

Chapter 15

Kyle found a parking space around the corner from the house where Micah and Tessa Sanborn lived in a Brooklyn Heights brownstone. He shut off the engine to the brand new Maxima and came around to assist Ava.

"I like driving your car."

Ava gave him a sensual smile. "Would you like to trade?"

"I don't think so," he drawled, reaching into the backseat for the bag with two bottles of premium champagne. He liked her car, but he liked his better.

"I don't think I've been to Brooklyn more than half a dozen times, and never to Brooklyn Heights," Ava admitted.

Kyle threaded his fingers through hers. "It took years before I learned every neighborhood in this borough. It's like a city within a city."

"I've always wanted to walk across the Brooklyn Bridge."

"We can do that."

Ava fell silent as they strolled along tree-lined streets with stately brownstones and townhouses that reminded her of the Mount Morris Historic District. What she'd shared with Kyle the night before was still too new for her to take in. They'd spent the night in the guest bedroom, and when she woke she'd found Kyle sitting in bed watching her. He appeared more like a stranger than a lover and they spent the day seemingly tiptoeing around each other.

"Are you going to take any vacation time this summer?" she asked him.

"I hadn't planned to, but if you want to go somewhere or do something, then let me know. My associate can hold down the fort whenever I'm not there."

"I'm scheduled to take another two weeks at the end of the year, but I've accumulated a lot of compensatory time. I have to use the comp time during the calendar year, otherwise I'll lose it. If I don't take vacation time it can be rolled over for three years."

"Maybe we can take either Fridays or Mondays off and go somewhere."

Ava gave Kyle a sidelong glance. He looked wonderfully casual in a pair of taupe tailored slacks, a navy blazer and a white shirt sans tie. She'd selected a pair of white linen slacks, a blue-and-white striped boatneck cotton sweater and navy leather mules.

"Where would we go?"

Kyle gave her fingers a gentle squeeze. "Have you ever been to Montreal?"

"No, I haven't."

"Would you go with me?"

Ava's smile was dazzling. "I'd love to go with you." The instant the word *love* slipped past her lips she regretted it.

"And I'd love to take you." Kyle slowed as they neared the brownstone with the shiny brass plaque advertising Signature Bridals. "Micah and Tessa live here." They climbed the steps to a door with stained-glass inserts. He rang the bell and it was opened by a tall, slender, dark-skinned man with a beguiling smile. He wore a white golf shirt, khakis and slip-ons.

Micah Sanborn waved a hand. "Please come in." Light from a table lamp in the foyer glinted off the shiny gold band on his left hand.

Kyle placed the decorative shopping bag on a table with a vase of exquisite exotic flowers. Then he and Micah exchanged rough hugs, pounding each other's backs. "Congratulations again."

Micah flashed his large, straight white teeth. "Thanks."

"How's married life?"

"The best. You should try it."

Kyle's smile was still in place when he wrapped an

arm around Ava's waist. "I'd like you to meet someone who's very special to me. Ava, this is Micah Sanborn. Micah, Ava Warrick."

Ava offered her hand. "My pleasure, Micah." Masculinity radiated off the man.

Micah, ignoring her proffered hand, dipped his head and kissed her cheek. "It's my pleasure to meet you. I don't know if your boyfriend told you, but he was my law-school mentor. It took me six years, attending part-time, to finish, but I finished with Kyle's help."

"Don't let Micah fool you. He would've graduated at the top of his class even if we never met. Both his parents are attorneys."

"Neither of them are practicing law now."

Kyle turned to Ava. "My friend here is a little too modest."

Micah peered into the shopping bag. "What did you bring?"

"Champagne."

"Excellent. Tessa's going to have my head if I don't bring you guys out back. We decided to set up outside because the weather this summer is nothing short of perfection."

Ava reached for Kyle's hand as they followed Micah down a hallway, into the kitchen and down several steps into the backyard. Dozens of votives and lamps affixed to the rear of the brownstone illuminated the area.

"Surprise!"

She jumped, startled when a roar went up from the

people who'd assembled in the back of the house. Kyle turned his back, while shaking his head. The dinner party wasn't to celebrate their first gathering as a married couple but for his thirty-ninth birthday.

He leaned into Micah whispering, "I should kick your ass for this."

"And I'll have you arrested for assaulting an officer of the law," Micah teased. Dropping an arm over his former mentor's shoulders, he winked at him. "Come and meet your guests."

When Micah mentioned guests Ava saw Ivan and Duncan with their arms around the waists of pretty young women who looked enough alike to be sisters. It was apparent they were in on the surprise. She stood off to the side while Kyle's friends came over to offer their good wishes.

"Are you Kyle's girlfriend?"

Ava turned to find an attractive woman with short curly hair, a deeply tanned gold-brown complexion and slanting eyes. "Yes," she answered confidently.

The woman extended her hand. "I'm Tessa Whitfield-Sanborn."

The two women shook hands. "Ava Warrick."

"I love your haircut, Ava."

She touched the tapered strands on the nape of her neck. "Thank you. I noticed the plaque on the front of house. Are you a wedding planner?"

Tessa smiled. "Yes. My sister and cousin and I make up Signature Bridals. I'm a planner and an occasional wedding-gown designer. Faith is a pastry chef specializing in wedding cakes and my sister Simone is a floral designer."

"How exciting. It's like one-stop shopping."

Tessa rested a hand on Ava's shoulder. "Once you and Kyle decide to marry I'd love to plan your wedding. And because Kyle was Micah's mentor you'll get the family rate."

Ava wanted to tell the wedding planner it wasn't happening. Just because she and Kyle had professed their love for each other, their relationship didn't have to culminate in a marriage.

What she shared with Kyle was perfect. He had his own place and she hers. She was independent, free to come and go without having to check in with him, and whenever they got together it was quality time. They cooked and ate together, listened to music and danced under the stars, and whenever they made love it was nothing short of perfection. He brought her to climax every time, something that hadn't happened with the other men in her life.

"I'll keep that in mind, Tessa."

"Come and get something to eat. Faith has outdone herself with the menu. Here's Faith."

Ava saw a tall woman with short hair and an incredibly beautiful face making her way towards them. The white apron tied around her waist accentuated a baby bump. She wondered if Faith had been a Signature bride. Tessa introduced her to the pastry chef.

"So, you're the birthday boy's girlfriend," Faith Whitfield-McMillan said, smiling.

"That I am," Ava confirmed.

She didn't know why her coming with Kyle Chatham made her the focus of attention. It made her wonder about the women in Kyle's past. Had he introduced them as someone who was very special to him? Was she one in a long line of women Kyle had dated, bedded but wouldn't wed?

"Don't move. I want to introduce you to my husband." Faith beckoned to a slender man a few feet away. He approached her and put both arms around her thickening waist. "Ethan, this is Kyle Chatham's girlfriend, Ava Warrick."

Ethan lowered one hand, offering it to Ava. "Ethan McMillan. You'd better go and get something to eat and drink before everything's gone. We had everyone show up at seven so as not to spoil the surprise."

Ava was mesmerized by Faith's husband's resonant voice and the deep slashes in his lean cheeks. The Whitfield women had married the kind of men most women spent their adult lives searching for. She had to acknowledge that she had a good man, but he wasn't *her* husband, and she feared if she did marry Kyle everything would change. It'd happened with the love of her life—a fellow college student who had professed to love her *and* another coed. Only Ava didn't know it until days before graduation when he'd told her he was getting married, but not to her.

Six years later she'd made the same mistake; she'd picked the wrong man. Her college lover had left her, and she'd *had* to leave Will or become a statistic of domestic violence.

Kyle had asked whether she would ever propose to him. In fact she was afraid to—afraid her husband would become a Jekyll and Hyde and she'd end up like Julie Nichols. Ava met Kyle as he headed toward her with a plate in his hand.

"I got you something to eat. Grab a chair and sit down."

Going on tiptoe, she kissed him. She took the plate and sat down. "Thank you. I'm going to get you for not telling me that today's your birthday."

"Why?"

"Because I would've bought you something."

He leaned closer. "That's why I didn't tell you, because I didn't want you to buy me anything. I have everything I want. I have Ava Warrick."

"Don't, Kyle. Not here."

"Where, baby?"

"Just don't make me cry in front of your friends."

He pressed his mouth to her ear. "You're only permitted to cry happy tears."

"Do I make you happy, Kyle?"

"No."

She pulled away from him. "No?"

"No. You make me delirious, crazy. When I'm with you I feel invincible. That there's nothing I can't do."

Ava kissed him again. "We'll talk about this later."

"Yo, birthday boy! Get a room!"

Kyle straightened, turning around when he recognized Ivan's voice. "There's only grown folks here whom I'm sure have seen and performed unspeakable acts." Everyone laughed loudly at Kyle's rejoinder, setting the stage for an evening of good food, drink and unrestrained frivolity. "I'll be back with something for you to drink."

Duncan Gilmore wended his way through the throng, a woman clinging possessively to his arm, and kissed Ava's cheek. "It's nice seeing you again."

She smiled up at the luscious-looking financial planner. "Same here. How have you been?"

"DG, I thought you were going to get me something to drink," whined the pretty woman in a voice that reminded Ava of fingernails on a chalkboard. "I am *so* parched that my throat feels as if it's closing up."

Duncan reached over and extracted the woman's hand from his arm. "I suggest you go and find something to drink before you expire. I'm not certain if there are any doctors or nurses here who would be able to resuscitate you."

The woman stomped her foot. "Duncan, how can you be so cruel?"

Giving her a look of sheer exasperation, Duncan said, "What I am is realistic, Monica. You don't need me to get you something to drink, *if* that's what you actually need. Now, if you don't mind I'd like to have few words with Kyle's girlfriend."

Monica's expression brightened when Duncan mentioned *Kyle's girlfriend.* "I'll be at the bar, *darling.*"

Ava watched her walk. "I'm sorry about your date."

A slight frown marred Duncan's smooth forehead when he sat down next to Ava. "She's not my date. Monica and Monique are neighbors of Tessa and Micah. And don't go there."

"What are you talking about?"

"I recognize that look on your face." Duncan was smiling.

"What look is that?" Ava asked.

"That I should give her a chance. You sisters all stick together."

"And you brothers don't," she countered. "You stick up for one another and, let's not forget, lie through the teeth for one another."

"You've got it all wrong, Ava. Kyle, Ivan and I have never lied for one another."

"Maybe the three of you are the exception."

"We're known around the way as the best men."

"Define *best.*"

"Good black men."

Duncan intrigued Ava. He hadn't boasted when he'd referred to himself as a good black man, but had said it rather matter-of-factly, as if it was his inherent right to refer to himself, Ivan and Kyle as such.

"Unfortunately there aren't enough best men available for sisters."

"There's plenty of them around, Ava. It's just that

women have a certain standard where they want every brother to look like Denzel Washington. Most of them don't realize there's only one Denzel."

"Are you saying we're superficial because we're only attracted to a man because of his looks?"

"Women are no more superficial than men when it comes to what they want their men to look like. All you have to do is look at the wives of professional athletes. Whether it's NASCAR, the NBA, NFL or major-league baseball, all of the ladies are a *type*."

"Am I a type, Duncan?"

Ava wanted to know if she looked like Kyle's former girlfriends. Whether she was *his* type.

"You're definitely not a type for Kyle. I suppose you can say that he's gone out with a number of women but has had few serious relationships. And of the two that I can remember, neither of them even remotely resembles you. You're much prettier."

Kyle returned, carrying a cup in each hand. "What's up, DG?"

"I'm trying to hit on your woman," Duncan said, deadpan.

Kyle handed Ava one of the cups. "Give it up, brother. She's not going to bite."

"Are you that certain, my brother?"

A smile crinkled the skin around Kyle's eyes. "So certain that I'm willing to wager all I have on it."

"Those stakes are a little too rich for my blood."

Kyle winked at Ava. "Don't let Duncan try and

fool you. He can buy and sell Ivan and me three or four times."

"Yeah, right." Duncan reached for Kyle's cup. "What are you drinking?"

"Take it. I'll get another one."

Duncan took a sip and screwed up his face. "What the hell is this?"

"Hawaiian punch."

"You're kidding?"

"No. I'm the designated driver."

"Brother, falling in love has made you soft."

Ava stared at Kyle, wondering if he'd mentioned to Duncan or Ivan that he was in love with her. She asked him the question when Duncan walked away.

"No, Ava. I don't make a habit of discussing the intimate details of my life with Duncan and Ivan."

"But why would he assume you are in love with me?"

"Maybe he can see something we're not aware of. Remember I've grown up with Ivan and Duncan, and in thirty years you can learn a lot about another person."

"Thirty years is a long time."

"I trust Duncan to look after my investments and I trust him and Ivan with my life. We made a pact years ago never to go after each other's women—even if they became an ex. There isn't anything I wouldn't do for them and vice versa. Maybe it's because we don't share blood that we're so loyal to one another."

"Have either of them been married?"

Kyle shook his head. "Duncan is the only who's

come close. He was engaged, but his fiancée died during the World Trade Center tragedy. They were to be married that coming weekend. To say he was devastated is an understatement. DG grieved hard for more than a year and he's still grieving."

Ava had listened to Duncan's exchange with Monica. He hadn't been rude or disrespectful to her, but cold and indifferent. It was as if he didn't care what she wanted. "Is he seeing someone now?"

"I don't know. As I said, we usually don't delve too deeply into one another's love lives."

"In other words, you respect one another's boundaries."

"Exactly, and it seems to work."

"Have you ever all gone out together with your respective women?"

"What's with the interrogation, Ava?"

"I need to know where I stand with your friends. I've known a lot of friendships break up because a man or woman starts seeing someone. I don't want to be the one responsible for monopolizing your time when you were supposed to be hanging with Ivan or Duncan."

"That's never going to happen."

"And why not, Kyle?"

"Because I'm sleeping with you, not Ivan and Duncan."

Ava almost choked on the sweet liquid in her cup. Picking up the napkin on her lap, she touched it to her lips. "No, you didn't say that."

"Yes, I did."

"So, it's all about the sex?"

Kyle stared at Ava as if she had taken leave of her senses. "Is that what you believe? That I'm with you because of sex?"

"You were the one who said you're sleeping with me and not your friends."

"Don't try and twist my words, Ava. I remember telling you that if I want a woman I know where to go to find one. And if I need to relieve myself I'm quite experienced in that department, too. So don't ever tell me that I'm with you for sex."

Ava wanted to come back at him but knew it wasn't the time or the place for a verbal confrontation. He'd been granted a reprieve because it was his birthday and they weren't alone.

She handed him the cup instead. "Could you please get me something a little stronger?"

"How strong do you want it?"

"Very strong."

"Are you angry with me, Ava?"

Her eyes narrowed. "No, darling. Right now I'm real pissed at you."

Smiling, Kyle leaned in and kissed her. "You're magnificent when you're pissed off. Your eyes get a little squinty and your chest heaves just enough to draw attention to your breasts."

She slapped at him with her napkin. "Get outta here, Kyle Chatham."

He pointed at her. "See. I got you to smile."

Ava compressed her lips. "I'm not smiling."

"Yeah, you are."

This time she did smile. "Please go and get my drink."

"If I get you a little tipsy will you allow me to take advantage of you? After all, it's my birthday and I should be entitled to a very special wish."

"How many wishes do you want? I've already given you at least twenty. You keep rubbing this genie and she's going on strike."

His forefinger traced the outline of the wishbone hanging around her neck. "I know a place I can rub and get the genie to give me everything I want."

Rolling her eyes, Ava turned her back on him. When she turned around the chair beside her was empty.

Chapter 16

Ava walked into the house on Strivers' Row, heading for the staircase. She was exhausted and slightly inebriated. Kyle had brought her a martini and she'd nursed it for an hour before putting the glass aside. The food Faith McMillan had prepared for the party was superb. She'd had two helpings of cold fish appetizers and eaten sparingly to sample roast pork, cold and hot salads, steak and salmon tartare, crudités, wraps and rolls.

A cake decorated with replicas of law books and a topper of blind justice was rolled around at eleven. Kyle appeared genuinely moved when everyone sang "Happy Birthday." Each guest was served cake and given souvenir slices in pale blue boxes. Micah, Duncan and

Ivan handed Kyle envelopes with gift checks to his favorite clothier.

Kyle personally thanked everyone for their good wishes as he was another year closer to the big four-oh. He teased Ivan and Duncan, saying he would still be thirty-nine when they turned forty.

It was after midnight when everyone started drifting off to their respective homes. Tessa took Ava aside, promising to invite her and Kyle for a small intimate dinner before the end of summer.

Now she walked through the master bedroom and into the en suite bath. Ava wanted to cleanse the makeup off her face, brush her teeth and shower before she fell asleep standing up. She was standing under the spray of the shower when the door opened and Kyle walked in. The emerging stubble on his jaw served to enhance his masculine sensuality.

"What are you doing?" she asked when Kyle eased the retractable nozzle from her grip.

He moved closer and she could smell mouthwash on his breath. "I'm going to help you wash your back."

Taking a step, she pressed her wet breasts to his chest. "It's your birthday, so I should be the one washing your back."

Kyle slowly shook his head. "It's after midnight so it's no longer my birthday."

Ava backed up until she couldn't go any farther. "I don't like the way you're looking at me."

"How am I looking at you, baby?"

Water had curled her hair and spiked her lashes. Ava's wet body glistened like liquid milk chocolate. Never had he seen her look so alluring.

"Like you want to do something to me."

"Oh, but I do, darling. I'm going to wash your back. Now turn around."

She presented him with her back. Bracing her hands against the wall, Ava closed her eyes. Kyle started at the nape of her neck with a bath sponge filled with her favorite shower gel. She moaned softly when he made circular motions along her spine and lower to her buttocks.

A shudder rippled through her when he began with small circles then widened them until he covered every inch of skin from head to toe. Tiny bubbles shimmered on her body like precious gems.

A sigh of ecstasy escaped her when Kyle changed the flow of water on the nozzle to pulsing. The tiny pulse beats heated and sped up her blood. There was a heaviness in her lower belly. He rinsed her feet, legs, thighs.

Then, without warning, Kyle eased down to sit on the floor of the shower stall. Slowly, methodically, he spread her legs and placed the nozzle inches from her vagina, rinsing away the residue of soap clinging to her pubis.

His fingers searched the folds, separating them and directing the pulsing flow to the delicate area with overly sensitive nerve endings. The light in the shower stall gave Kyle an up-close view of the area that gave him so much pleasure. He positioned the nozzle near her inner thigh and knelt forward. Spreading the folds again, he pressed his face against her mound and tasted her. He began tentatively, as if sampling a new dish. He increased the pressure until his face was flush against her vagina and he ate with the relish of a starving man eating after a prolonged fast.

Ava tried escaping his rapacious tongue, but the hand on her belly wouldn't permit movement. She cried, screamed and begged for him to let her go, but Kyle was relentless. His tongue moved in and out of her body until she was helpless to control the shudders shaking her as if she were experiencing a seizure.

Unable to stop the assault, she surrendered as orgasms overlapped themselves. As she braced herself for another one, Kyle pushed into her and released his own passions. Spent, they lay together, waiting for their hearts to slow down to a normal rate.

He washed between her thighs, then between his own. No words were necessary when they went into the bedroom and climbed into bed together. Ava curled into the hard contours of Kyle's body and went to sleep.

For Kyle, his thirty-ninth birthday would be one he would remember—forever.

Wyatt Wainwright had agreed to a meeting. Kyle wanted the real estate mogul to come to Harlem, but he refused, declaring he rarely ventured uptown to do business.

Jordan was angry because he felt they were giving

Wyatt the upper hand, but Kyle was quick to remind him that *they* were in control because Wyatt had come around enough to agree to meet.

Jordan was waiting outside the Wainwright building when Kyle stepped out of a taxi at seven-fifty. It was just like his grandfather to schedule a breakfast meeting. And with the meeting had come a condition: Wyatt refused to meet with the tenants' committee.

Moving forward, Jordan met Kyle and shook his hand. "Good morning."

Kyle noticed lines of stress ringing his associate's mouth and a slight puffiness under his eyes. "Is it a good morning?"

"You noticed?"

"Yes. How much sleep did you get last night?" he asked perceptively.

"I managed to get about two hours."

"It shows."

"Thank you for the compliment."

"You're welcome, Jordan. Are you sure you're ready for this?"

"I'm ready."

Kyle patted Jordan's back. "Let's go do battle."

The two men walked into the revolving door and out into an opulent lobby. The guard standing behind a desk straightened when he recognized his boss's grandson. "Good morning, Mr. Wainwright."

"Good morning. I'm going up to see my grandfather. Mr. Chatham is with me."

"No problem, Mr. Wainwright."

"I guess it pays to have your name on the building," Kyle teased Jordan after the doors to a private elevator closed behind them. If he'd come alone he would've had to be announced and cleared by building security.

"It doesn't mean jack. It's all for show."

"Don't knock it, Jordan. Being a Wainwright gave you a prep-school education, entrée to Harvard and their law school. And I doubt after you graduated you were burdened by thousands in student loans. If I hadn't worked for TCB I still would be paying off my loans."

"So you think I'm a whiney little rich boy?"

"You said it, Jordan. Not me."

"Being rich isn't all that it's cracked up to be."

"It's better than being poor. If those people involved in the rent strike could afford to live elsewhere they would. But right now they're stuck. At least they know they can afford to pay the rent where they are."

The elevator stopped and the doors opened to an area with a massive table with miniature models of buildings owned, designed or purchased by Wainwright Developers Group.

Very nice, Kyle mused as he followed Jordan down a hallway with walls of glass. The view from fifty-five stories above the Manhattan streets was breathtaking. Their footsteps were muffled in priceless Persian carpet as they stepped through double doors leading into Wyatt Wainwright's private office.

"Good morning, Rebecca."

A young woman with long auburn hair spun around in her chair at Jordan's greeting. A bright smile reached her sea-green eyes. "Jordan. What a wonderful surprise."

Jordan barely glanced at his grandfather's latest sex toy. "Is Wyatt in?"

"Yes. He's expecting you and…" Her professionally waxed eyebrows lifted slightly when she focused her full attention on Kyle. She ran the tip of her tongue over her glossy lips. "It is Mr. Chatham?"

Kyle's expression was as immobile as dried concrete. He'd gotten up at five and flagged down a taxi to take him downtown for an eight o'clock meeting to conduct business and, he hoped, settle a score, not flirt.

"Yes, *it* is," he drawled sarcastically.

Rebecca had the wherewithal to blush. "Please go in, gentlemen."

Jordan and Kyle walked into Wyatt's private office. The tall, slender man with a silver mane stood at a table with china, silver, crystal and cellophane-covered trays of sliced fruit, mini pastries and jars of yogurt. Pitchers of orange, apple and grapefruit juice, along with carafes of coffee and hot water for tea, rested on another table.

Wyatt flashed a cold smile. "Please come in. Jordan, I must say you're looking rather well."

"Thank you, sir."

Taking a step forward, Wyatt offered his hand to Kyle. "Mr. Chatham."

Kyle shook his callused palm. "Mr. Wainwright."

"May I call you Kyle?"

"Yes, you may, Wyatt."

Wyatt's eyes narrowed as he studied the man who'd enthralled his grandson. He'd had Kyle Chatham investigated and had to admit to being impressed by his curriculum vitae and illustrious tenure at Trilling, Carlyle and Browne.

Chatham was the total package from the top of his close-cropped hair to his imported-soled feet. His suit was a perfect fit, the hem of his trousers falling into a precise break at his shoes. What he couldn't understand was why Chatham would leave a firm paying him seven figures to hustle like an itinerant peddler for nickels.

Wyatt inclined his leonine head when he gestured to the table. "Please serve yourselves. We'll talk after we've eaten."

"I'd rather we talk *while* we eat," Jordan said.

Kyle rested an arm over Jordan's shoulder. "It's all right, Jordan. We have all morning. We'll eat first, and then we'll talk."

He unbuttoned his suit jacket and sat, waiting for Jordan to follow suit. He wanted to thump the younger man for his impertinence. Kyle had instructed Jordan that he would chair the meeting.

When Wyatt took a chair across from Kyle the slight resemblance between grandfather and grandson was obvious: height, lean face and stubborn chin. Jordan was probably more like his grandfather than he cared to admit.

Wyatt's brilliant blue eyes lingered on his first grandchild before he picked up a fragile cup, filling it with steaming, fragrant coffee. "We expected you to come down to the summer house last weekend."

Jordan reached for a napkin, unfolded it and placed it across his lap. "I had prior plans."

"I hope those plans included a woman. You know how spastic your mother has become because you're still single. In fact, I think she would calm down even if you were seeing someone on a steady basis."

"Sorry, Grandfather. I don't live my life for Mother. Perhaps she will have more luck with Noah."

Wyatt scowled. "Noah doesn't even like women."

Jordan smiled for the first time that morning. "Oh, that's where you're wrong, Grandfather. My brother likes women, just not the ones you parade in front of him or try to hook him up with."

Wyatt's frown deepened. "He could've said something rather than act like a fruit."

"The politically correct term is *gay,*" Jordan insisted.

Kyle spread a napkin over his knees. He was enjoying the sharp interchange between Jordan and Wyatt. The sarcasm was thick enough to cut with a knife, but at least they were talking.

He selected a small portion of fruit, coffee and yogurt with a topping of wheat germ. Kyle had met more Wyatt Wainwrights than he wanted to. Pompous men filled with their own self-importance. Wealthy men who thought everyone had a price. Sanctimonious men who believed everything they did was right, that they didn't have to answer to anyone but themselves.

Kyle glanced at his watch. "Wyatt, I'd like to get started."

"But you've hardly eaten."

"I've eaten all I'm going to eat. Now, if you don't mind I want to begin by saying I'm sorry we have to meet like this. I would've much preferred inviting your family to a soirée to celebrate your grandson making partner."

Wyatt choked, coughing violently when he attempted to swallow while sipping coffee. "You're making Jordan a partner?" he asked after he'd recovered from his coughing jag.

Kyle nodded. "He's earned it."

"He humiliates me and you reward him by making him a partner."

"You humiliated yourself by hiring incompetents to oversee your holding companies. They dropped the ball. Is your empire so vast that you don't know what's going on?"

Thick black eyebrows lowered as Wyatt appeared deep in thought. "I wasn't aware of the conditions in those buildings until I saw that news footage."

"Are you saying no one told you about the violations?"

Wyatt combed his fingers through his thick, wiry hair. "No. When I asked about it I was told the building manager didn't want to bother me with trivial problems."

Kyle shook his head. "Trivial problems that jumped up to bite you in the ass."

Lacing his fingers together, Wyatt glared at Kyle. "You must think I don't care about the people that live in my buildings. Well, let me tell you something. I do care, because I was once one of those very people who stood on that street basking in their fifteen minutes of fame.

"I lived in a stinking tenement with shotgun apartments. I know what it was like to have to heat water to take a bath or wash dishes, what it was to look out the windows and see a backyard filled with so much debris that if someone fell off the roof the garbage would act as a buffer against serious injury.

"If my grandson had come to me instead of posturing before a television camera I would've taken care of everything."

"It wouldn't have mattered, Wyatt. Even if Jordan hadn't come to work for me I still would've called you out," Kyle countered. "This has nothing to do with the manner or approach he utilizes to protect the rights of his clients and everything to do with you not taking care of your business."

A flush of red crept from Wyatt's throat to his hairline at the same time a large vein pulsed in his forehead. "Who the hell do you think you are to lecture me on how I should run my business?"

Kyle smiled, knowing he'd rattled the older man. "I'm not lecturing, but I am warning you. I'm the one who will have the ultimate pleasure of ruining your reputation if you don't correct those violations before the

Labor Day weekend. And I don't give a damn how many people you have to hire to get the job done."

Wyatt snorted sarcastically. "You ruin me? Surely you jest."

"I wonder how the members of your country club would react if each received photographs of the squalor in your buildings. Most of the people living in unsanitary and unsafe condition are children. How would it look if one of those children were to die or suffer serious injury because of your neglect? In case you've forgotten, your tenants do pay rent every month. Meanwhile, during the Christmas season you dress up like Santa to give away gifts and money to needy families. Have you heard that charity begins at home?" He leaned over the table. "Take care of your home." Silence descended like a shroud on the room's three occupants. The hostility was so thick it was palpable.

It was Jordan who finally broke the impasse. "He's not bluffing, Grandpa."

Wyatt slumped in his chair. He'd waited more than a year for Jordan to call him *Grandpa,* and not *Sir* or the more formal *Grandfather.* "What do you want?" His query was filled with defeat *and* resignation. He would do anything and give up everything to reestablish a relationship with his grandson.

Pushing back from the table, Kyle looped one leg over the opposite knee. "I told you what our clients want. They want their apartments brought up to code."

"Consider it done."

Rising, Kyle extended his hand to Wyatt. "Thank you."

"It's been a pleasure," Wyatt said facetiously when he took Kyle's hand. He turned to Jordan. "Call me at home tonight."

Jordan's gaze softened when he stared at his grandfather. He nodded. "Okay." Rising to his feet, he walked out of the office to wait near the elevator for Kyle. The tenants' association had gotten what they wanted, Kyle had gotten what he wanted and, at the mention of becoming a partner, Jordan had gotten what he wanted.

Kyle met Jordan at the elevator, both men sporting wide grins. "Who were you calling *gangsta?*" Jordan teased.

"I didn't want to believe it when the old man rolled up on me like that."

"You're lucky the old man didn't draw down on you. I've never seen it, but there are rumors that he carries a small automatic concealed on his person. It's totally unnecessary because he has a driver who doubles as his bodyguard."

"Maybe he doesn't trust his bodyguard."

Jordan pushed the button for the elevator, and the doors opened silently. "My grandfather doesn't trust anyone." He stood off to the side and waited for Kyle to enter the car, then followed. "Were you serious when you mentioned me becoming a partner?"

Kyle stared at Jordan, recognizing his hunger for success and the need to prove his worthiness. The question was: to whom? "Yes, Jordan, I am quite serious about making you partner. I've already instructed the office manager to change the letterhead to read Chatham and Wainwright."

Jordan closed his eyes and said a silent prayer of thanks. He liked working for and with Kyle, enjoyed advocating for the firm's clients and he liked Harlem. Many times he took his lunch outside the office and wound up touring the neighborhood.

He opened his eyes. "Thank you, Kyle."

"There's no need to thank me. You've earned it. You've been putting in a lot of hours."

"I feel like celebrating. Why don't you come by and see my new place? I'm seeing a girl who's in culinary school and I get to test everything she prepares. I'll ask her to put something together and we can toast my good fortune over drinks."

"I'd like to, but I promised my girlfriend that we would go out for dinner."

"Why don't you come and bring her with you? I'm certain anything Natasha would prepare would equal or surpass a restaurant meal."

"Okay, Jordan. Ava and I will come see your new house and toast your success. I want you to take the rest of the day off. You'll have just twenty-four hours to bask in your newfound success, because tomorrow you'll have to jump back on the treadmill." He and his new partner shared a smile. "What time is your soirée?"

"Cocktails will be served at seven and dinner at eight."

The elevator arrived at the lobby, and Kyle and

Jordan stood outside the steel-and-glass building talking for a few minutes before parting with a promise to see one another later that evening.

Chapter 17

"Do you have me on speaker, Kyle?"

"Yes, I do, Mom."

"You know I hate it when you do that. You sound as if you're in a tunnel."

"I can't hold the phone, talk to you and dress myself at the same time." Kyle tightened the knot in his tie and then turned down the shirt collar.

"Do you want me to call you back at another time?" Frances Chatham asked.

Picking up the cordless instrument, Kyle deactivated the speaker. "No, Mom."

"I just called to thank you for the anniversary gift. The gift certificate from that Arizona spa arrived today.

Elwin complained about going to a place where women sat around in fluffy white bathrobes with mudpacks on their faces until I told him there were spa packages for men, too, that include massages, facials and golfing. I think it was the mention of golf that made him change his mind about going with me. I want to thank you for thinking of us, Kyle. Sedona isn't that far from Phoenix, so after we leave the spa we're going to spend a couple of days with Sandra and the grandbabies."

"You don't have to thank me, Mom."

"Yes, I do, Kyle. You always remember our anniversary."

Kyle smiled. "It's kind of hard not to remember when it falls on my birthday. And, I'd like to thank *you* for the wonderful card."

"You are quite welcome, son. How does it feel to be thirty-nine?"

"I feel good. In fact, I feel very, very good." Kyle adjusted the receiver between his chin and shoulder as he sat down on a padded bench to slip into his shoes. He told his mother about the surprise birthday celebration at Micah's house.

"That was very generous of him to do that," Frances said. "I still can't believe that Micah is a married man. I remember him saying he would never get married. If he can do it, so can you."

"The difference between Micah and me is that Micah said he was never going to marry. I've never said that."

"Do you think you'll ever get married, son?"

Leaning over, Kyle tied his shoelaces. "I'm sure I will. But she has to be the right woman."

"There are no right and wrong women, Kyle. What you're looking for is perfection, and there are no perfect women in the world, just like there're no perfect men. We all come with flaws. What you have to do is ignore or overlook the flaws to appreciate the better qualities."

He smiled. "It all sounds good, Mom. You'll be the first to know when I find that almost perfect, slightly flawed woman who makes me consider putting a ring on her finger. Right now it's not going to happen."

"Why are you always so cynical when it comes to the topic of marriage?"

"I'm not cynical, Mom. Marriage is an important *and* sacred institution, but you'd never know it by the soaring divorce rates. When I commit to marrying a woman I don't want it to be like test-driving a car. Either I'm in it for the duration or I'm going to stay single. I have no qualms about ending a relationship if it means saving myself from an emotional breakdown. Ivan has enough screwed-up folks on his couch crying about their messed-up marriages and relationships. I don't intend to become one of them."

"Are you looking for someone?"

"Unconsciously I'm always looking for the woman who'll become the *one*. The ultimate challenge is finding her."

Kyle saw movement out the corner of his eye. Turning, he saw Ava standing in the doorway to his dressing room.

Smiling, he beckoned her closer. He'd called to ask her
if she wouldn't mind a change of plans for the evening,
and she'd agreed to accompany him to Jordan's rather
than have dinner at local restaurant. He'd given her a set
of keys to his house and told her to hold on to them. It
was apparent she'd used them to let herself in.

"Mom, I'd love to talk some more, but I have to go
or I'm going to be late for an appointment."

"Thanks again for the anniversary gift."

"You're welcome. I'll call you in a couple of days."

"Goodbye, son. I love you."

"I love you, too, Mom."

A sheepish grin crossed his face as he hung up. "That
was my mother."

Ava forced a brittle smile. Her mouth was smiling,
but inside, her stomach muscles felt as if they were tied
into knots. She'd walked in on Kyle in time to hear him
say he was always subconsciously looking for the right
woman. What a fool she'd been, because she'd believed
that she *was* that woman.

It was a case of history repeating itself. She'd dated
Anthony exclusively during college, believing they were
going to marry following graduation, but it hadn't happened because Anthony claimed he'd found someone
else better suited to his temperament.

Ava had met Anthony King her first week at
Columbia and it was as if she'd been struck by a bolt of
lightning. The psychology major was sitting in a coffee
shop with a group of boys and when she'd walked in to

find every seat occupied, he got up and offered her his seat. Of course, he became the butt of jokes when his friends called him Sir Anthony because of his chivalrous exhibition. They laughed while she was impressed.

Both were considered nerds, and this suited Ava just fine because she'd come to New York's Columbia University to study, not party.

Anthony lived in a small dorm room while she shared a two-bedroom apartment with her Iowan roommate. Anthony stayed over so often that Ava felt as if they were living together. What she hadn't known until it was too late was that the nights he didn't stay over he was sleeping with another student at his dorm—a girl better suited to his temperament.

His announcement had caught her completely by surprise, and she'd walked around shell-shocked for months. Thankfully she'd secured a teaching position in a school in Alphabet City and having to deal with a classroom of noisy, hyperactive first-graders forced the focus on her career.

Kyle claimed he loved her, wanted to take care of her, yet unconsciously he was looking for a woman to replace her.

Fool me once, shame on you. Fool me twice, shame on me. Ava Warrick had no intention of playing the fool to a man to whom she'd given her heart. At least with William Marshall she didn't have to deal with another woman. It was just him and his crazy perception of life.

She walked over and touched her cheek to his. "You smell nice."

Damn, I'm good. Ava couldn't believe what a consummate actress she'd become. She'd promised Kyle that she would go with him to his law associate's home for an informal cocktail party and she planned to follow through on her promise. She'd also promised to sleep over and she would follow through on that promise, too.

Tonight was already scripted, but she wasn't so certain about tomorrow. What Ava had to decide was whether to walk out of Kyle's life as she'd done with Will, or to confront him about what she'd overheard him tell his mother. The latter posed a problem because he could accuse her of eavesdropping.

Then there was always the wait-and-see method. Wait to see if what they had was worth fighting for before she decided to let it go. Her internal struggle was that she loved Kyle, loved him more than she'd loved any other man in her life.

Kyle smiled at the woman who made him feel like a kid with a crush on a girl who wouldn't give him a glance or the time of day, a woman who had him craving her like an addiction and a woman who had him thinking about sharing his future with her. He'd lied to his mother when he'd told her he was looking for a woman he wanted to marry, because he didn't want Frances to become the town crier, calling every family member to tell them her firstborn was going to jump the broom.

"You look incredible, darling." And she did. Ava wore a little black dress that hugged every curve of her sexy body. The squared neckline, capped sleeves and hem ending at her knees were simple and elegant. His gaze moved down to her smooth, bare legs and groomed feet in a pair of strappy black stilettos.

Ava lowered her gaze, peering up at him through her lashes. "Thank you."

Dipping his head, Kyle kissed her cheek. "I love taking you out and showing you off."

"Like a hood ornament?"

A frown settled into his features. "Why would you say something like that, Ava?"

"Didn't you say you like showing me off? Isn't that what men do with women they think of as eye candy?"

"You're a lot more than eye candy."

"What am I, Kyle?"

"You're the love of my life."

"But for how long?"

"What!"

"You heard me, Kyle. How long will I remain the love of your life?"

"I'd like to believe I'd be around after the end of September."

"What are you talking about?" Ava had never known Kyle to talk in riddles.

"Wasn't it you who said we'd only be together for three months? Then my very beautiful genie granted me an additional month."

"Did I say that?"

"Yes, you did." Pushing back his shirt cuff, Kyle

looked at his watch. "We have to go or we're going to be late."

Ava was more confused now than she'd been when she'd walked in and overheard Kyle talking to his mother. She hadn't thought Kyle would take her seriously when she'd said they would be together for three months. It was something that had come to mind at that moment.

Maybe, just maybe, Kyle Chatham could become the last man in her life. She would celebrate her thirty-fifth birthday in December and she hadn't wanted to start over looking for a man.

Before meeting Kyle, Ava had believed she didn't need to be married and that not bearing a child could still make her feel like a complete woman, but she'd lied to herself. Maybe her change of heart had come from spending the two weeks with her sister. After several false starts, Aisha had finally found the love of her life. She lived in a beautiful home, had a loving and protective husband and a new baby.

Ava knew she was in denial.

Ava wanted to be married.

Ava wanted Kyle Chatham.

Ava Warrick wanted to become the mother of Kyle Chatham's babies.

Kyle waved a hand in front Ava's face. "Where were you?"

Her eyelids fluttered. "What?"

"You just zoned out on me. I said we have to leave or we're going to be late."

"Where are we going?"

"Ninety-eighth and Fifth."

"That's not too far."

Kyle, resting his hand in the small of Ava's back, steered her out of the dressing room. "I'm not driving."

"How are we getting there?"

"Jordan's sending a car."

A black-suited driver, leaning against the bumper of a Town Car, straightened when Kyle and Ava descended the steps to the street. He opened the rear door, waiting until his passengers were seated before closing the door and sitting down behind the wheel.

Kyle held on to Ava's hand during the short ride until the driver maneuvered in front of the prewar highrise steps from Central Park and Mount Sinai Hospital. The building's doorman opened the door, assisting Ava when she placed one foot on the sidewalk, then the other. Kyle surreptitiously slipped the driver a bill, then took Ava's arm and led her into the opulently appointed lobby.

He gave the doorman his name and who he was visiting, and they were escorted to Jordan's maisonette. A passing elevator attendant slowed to take furtive glances at Ava's legs. *Yes,* he thought, *she's all mine.*

Jordan stood in the doorway, smiling. "Welcome, welcome."

Kyle exchanged a handshake and embrace with his law partner. Reaching into the breast pocket of his jacket, he handed Jordan a small, silver-wrapped box. "Here's a little something to commemorate your new position."

Jordan slapped Kyle's broad back. "Thanks, partner. Please come in so I can make the proper introductions before showing you around the place."

Ava gaped at the tall, tanned and incredibly handsome man who had become Kyle's law partner. K. E. Chatham Legal Services was now Chatham and Wainwright, PC, Attorneys at Law. She felt a shiver go through her when Jordan focused his large hazel eyes on her. The recessed lighting in the spacious foyer glinted off the shimmering green.

Jordan extended a large, groomed hand. "Jordan Wainwright."

Ava placed her hand on his palm. "Ava Warrick."

He inclined his head in a gesture she interpreted as reverence. "It's my deepest pleasure to welcome you into my home."

Ava gave Kyle a sidelong glance, wanting to ask him if Jordan Wainwright was for real. The young attorney was the epitome of formality. "Thank you for inviting *us*."

"Jordan, darling, I see that our guests have arrived."

Kyle turned to find a petite, dark-skinned woman with a profusion of tiny twists of hair secured on the top of her head. Several of them had escaped to cascade on her nape and over her ears. She wore a white chef's tunic over black cropped pants. She'd pushed her tiny feet into black ballet-type shoes. He smiled as realization dawned. Jordan's rift with his grandfather was because he was dating an African-American woman.

Jordan held out his hand and she floated over to take

it. "Natasha, this is Kyle Chatham, whom I never stop talking about, and the beautiful lady with him is Ava Warrick. Kyle, Ava, this is Natasha Parker. She's putting together the most exquisite dinner." Ava and Kyle exchanged handshakes with Natasha.

Natasha rested a hand on Jordan's suit jacket. "Will you please serve the cocktails while I get the hors d'oeuvres?"

"Of course, honey. Kyle, Ava, please follow me."

Ava found herself in an enormous living room with twelve-foot ceilings and wall-to-wall windows. The apartment was filled with antiques and reproductions, reminding her of furnishings on display at museums.

"What are you drinking, Ava?"

She remembered the last time she had had an alcoholic drink, when she and Kyle had wound up copulating on the floor of the shower stall. "I'll have a white wine."

Jordan opened a built-in refrigerator and removed a bottle of wine. "How about you, Kyle?"

"I'll have a Scotch and soda."

"Good choice."

The three waited for Natasha to return before they toasted one another and the new partnership. The aspiring chef had prepared hot and cold hors d'oeuvres that demonstrated her unique cooking talent.

Jordan showed them around the apartment, which featured split bedrooms, two bathrooms, one with a Jacuzzi, and a gourmet kitchen with Miele appliances, a formal dining room and a spacious living room. A back-door entrance led into the kitchen and a maid's room and bath. The area also had a pantry and a laundry room with a washer and dryer.

The cocktail hour ended and at exactly eight o'clock they sat down to a dinner of crown rib roast, blanched green beans and saffron rice. A fragrant red wine accompanied the meal and after her second glass of wine that evening Ava wanted to curl up and go to sleep. When she'd remarked on the quality of the merlot, Jordan revealed that a case of red and white wines had arrived that afternoon, compliments of Kyle. Dinner ended with a dessert of meringues dusted with cinnamon, coffee and various cordials.

Jordan opened Kyle's gift; he held up the box with a solid gold tie tack that matched his cufflinks. He bowed his head. "Thanks, partner."

Kyle returned the nod. "You're most welcome, partner."

The dinner party ended at ten-thirty and the driver was waiting when Kyle and Ava left the maisonette for the ride back to Harlem.

Ava stood in front the mirror slathering her face with cold cream before she removed her makeup with a warm cloth. She smiled when Kyle appeared in the mirror behind her.

"I like Jordan and Natasha."

Kyle moved closer, pressing his bare chest to her back. "I like you."

Ava ducked her head as she splashed water on her face. Kyle handed her a towel. "Thanks." Straightening, she patted at the moisture on her face. Her gaze met his in the mirror. "I like you, too, Kyle."

"How well do you like me?"

She turned to stare up him. There was something in him that made her feel as if he were a stranger instead of the man whose bed she shared, on average, three times a week.

"I love you, Kyle."

He rested his hands on her shoulders. "Do you love me enough to go off the pill?"

Ava's eyes grew wide, wild. "I told you I had no intention of becoming a baby mama."

Kyle kissed her hair. "You wouldn't be a baby mama if you married me."

Ava froze, unable to believe that Kyle Chatham had proposed marriage. "What are you trying to say?"

Wrapping an arm around her neck, he held her captive. "I'm not *trying* to say anything, Ava. I said I want you to marry me."

"When do you want to get married?"

"That will be your call. You still haven't answered my question. Miss Ava Warrick, will you marry me?"

Turning in his loose embrace, Ava went on tiptoe and kissed him, gently at first, then she opened her mouth to devour his. "Yes, Mr. Kyle Chatham, I will marry you."

One moment she was standing and the next she was in bed, on her back, with Kyle's hardness moving inside her. They didn't have sex, but made slow, sensual love with each other. There was no need for a quick coupling because they had the rest of their lives to share a bed and share a future. They climaxed together but Kyle loathed pulling out.

"I was going to leave you after tonight," Ava confessed after her respiration had slowed to a normal rate.

Kyle raised his head to stare at her. "Why?"

She told him about overhearing the conversation he'd had with his mother. She also gave him the intimate details of her four-year relationship with Anthony. "I wasn't going to wait around to have you leave me if or when you found someone better."

Kyle kissed her forehead. "There's no one better for me than you. There were times when I felt I wasn't good enough for you."

"You must be kidding, darling. You are the best of the best."

He smiled. "What are your plans for tomorrow?"

"I don't have anything planned except to make my lunches for the week. Why?"

"How would you like to go look at rings?"

"You're really serious about this marriage thing, aren't you?"

"You just don't know how serious."

"Okay, we'll look at rings. I have to call my mother and sister to give them the news. Then I have to decide what type of wedding I want. We need to pick out a place for a reception—"

"Slow down, Ava. You'll have time and help planning a wedding. I'll have Tessa plan a wedding that will be spectacular."

Ava remembered Tessa offering her services if she and Kyle decided to marry. It was apparent the wedding planner had known something she hadn't. Even Duncan had seen that Kyle was in love with her.

It was obvious that Kyle had changed and that she had changed. She'd never known when she'd crashed into his car that they were fated to meet and share a future.

Kyle Chatham was her man of fate.

REQUEST YOUR FREE BOOKS!

2 FREE NOVELS
PLUS 2 FREE GIFTS!

KIMANI™
ROMANCE

Love's ultimate destination!

National bestselling author

ROCHELLE ALERS

Naughty

Parties, paparazzi, red-carpet catfights…

Wild child Breanna Parker's antics have
always been a ploy to gain attention from
her diva mother and record-producer father.
As her marriage implodes, Bree moves to
Rome. There she meets charismatic Reuben,
who becomes both her romantic and business
partner. But just as she's enjoying her
successful new life, Bree is confronted
with a devastating scandal that threatens
everything she's worked so hard for….

*Coming the first week of March 2009
wherever books are sold.*

KIMANI PRESS™

www.kimanipress.com
www.myspace.com/kimanipress

The thirteenth novel in
the successful *Hideaway* series...

NATIONAL BESTSELLING AUTHOR

ROCHELLE ALERS

Secret Agenda

When Vivienne Neal's "perfect life" is turned
upside down, she moves to Florida to take a job
with Diego Cole-Thomas, a powerful CEO with
an intimidating reputation. Vivienne's job skills
prove invaluable to Diego, and on a business trip,
their relationship takes a sensual turn. But when
threatening letters arrive at Diego's office, he
realizes a horrible secret can threaten both of
them—and their future together.

"There's no doubt that Rochelle Alers is a compelling
storyteller who has the ability to weave romance with
the delicate subtlety of Monet."
—*Romantic Times BOOKreviews* on *HIDEAWAY*

*Coming the first week of May 2009
wherever books are sold.*

ARABESQUE®